William Wordsworth

Poetical Works of William Wordsmith - With a Memoir

Vol. V

William Wordsworth

Poetical Works of William Wordsmith - With a Memoir
Vol. V

ISBN/EAN: 9783337093433

Printed in Europe, USA, Canada, Australia, Japan

Cover: Foto ©Andreas Hilbeck / pixelio.de

More available books at **www.hansebooks.com**

THE POETICAL WORKS

OF

WILLIAM WORDSWORTH.

WITH A MEMOIR.

VOL. V.

BOSTON:

JAMES R. OSGOOD AND COMPANY,

Late Ticknor & Fields, and Fields, Osgood, & Co.

1871.

CONTENTS.

VOL. V.

***

MISCELLANEOUS POEMS.

INSCRIPTIONS.

SELECTIONS FROM CHAUCER, MODERNIZED.

POEMS REFERRING TO THE PERIOD OF OLD AGE.

EPITAPHS AND ELEGIAC PIECES.

CONTENTS.

APPENDIX, PREFACES, ETC., ETC.

MISCELLANEOUS POEMS.

I.

EPISTLE

TO SIR GEORGE HOWLAND BEAUMONT, BART.

From the Southwest Coast of Cumberland. — 1811.

FAR from our home by Grasmere's quiet Lake,
From the Vale's peace which all her fields partake,
Here on the bleakest point of Cumbria's shore
We sojourn stunned by Ocean's ceaseless roar;
While, day by day, grim neighbor! huge Black
    Comb
Frowns, deepening visibly his native gloom,
Unless, perchance rejecting in despite
What on the Plain *we* have of warmth and light,
In his own storms he hides himself from sight.
Rough is the time; and thoughts, that would be
    free
From heaviness, oft fly, dear Friend, to thee;
Turn from a spot where neither sheltered road
Nor hedge-row screen invites my steps abroad;

Where one poor Plane-tree, having as it might
Attained a stature twice a tall man's height,
Hopeless of further growth, and brown and sere
Through half the summer, stands with top cut sheer,
Like an unshifting weathercock which proves
How cold the quarter that the wind best loves,
Or like a sentinel, that, evermore,
Darkening the window, ill defends the door
Of this unfinished house, — a Fortress bare,
Where strength has been the Builder's only care;
Whose rugged walls may still for years demand
The final polish of the Plasterer's hand.
— This Dwelling's Inmate more than three weeks'
          space
And oft a Prisoner in the cheerless place,
I — of whose touch the fiddle would complain,
Whose breath would labor at the flute in vain,
In music all unversed, nor blessed with skill
A bridge to copy, or to paint a mill,
Tired of my books, a scanty company !
And tired of listening to the boisterous sea —
Pace between door and window, muttering rhyme,
An old resource to cheat a froward time !
Though these dull hours (mine is it, or their
          shame ?)
Would tempt me to renounce that humble aim.
— But if there be a Muse who, free to take
Her seat upon Olympus, doth forsake
Those heights, (like Phœbus when his golden locks
He veiled, attendant on Thessalian flocks,)

And, in disguise, a Milkmaid with her pail
Trips down the pathways of some winding dale ;
Or, like a Mermaid, warbles on the shores
To fishers mending nets beside their doors ;
Or, Pilgrim-like, on forest moss reclined,
Gives plaintive ditties to the heedless wind,
Or listens to its play among the boughs
Above her head, and so forgets her vows, —
If such a Visitant of Earth there be,
And she would deign this day to smile on me
And aid my verse, content with local bounds
Of natural beauty and life's daily rounds,
Thoughts, chances, sights, or doings, which we tell
Without reserve to those whom we love well, —
Then haply, Beaumont ! words in current clear
Will flow, and on a welcome page appear
Duly before thy sight, unless they perish here.

What shall I treat of ?   News from Mona's Isle ?
Such have we, but unvaried in its style ;
No tales of Runagates fresh landed, whence
And wherefore fugitive or on what pretence ;
Of feasts, or scandal, eddying like the wind,
Most restlessly alive when most confined.
Ask not of me, whose tongue can best appease
The mighty tumults of the HOUSE OF KEYS ;
The last year's cup whose Ram or Heifer gained,
What slopes are planted, or what mosses drained :
An eye of fancy only can I cast
On that proud pageant now at hand or past,

When full five hundred boats in trim array,
With nets and sails outspread and streamers gay,
And chanted hymns and stiller voice of prayer,
For the old Manx-harvest to the Deep repair,
Soon as the herring-shoals at distance shine,
Like beds of moonlight shifting on the brine.

Mona from our abode is daily seen,
But with a wilderness of waves between;
And by conjecture only can we speak
Of aught transacted there in bay or creek;
No tidings reach us hence from town or field,
Only faint news her mountain sunbeams yield,
And some we gather from the misty air,
And some the hovering clouds, our telegraph, de-
    clare.
But these poetic mysteries I withhold;
For Fancy hath her fits both hot and cold,
And should the colder fit with you be on
When you might read, my credit would be gone.

Let more substantial themes the pen engage,
And nearer interests, culled from the opening stage
Of our migration. — Ere the welcome dawn
Had from the east her silver star withdrawn,
The Wain stood ready, at our Cottage-door,
Thoughtfully freighted with a various store;
And long or ere the uprising of the Sun,
O'er dew-damped dust our journey was begun,
A needful journey, under favoring skies,

Through peopled Vales ; yet something in the guise
Of those old Patriarchs when from well to well
They roamed through Wastes where now the
    tented Arabs dwell.

Say first, to whom did we the charge confide,
Who promptly undertook the Wain to guide
Up many a sharply twining road and down,
And over many a wide hill's craggy crown,
Through the quick turns of many a hollow nook,
And the rough bed of many an unbridged brook ?
A blooming Lass, — who in her better hand
Bore a light switch, her sceptre of command
When, yet a slender Girl, she often led,
Skilful and bold, the horse and burdened *sled* *
From the peat-yielding Moss on Gowdar's head.
What could go wrong with such a Charioteer
For goods and chattels, or those Infants dear,
A Pair who smilingly sat side by side,
Our hope confirming that the salt-sea tide,
Whose free embraces we were bound to seek,
Would their lost strength restore and freshen the
    pale cheek ?
Such hope did either Parent entertain
Pacing behind along the silent lane.

Blithe hopes and happy musings soon took flight,
For lo ! an uncouth, melancholy sight. —

* A local word for sledge.

On a green bank a creature stood forlorn,
Just half protruded to the light of morn,
Its hinder part concealed by hedge-row thorn.
The Figure called to mind a beast of prey
Stripped of its frightful powers by slow decay,
And, though no longer upon rapine bent,
Dim memory keeping of its old intent.
We started, looked again with anxious eyes,
And in that griesly object recognize
The Curate's Dog,— his long-tried friend, for they,
As well we knew, together had grown gray.
The Master died, his drooping servant's grief
Found at the Widow's feet some sad relief;
Yet still he lived in pining discontent,
Sadness which no indulgence could prevent;
Hence whole day wanderings, broken nightly sleeps,
And lonesome watch that out of doors he keeps;
Not oftentimes, I trust, as we, poor brute!
Espied him on his legs sustained, blank, mute,
And of all visible motion destitute,
So that the very heaving of his breath
Seemed stopped, though by some other power than
        death.
Long as we gazed upon the form and face,
A mild domestic pity kept its place,
Unscared by thronging fancies of strange hue
That haunted us in spite of what we knew.
Even now I sometimes think of him as lost
In second-sight appearances, or crost
By spectral shapes of guilt, or to the ground

On which he stood by spells unnatural bound,
Like a gaunt, shaggy Porter, forced to wait
In days of old romance at Archimago's gate.

Advancing Summer, Nature's law fulfilled,
The choristers in every grove had stilled ;
But we, we lacked not music of our own,
For lightsome Fanny had thus early thrown,
'Mid the gay prattle of those infant tongues,
Some notes prelusive, from the round of songs
With which, more zealous than the liveliest bird
That in wild Arden's brakes was ever heard,
Her work and her work's partners she can cheer
The whole day long, and all days of the year.

Thus gladdened, from our own dear Vale we pass,
And soon approach Diana's Looking-glass !
To Loughrigg Tarn, round, clear, and bright as
        heaven,
Such name Italian fancy would have given,
Ere on its banks the few gray cabins rose
That yet disturb not its concealed repose
More than the feeblest wind that idly blows.

Ah, Beaumont ! when an opening in the road
Stopped me at once by charm of what it showed,
The encircling region vividly exprest
Within the mirror's depth, a world at rest, —
Sky streaked with purple, grove and craggy *bield*,*

* A word common in the country, signifying shelter, as in
Scotland.

And the smooth green of many a pendent field,
And, quieted and soothed, a torrent small,
A little, daring would-be waterfall,
One chimney smoking and its azure wreath,
Associate all in the calm Pool beneath,
With here and there a faint imperfect gleam
Of water-lilies veiled in misty steam, —
What wonder, at this hour of stillness deep,
A shadowy link 'tween wakefulness and sleep,
When Nature's self, amid such blending, seems
To render visible her own soft dreams,
If, mixed with what appeared of rock, lawn, wood,
Fondly embosomed in the tranquil flood,
A glimpse I caught of that abode, by thee
Designed to rise in humble privacy.
A lowly dwelling, here to be outspread,
Like a small hamlet, with its bashful head
Half hid in native trees.   Alas! 't is not,
Nor ever was; I sighed, and left the spot
Unconscious of its own untoward lot,
And thought in silence, with regret too keen,
Of unexperienced joys that might have been;
Of neighborhood and intermingling arts,
And golden summer days uniting cheerful hearts.
But time, irrevocable time, is flown,
And let us utter thanks for blessings sown
And reaped, — what hath been, and what is, our own.

Not far we travelled ere a shout of glee,
Startling us all, dispersed my reverie;

Such shout as, many a sportive echo meeting,
Ofttimes from Alpine *chalets* sends a greeting.
Whence the blithe hail? behold a Peasant stand
On high, a kerchief waving in her hand!
Not unexpectant that by early day
Our little Band would thrid this mountain way,
Before her cottage on the bright hill-side
She hath advanced with hope to be descried.
Right gladly answering signals we displayed,
Moving along a tract of morning shade,
And vocal wishes sent of like good-will
To our kind Friend high on the sunny hill,—
Luminous region, fair as if the prime
Were tempting all astir to look aloft or climb;
Only the centre of the shining cot
With door left open makes a gloomy spot,
Emblem of those dark corners sometimes found
Within the happiest breast on earthly ground.

Rich prospect left behind of stream and vale,
And mountain-tops, a barren ridge we scale;
Descend and reach, in Yewdale's depths, a plain
With haycocks studded, striped with yellowing
    grain,—
An area level as a Lake, and spread
Under a rock too steep for man to tread,
Where, sheltered from the north and bleak north-
    west,
Aloft the Raven hangs a visible nest,
Fearless of all assaults that would her brood molest.

Hot sunbeams fill the steaming vale; but hark,
At our approach, a jealous watch-dog's bark,
Noise that brings forth no liveried Page of state,
But the whole household, that our coming wait.
With Young and Old warm greetings we exchange,
And jocund smiles, and toward the lowly Grange
Press forward, by the teasing dogs unscared.
Entering, we find the morning meal prepared:
So down we sit, though not till each had cast
Pleased looks around the delicate repast,—
Rich cream, and snow-white eggs fresh from the nest,
With amber honey from the mountain's breast;
Strawberries from lane or woodland, offering wild
Of children's industry, in hillocks piled;
Cakes for the nonce, and butter fit to lie
Upon a lordly dish; frank hospitality
Where simple art with bounteous nature vied,
And cottage comfort shunned not seemly pride.

Kind Hostess! Handmaid also of the feast,
If thou be lovelier than the kindling East,
Words by thy presence unrestrained may speak
Of a perpetual dawn from brow and cheek
Instinct with light whose sweetest promise lies,
Never retiring, in thy large, dark eyes,—
Dark, but to every gentle feeling true,
As if their lustre flowed from ether's purest blue.

Let me not ask what tears may have been wept
By those bright eyes, what weary vigils kept,

Beside that hearth what sighs may have been heaved
For wounds inflicted, nor what toil relieved
By fortitude and patience, and the grace
Of Heaven in pity visiting the place.
Not unadvisedly those secret springs
I leave unsearched : enough that memory clings,
Here as elsewhere, to notices that make
Their own significance for hearts awake,
To rural incidents, whose genial powers
Filled with delight three summer morning hours.

More could my pen report of grave or gay
That through our gypsy travel cheered the way ;
But, bursting forth above the waves, the Sun
Laughs at my pains, and seems to say, " Be done."
Yet, Beaumont, thou wilt not, I trust, reprove
This humble offering made by Truth to Love,
Nor chide the Muse that stooped to break a spell
Which might have else been on me yet : —

FAREWELL.

Note. — LOUGHRIGG TARN, alluded to in the foregoing Epistle, resembles, though much smaller in compass, the Lake
Nemi, or *Speculum Dianæ* as it is often called, not only in its
clear waters and circular form, and the beauty immediately
surrounding it, but also as being overlooked by the eminence
of Langdale Pikes, as Lake Nemi is by that of Monte Calvo.
Since this Epistle was written, Loughrigg Tarn has lost much
of its beauty by the felling of many natural clumps of wood,
relics of the old forest, particularly upon the farm called " The
Oaks," from the abundance of that tree which grew there.

It is to be regretted, upon public grounds, that Sir George
Beaumont did not carry into effect his intention of constructing

UPON PERUSING THE FOREGOING EPISTLE THIRTY YEARS AFTER ITS COMPOSITION.

Soon did the Almighty Giver of all rest
Take those dear young Ones to a fearless nest;
And in Death's arms has long reposed the Friend
For whom this simple Register was penned.
Thanks to the moth that spared it for our eyes;
And Strangers even the slighted Scroll may prize,
Moved by the touch of kindred sympathies.
For, save the calm repentance sheds o'er strife
Raised by remembrances of misused life,
The light from past endeavors purely willed
And by Heaven's favor happily fulfilled, —
Save hope that we, yet bound to Earth, may share
The joys of the Departed, — what so fair
As blameless pleasure, not without some tears,
Reviewed through Love's transparent veil of years?

here a summer retreat in the style I have described; as his
taste would have set an example how buildings, with all the
accommodations modern society requires, might be introduced
even into the most secluded parts of this country without in-
juring their native character. The design was not abandoned
from failure of inclination on his part, but in consequence of
local untowardness which need not be particularized.

II.

GOLD AND SILVER FISHES IN A VASE.

THE soaring lark is blest as proud
   When at heaven's gate she sings;
The roving bee proclaims aloud
   Her flight by vocal wings;
While ye, in lasting durance pent,
   Your silent lives employ
For something more than dull content,
,   Though haply less than joy.

Yet might your glassy prison seem
   A place where joy is known,
Where golden flash and silver gleam
   Have meanings of their own;
While, high and low, and all about,
   Your motions, glittering Elves!
Ye weave,— no danger from without,
   And peace among yourselves.

Type of a sunny human breast
   Is your transparent cell;
Where Fear is but a transient guest,
   No sullen Humors dwell;
Where, sensitive of every ray
   That smites this tiny sea,
Your scaly panoplies repay
   The loan with usury.

How beautiful!—Yet none knows why
  This ever-graceful change,
Renewed, renewed incessantly,
  Within your quiet range.
Is it that ye with conscious skill
  For mutual pleasure glide;
And sometimes, not without your will,
  Are dwarfed, or magnified?

Fays, Genii of gigantic size!
  And now, in twilight dim,
Clustering like constellated eyes,
  In wings of Cherubim,
When the fierce orbs abate their glare;—
  Whate'er your forms express,
Whate'er ye seem, whate'er ye are,—
  All leads to gentleness.

Cold though your nature be, 't is pure;
  Your birthright is a fence
From all that haughtier kinds endure
  Through tyranny of sense.
Ah! not alone by colors bright
  Are ye to heaven allied,
When, like essential forms of light,
  Ye mingle, or divide.

For day-dreams soft as e'er beguiled
  Day-thoughts while limbs repose;
For moonlight fascinations mild,
  Your gift, ere shutters close,—

Accept, mute Captives ! thanks and praise ;
And may this tribute prove
That gentle admirations raise
Delight resembling love.

1828.

III.

LIBERTY.

(SEQUEL TO THE PRECEDING.)

[Addressed to a friend; the gold and silver fishes having
been removed to a pool in the pleasure-ground of Rydal
Mount.]

" The liberty of a people consists in being governed by laws
which they have made for themselves, under whatever form it
be of government. The liberty of a private man, in being
master of his own time and actions, as far as may consist with
the laws of God and of his country. Of this latter we are here
to discourse." — COWLEY.

THOSE breathing Tokens of your kind regard,
(Suspect not, Anna, that their fate is hard ;
Not soon does aught to which mild fancies cling
In lonely spots, become a slighted thing,)
Those silent Inmates now no longer share,
Nor do they need, our hospitable care,
Removed in kindness from their glassy Cell
To the fresh waters of a living Well,—
An elfin pool so sheltered that its rest
No winds disturb ; the mirror of whose breast
Is smooth as clear, save where with dimples small

A fly may settle, or a blossom fall.
— *There* swims, of blazing sun and beating shower
Fearless, (but how obscured!) the golden Power,
That from this bauble prison used to cast
Gleams by the richest jewel unsurpast;
And near him, darkling like a sullen Gnome,
The silver Tenant of the crystal dome;
Dissevered both from all the mysteries
Of hue and altering shape that charmed all eyes.
Alas! they pined, they languished while they
     shone;
And, if not so, what matters beauty gone
And admiration lost, by change of place
That brings to the inward creature no disgrace?
But if the change restore his birthright, then,
Whate'er the difference, boundless is the gain.
Who can divine what impulses from God
Reach the caged lark, within a town abode,
From his poor inch or two of daisied sod?
O yield him back his privilege! — No sea .
Swells like the bosom of a man set free;
A wilderness is rich with liberty.
Roll on, ye spouting whales, who die or keep
Your independence in the fathomless Deep!
Spread, tiny nautilus, the living sail;
Dive, at thy choice, or brave the freshening gale!
If unreproved the ambitious eagle mount
Sunward to seek the daylight in its fount,
Bays, gulfs, and ocean's Indian width shall be,
Till the world perishes, a field for thee!

While musing here I sit in shadow cool,
And watch these mute Companions, in the pool
(Among reflected boughs of leafy trees)
By glimpses caught, disporting at their ease,
Enlivened, braced, by hardy luxuries,
I ask what warrant fixed them (like a spell
Of witchcraft fixed them) in the crystal cell ;
To wheel with languid motion round and round,
Beautiful, yet in mournful durance bound.
Their peace, perhaps, our lightest footfall marred ;
On their quick sense our sweetest music jarred ;
And whither could they dart, if seized with fear ?
No sheltering stone, no tangled root was near.
When fire or taper ceased to cheer the room,
They wore away the night in starless gloom ;
And, when the sun first dawned upon the streams,
How faint their portion of his vital beams !
Thus, and unable to complain, they fared,
While not one joy of ours by them was shared.

Is there a cherished bird (I venture now
To snatch a sprig from Chaucer's reverend brow) —
Is there a brilliant fondling of the cage,
Though sure of plaudits on his costly stage,
Though fed with dainties from the snow-white hand
Of a kind mistress, fairest of the land,
But gladly would escape ; and, if need were,
Scatter the colors from the plumes that bear
The emancipated captive through blithe air
Into strange woods, where he at large may live

On best or worst which they and Nature give?
The beetle loves his unpretending track,
The snail the house he carries on his back;
The far-fetched worm with pleasure would disown
The bed we give him, though of softest down;
A noble instinct; in all kinds the same,
All ranks!   What Sovereign, worthy of the name,
If doomed to breathe against his lawful will
An element that flatters him — to kill,
But would rejoice to barter outward show
For the least boon that freedom can bestow?

But most the Bard is true to inborn right,
Lark of the dawn, and Philomel of night,
Exults in freedom, can with rapture vouch
For the dear blessings of a lowly couch,
A natural meal,—days, months, from Nature's hand;
Time, place, and business, all at his command! —
Who bends to happier duties, who more wise,
Than the industrious Poet, taught to prize
Above all grandeur a pure life uncrossed
By cares in which simplicity is lost?
That life, the flowery path that winds by stealth,
Which Horace needed for his spirit's health;
Sighed for, in heart and genius, overcome
By noise and strife, and questions wearisome,
And the vain splendors of Imperial Rome? —
Let easy mirth his social hours inspire,
And fiction animate his sportive lyre,
Attuned to verse that, crowning light Distress

With garlands, cheats her into happiness;
Give *me* the humblest note of those sad strains
Drawn forth by pressure of his gilded chains,
As a chance sunbeam from his memory fell
Upon the Sabine farm he loved so well;
Or when the prattle of Blandusia's spring
Haunted his ear, — he only listening, —
He proud to please, above all rivals, fit
To win the palm of gayety and wit;
He, doubt not, with involuntary dread,
Shrinking from each new favor to be shed,
By the world's Ruler, on his honored head!

In a deep vision's intellectual scene,
Such earnest longings and regrets as keen
Depressed the melancholy Cowley, laid
Under a fancied yew-tree's luckless shade;
A doleful bower for penitential song,
Where Man and Muse complained of mutual wrong
While Cam's ideal current glided by,
And antique towers nodded their foreheads high,
Citadels dear to studious privacy.
But Fortune, who had long been used to sport
With this tried Servant of a thankless Court,
Relenting met his wishes; and to you
The remnant of his days at least was true;
You, whom, though long deserted, he loved best;
You, Muses, books, fields, liberty, and rest!

Far happier they who, fixing hope and aim
On the humanities of peaceful fame,

Enter betimes with more than martial fire
The generous course, aspire, and still aspire;
Upheld by warnings heeded not too late,
Stifle the contradictions of their fate,
And to one purpose cleave, their Being's godlike
     mate !

   Thus, gifted Friend, but with the placid brow
That woman ne'er should forfeit, keep *thy* vow;
With modest scorn reject whate'er would blind
The ethereal eyesight, cramp the wingèd mind !
Then, with a blessing granted from above
To every act, word, thought, and look of love,
Life's book for Thee may lie unclosed, till age
Shall with a thankful tear bedrop its latest page.*
                      1829.

* There is now, alas! no possibility of the anticipation,
with which the above Epistle concludes, being realized: nor
were the verses ever seen by the Individual for whom they
were intended.   She accompanied her husband, the Rev. Wm.
Fletcher, to India, and died of cholera, at the age of thirty-two
or thirty-three years, on her way from Shalapore to Bombay,
deeply lamented by all who knew her.

Her enthusiasm was ardent, her piety steadfast; and her
great talents would have enabled her to be eminently useful
in the difficult path of life to which she had been called.   The
opinion she entertained of her own performances, given to the
world under her maiden name, Jewsbury, was modest and
humble, and, indeed, far below their merits; as is often the
case with those who are making trial of their powers, with a
hope to discover what they are best fitted for.   In one quality
namely, quickness in the motions of her mind, she had, within
the range of the Author's acquaintance, no equal.

IV.

POOR ROBIN.*

Now when the primrose makes a splendid show,
And lilies face the March-winds in full blow,
And humbler growths, as moved with one desire,
Put on, to welcome spring, their best attire,
Poor Robin is yet flowerless ; but how gay
With his red stalks upon this sunny day !
And, as his tufts of leaves he spreads, content
With a hard bed and scanty nourishment,
Mixed with the green, some shine not lacking power
To rival summer's brightest scarlet flower ;
And flowers they well might seem to passers-by
If looked at only with a careless eye ;
Flowers, — or a richer produce (did it suit
The season), sprinklings of ripe strawberry fruit.

But while a thousand pleasures come unsought,
Why fix upon his wealth or want a thought ?
Is the string touched in prelude to a lay
Of pretty fancies that would round him play
When all the world acknowledged elfin sway ?
Or does it suit our humor to commend
Poor Robin as a sure and crafty friend,
Whose practice teaches, spite of names to show
Bright colors whether they deceive or no ? —

* The small wild Geranium known by that name.

Nay, we would simply praise the free good-will
With which, though slighted, he, on naked hill
Or in warm valley, seeks his part to fill;
Cheerful alike if bare of flowers as now,
Or when his tiny gems shall deck his brow:
Yet more, we wish that men by men despised,
And such as lift their foreheads overprized,
Should sometimes think, where'er they chance to spy
This child of Nature's own humility,
What recompense is kept in store or left
For all that seem neglected or bereft;
With what nice care equivalents are given;
How just, how bountiful, the hand of Heaven.

MARCH, 1840.

V.

THE GLEANER.

(SUGGESTED BY A PICTURE.)

THAT happy gleam of vernal eyes,
Those locks from summer's golden skies,
    That o'er thy brow are shed;
That cheek, — a kindling of the morn, —
That lip, — a rose-bud from the thorn, —
    I saw; and Fancy sped
To scenes Arcadian, whispering, through soft air,
Of bliss that grows without a care,

And happiness that never flies, —
(How can it where love never dies ?) —
Whispering of promise, where no blight
Can reach the innocent delight ;
Where pity, to the mind conveyed
In pleasure, is the darkest shade
That Time, unwrinkled grandsire, flings
From his smoothly gliding wings.

What mortal form, what earthly face,
Inspired the pencil, lines to trace,
And mingle colors, that should breed
Such rapture, nor want power to feed ;
For had thy charge been idle flowers,
Fair Damsel ! o'er my captive mind,
To truth and sober reason blind,
'Mid that soft air, those long-lost bowers,
The sweet illusion might have hung, for hours.

Thanks to this tell-tale sheaf of corn,
That touchingly bespeaks thee born
Life's daily tasks with them to share
Who, whether from their lowly bed
They rise, or rest the weary head,
Ponder the blessing they entreat
From Heaven, and *feel* what they repeat,
While they give utterance to the prayer
That asks for daily bread.

1823.

VI.

TO A REDBREAST — (IN SICKNESS).

STAY, little cheerful Robin! stay,
  And at my casement sing,
Though it should prove a farewell lay
  And this our parting spring.

Though I, alas! may ne'er enjoy
  The promise in thy song,
A charm, *that* thought cannot destroy,
  Doth to thy strain belong.

Methinks that in my dying hour
  Thy song would still be dear,
And with a more than earthly power
  My passing Spirit cheer.

Then, little Bird, this boon confer:
  Come, and my requiem sing,
Nor fail to be the harbinger
  Of everlasting Spring.

S. H.

VII.

I KNOW an aged Man constrained to dwell
In a large house of public charity,

Where he abides, as in a Prisoner's cell,
With numbers near, alas! no company.

When he could creep about, at will, though poor
And forced to live on alms, this old Man fed
A Redbreast, one that to his cottage door
Came not, but in a lane partook his bread.

There, at the root of one particular tree,
An easy seat this worn-out Laborer found,
While Robin pecked the crumbs upon his knee
Laid one by one, or scattered on the ground.

Dear intercourse was theirs, day after day;
What signs of mutual gladness when they met!
Think of their common peace, their simple play,
The parting moment and its fond regret.

Months passed in love that failed not to fulfil,
In spite of season's change, its own demand,
By fluttering pinions here and busy bill;
There by caresses from a tremulous hand.

Thus in the chosen spot a tie so strong
Was formed between the solitary pair,
That, when his fate had housed him 'mid a throng,
The Captive shunned all converse proffered there.

Wife, children, kindred, they were dead and gone;
But, if no evil hap his wishes crossed,

One living Stay was left, and on that one
Some recompense for all that he had lost.

O that the good old Man had power to prove,
By message sent through air or visible token,
That still he loves the Bird, and still must love;
That friendship lasts though fellowship is broken!

1846.

VIII.

SONNET.

(TO AN OCTOGENARIAN.)

AFFECTIONS lose their object; Time brings forth
No successors; and, lodged in memory,
If love exist no longer, it must die, —
Wanting accustomed food, must pass from earth,
Or never hope to reach a second birth.
This sad belief, the happiest that is left
To thousands, share not thou; howe'er bereft,
Scorned, or neglected, fear not such a dearth.
Though poor and destitute of friends thou art,
Perhaps the sole survivor of thy race,
One to whom Heaven assigns that mournful part
The utmost solitude of age to face,
Still shall be left some corner of the heart
Where Love for living Thing can find a place.

1846.

IX.

FLOATING ISLAND

These lines are by the Author of the Address to the Wind,
&c., published heretofore along with my Poems.   Those to a
Redbreast are by a deceased female Relative.

HARMONIOUS Powers with Nature work
On sky, earth, river, lake, and sea ;
Sunshine and cloud, whirlwind and breeze,
All in one duteous task agree.

Once did I see a slip of earth
(By throbbing waves long undermined)
Loosed from its hold ; how, no one knew,
But all might see it float, obedient to the wind ;

Might see it, from the mossy shore
Dissevered, float upon the Lake,
Float with its crest of trees adorned
On which the warbling birds their pastime take.

Food, shelter, safety, there they find ;
There berries ripen, flowerets bloom ;
There insects live their lives, and die :
A peopled world it is ; in size a tiny room.

And thus through many seasons' space
This little Island may survive ;
But Nature, though we mark her not,
Will take away, may cease to give.

Perchance when you are wandering forth
Upon some vacant sunny day,
Without an object, hope, or fear,
Thither your eyes may turn, — the Isle is passed
    away ;

Buried beneath the glittering Lake,
Its place no longer to be found ;
Yet the lost fragments shall remain
To fertilize some other ground.

D. W.

X.

How beautiful the Queen of Night, on high
Her way pursuing among scattered clouds,
Where, ever and anon, her head she shrouds,
Hidden from view in dense obscurity.
But look, and to the watchful eye
A brightening edge will indicate that soon
We shall behold the struggling Moon
Break forth, again to walk the clear blue sky.

XI.

" Late, late yestreen I saw the new moone
  Wi' the auld moone in hir arme."
Ballad of Sir Patrick Spence, Percy's Reliques.

ONCE I could hail (howe'er serene the sky)
The moon re-entering her monthly round,

No faculty yet given me to espy
The dusky Shape within her arms imbound,
That thin memento of effulgence lost
Which some have named her Predecessor's ghost.

Young, like the Crescent that above me shone,
Naught I perceived within it dull or dim ;
All that appeared was suitable to one
Whose fancy had a thousand fields to skim ;
To expectations spreading with wild growth,
And hope that kept with me her plighted troth.

I saw (ambition quickening at the view)
A silver boat launched on a boundless flood ;
A pearly crest, like Dian's when it threw
Its brightest splendor round a leafy wood ;
But not a hint from under-ground, no sign
Fit for the glimmering brow of Proserpine.

Or was it Dian's self that seemed to move
Before me ? — nothing blemished the fair sight ;
On her I looked whom jocund Fairies love,
Cynthia, who puts the *little* stars to flight,
And by that thinning magnifies the great,
For exaltation of her sovereign state.

And when I learned to mark the spectral Shape
As each new Moon obeyed the call of time,
If gloom fell on me, swift was my escape ;
Such happy privilege hath life's gay Prime,

To see or not to see, as best may please
A buoyant Spirit, and a heart at ease.

Now, dazzling Stranger ! when thou meet'st my
          glance,
Thy dark Associate ever I discern ;
Emblem of thoughts too eager to advance
While I salute my joys, thoughts sad or stern ;
Shades of past bliss, or phantoms that, to gain
Their fill of promised lustre, wait in vain.

So changes mortal Life with fleeting years ;
A mournful change, should Reason fail to bring
The timely insight that can temper fears,
And from vicissitude remove its sting ;
While Faith aspires to seats in that domain
Where joys are perfect, — neither wax nor wane.

                                        1826.

XII.

TO THE LADY FLEMING,

ON SEEING THE FOUNDATION PREPARING FOR THE EREC-
TION OF RYDAL CHAPEL, WESTMORELAND.

I.

BLEST is this Isle, — our native Land ;
Where battlement and moated gate
Are objects only for the hand

Of hoary Time to decorate;
Where shady hamlet, town that breathes
Its busy smoke in social wreaths,
No rampart's stern defence require,
Naught but the heaven-directed spire,
And steeple tower (with pealing bells
Far heard), — our only citadels.

II.

O Lady! from a noble line
Of chieftains sprung, who stoutly bore
The spear, yet gave to works divine
A bounteous help in days of yore,
(As records mouldering in the Dell
Of Nightshade * haply yet may tell,)
Thee kindred aspirations moved
To build, within a vale beloved,
For Him upon whose high behests
All peace depends, all safety rests.

III.

How fondly will the woods embrace
This daughter of thy pious care,
Lifting her front with modest grace
To make a fair recess more fair,
And to exalt the passing hour,
Or soothe it with a healing power
Drawn from the Sacrifice fulfilled,

* Bekangs Ghyll, — or the dell of Nightshade, — in which
stands St. Mary's Abbey in Low Furness.

Before this rugged soil was tilled,
Or human habitation rose
To interrupt the deep repose !

IV.

Well may the villagers rejoice !
Nor heat, nor cold, nor weary ways,
Will be a hindrance to the voice
That would unite in prayer and praise ;
More duly shall wild, wandering Youth
Receive the curb of sacred truth,
Shall tottering Age, bent earthward, hear
The Promise, with uplifted ear ;
And all shall welcome the new ray
Imparted to their Sabbath-day.

V.

Nor deem the Poet's hope misplaced,
His fancy cheated, that can see
A shade upon the future cast,
Of time's pathetic sanctity ;
Can hear the monitory clock
Sound o'er the lake with gentle shock
At evening, when the ground beneath
Is ruffled o'er with cells of death ;
Where happy generations lie,
Here tutored for eternity.

VI.

Lives there a man whose sole delights
Are trivial pomp and city noise,

Hardening a heart that loathes or slights
What every natural heart enjoys?
Who never caught a noontide dream
From murmur of a running stream ·
Could strip, for aught the prospect yields
To him, their verdure from the fields;
And take the radiance from the clouds
In which the sun his setting shrouds?

VII.

A soul so pitiably forlorn,
If such do on this earth abide,
May season apathy with scorn,
May turn indifference to pride;
And still be not unblest, compared
With him who grovels, self-debarred
From all that lies within the scope
Of holy faith and Christian hope;
Or, shipwrecked, kindles on the coast
False fires, that others may be lost.

VIII.

Alas that such perverted zeal
Should spread on Britain's favored ground!
That public order, private weal,
Should e'er have felt or feared a wound
From champions of the desperate law
Which from their own blind hearts they draw;
Who tempt their reason to deny
God, whom their passions dare defy,

And boast that they alone are free
Who reach this dire extremity

IX.

But turn we from these "bold, bad " men;
The way, mild Lady! that hath led
Down to their " dark, opprobrious den,"
Is all too rough for thee to tread.
Softly as morning vapors glide
Down Rydal Cove from Fairfield's side,
Should move the tenor of *his* song
Who means to charity no wrong;
Whose offering gladly would accord
With this day's work, in thought and word.

X.

Heaven prosper it! may peace, and love,
And hope, and consolation, fall,
Through its meek influence, from above,
And penetrate the hearts of all;
All who, around the hallowed Fane,
Shall sojourn in this fair domain;
Grateful to thee, while service pure,
And ancient ordinance, shall endure,
For opportunity bestowed
To kneel together, and adore their God .

1823.

XIII.

ON THE SAME OCCASION.

Oh! gather whencesoe'er ye safely may
The help which slackening Piety requires;
Nor deem that he perforce must go astray
Who treads upon the footmarks of his sires.

Our churches, invariably perhaps, stand east and west, but *why* is by few persons *exactly* known; nor, that the degree of deviation from *due* east often noticeable in the ancient ones was determined, in each particular case, by the point in the hori zon at which the sun rose upon the day of the saint to whom the church was dedicated. These observances of our ancestors, and the causes of them, are the subject of the following stanzas.

WHEN, in the antique age of bow and spear
And feudal rapine clothed with iron mail,
Came ministers of peace intent to rear
The Mother Church in yon sequestered vale, —

Then to her Patron Saint a previous rite
Resounded with deep swell and solemn close,
Through unremitting vigils of the night,
Till from his couch the wished-for Sun uprose.

He rose, and straight, as by divine command,
They, who had waited for that sign to trace
Their work's foundation, gave with careful hand
To the high altar its determined place ; —

Mindful of Him who, in the Orient born,
There lived, and on the cross his life resigned,
And who, from out the regions of the morn,
Issuing in pomp, shall come to judge mankind.

So taught *their* creed;—nor failed the eastern sky,
'Mid these more awful feelings, to infuse
The sweet and natural hopes that shall not die,
Long as the sun his gladsome course renews.

For us hath such prelusive vigil ceased;
Yet still we plant, like men of elder days,
Our Christian altar faithful to the east,
Whence the tall window drinks the morning rays;

That obvious emblem giving to the eye
Of meek devotion, which erewhile it gave,
That symbol of the day-spring from on high,
Triumphant o'er the darkness of the grave.

1822.

XIV

THE HORN OF EGREMONT CASTLE.

Ere the Brothers through the gateway
Issued forth with old and young,
To the Horn Sir Eustace pointed,
Which for ages there had hung.

Horn it was which none could sound,
No one upon living ground,
Save he who came as rightful Heir
To Egremont's Domains and Castle fair.

Heirs from times of earliest record
Had the House of Lucie born,
Who of right had held the Lordship
Claimed by proof upon the Horn:
Each at the appointed hour
Tried the Horn, — it owned his power;
He was acknowledged: and the blast
Which good Sir Eustace sounded was the last.

With his lance Sir Eustace pointed,
And to Hubert thus said he:
" What I speak this horn shall witness
For thy better memory.
Hear, then, and neglect me not!
At this time, and on this spot,
The words are uttered from my heart,
As my last earnest prayer ere we depart.

" On good service we are going
Life to risk by sea and land,
In which course if Christ our Saviour
Do my sinful soul demand,
Hither come thou back straightway,
Hubert, if alive that day;
Return, and sound the Horn, that we
May have a living House still left in thee ! "

" Fear not," quickly answered Hubert ;
" As I am thy father's son,
What thou askest, noble Brother,
With God's favor shall be done."
So were both right well content :
Forth they from the Castle went,
And at the head of their array
To Palestine the Brothers took their **way.**

Side by side they fought, (the Lucies
Were a line for valor famed,)
And where'er their strokes alighted,
There the Saracens were tamed.
Whence, then, could it come, — the thought, —
By what evil spirit brought ?
O, can a brave Man wish to take
His Brother's life, for Lands' and Castle's **sake** ?

" Sir ! " the Ruffians said to Hubert,
" Deep he lies in Jordan flood."
Stricken by this ill assurance,
Pale and trembling Hubert stood.
" Take your earnings." — O that I
Could have *seen* my Brother die !
It was a pang that vexed him then ;
And oft returned, again, and yet again.

Months passed on, and no Sir Eustace !
Nor of him were tidings heard.
Wherefore, bold as day, the Murderer
Back again to England steered.

To his Castle Hubert sped ;
Nothing has he now to dread.
But silent and by stealth he came,
And at an hour which nobody could name.

None could tell if it were night-time,
Night or day, at even or morn ;
No one's eye had seen him enter,
No one's ear had heard the Horn.
But bold Hubert lives in glee :
Months and years went smilingly ;
With plenty was his table spread,
And bright the Lady is who shares his bed.

Likewise he had sons and daughters ;
And, as good men do, he sate
At his board by these surrounded,
Flourishing in fair estate.
And while thus in open day
Once he sate, as old books say,
A blast was uttered from the Horn,
Where by the Castle gate it hung forlorn.

'T is the breath of good Sir Eustace !
He is come to claim his right :
Ancient castle, woods, and mountains
Hear the challenge with delight.
Hubert ! though the blast be blown,
He is helpless and alone :
Thou hast a dungeon ; speak the word !
And there he may be lodged, and thou be Lord.

Speak ! — astounded Hubert cannot ;
And, if power to speak he had,
All are daunted, all the household
Smitten to the heart, and sad.
'T is Sir Eustace ; if it be
Living man, it must be he !
Thus Hubert thought in his dismay,
And by a postern gate he slunk away.

Long and long was he unheard of :
To his Brother then he came,
Made confession, asked forgiveness,
Asked it by a brother's name,
And by all the saints in heaven ;
And of Eustace was forgiven :
Then in a convent went to hide
His melancholy head, and there he died.

But Sir Eustace, whom good angels
Had preserved from murderers' hands,
And from Pagan chains had rescued,
Lived with honor on his lands.
Sons he had, saw sons of theirs,
And through ages, heirs of heirs,
A long posterity renowned,
Sounded the Horn which they alone could sound.

1806.

XV.

GOODY BLAKE AND HARRY GILL.

A TRUE STORY.

O, WHAT 's the matter ? what 's the matter ?
What is 't that ails young Harry Gill ?
That evermore his teeth they chatter,
Chatter, chatter, chatter still !
Of waistcoats Harry has no lack,
Good duffle gray, and flannel fine ;
He has a blanket on his back,
And coats enough to smother nine.

In March, December, and in July,
'T is all the same with Harry Gill ;
The neighbors tell, and tell you truly,
His teeth they chatter, chatter still.
At night, at morning, and at noon,
'T is all the same with Harry Gill ;
Beneath the sun, beneath the moon,
His teeth they chatter, chatter still !

Young Harry was a lusty drover,
And who so stout of limb as he ?
His cheeks were red as ruddy clover ;
His voice was like the voice of three.
Old Goody Blake was old and poor ;
Ill fed she was and thinly clad ;
And any man who passed her door
Might see how poor a hut she had.

All day she spun in her poor dwelling :
And then her three hours' work at night,
Alas ! 't was hardly worth the telling,
It would not pay for candle-light.
Remote from sheltered village-green,
On a hill's northern side she dwelt,
Where from sea-blasts the hawthorns lean,
And hoary dews are slow to melt.

By the same fire to boil their pottage,
Two poor old Dames, as I have known,
Will often live in one small cottage ;
But she, poor Woman ! housed alone.
'T was well enough when summer came,
The long, warm, lightsome summer-day ;
Then at her door the *canty* Dame
Would sit, as any linnet gay.

But when the ice our streams did fetter,
O then how her old bones would shake !
You would have said, if you had met her,
'T was a hard time for Goody Blake.
Her evenings then were dull and dead :
Sad case it was, as you may think,
For very cold to go to bed,
And then for cold not sleep a wink.

O joy for her ! whene'er in winter
The winds at night had made a rout,
And scattered many a lusty splinter
And many a rotten bough about.

Yet never had she, well or sick,
As every man who knew her says,
A pile beforehand, turf or stick,
Enough to warm her for three days.

Now, when the frost was past enduring,
And made her poor old bones to ache,
Could anything be more alluring
Than an old hedge to Goody Blake?
And, now and then, it must be said,
When her old bones were cold and chill,
She left her fire, or left her bed,
To seek the hedge of Harry Gill!

Now Harry he had long suspected
This trespass of old Goody Blake;
And vowed that she should be detected,—
That he on her would vengeance take.
And oft from his warm fire he 'd go,
And to the fields his road would take;
And there, at night, in frost and snow,
He watched to seize old Goody Blake.

And once, behind a rick of barley,
Thus looking out did Harry stand:
The moon was full and shining clearly,
And crisp with frost the stubble land.
— He hears a noise, — he 's all awake, —
Again? — on tiptoe down the hill
He softly creeps, — 't is Goody Blake;
She 's at the hedge of Harry Gill!

Right glad was he when he beheld her:
Stick after stick did Goody pull:
He stood behind a bush of elder,
Till she had filled her apron full.
When with her load she turned about,
The by-way back again to take,
He started forward with a shout,
And sprang upon poor Goody Blake.

And fiercely by the arm he took her,
And by the arm he held her fast,
And fiercely by the arm he shook her,
And cried, " I 've caught you then at last!"
Then Goody, who had nothing said,
Her bundle from her lap let fall;
And, kneeling on the sticks, she prayed
To God that is the judge of all.

She prayed, her withered hand uprearing,
While Harry held her by the arm, —
" God! who art never out of hearing,
O may he never more be warm!"
The cold, cold moon above her head,
Thus on her knees did Goody pray:
Young Harry heard what she had said;
And icy cold he turned away.

He went complaining all the morrow
That he was cold and very chill:
His face was gloom, his heart was sorrow,
Alas! that day for Harry Gill!

That day he wore a riding-coat,
But not a whit the warmer he:
Another was on Thursday brought,
And ere the Sabbath he had three.

'T was all in vain, a useless matter,
And blankets were about him pinned;
Yet still his jaws and teeth they clatter,
Like a loose casement in the wind.
And Harry's flesh it fell away;
And all who see him say 't is plain,
That, live as long as live he may,
He never will be warm again.

No word to any man he utters,
Abed or up, to young or old;
But ever to himself he mutters,
" Poor Harry Gill is very cold."
Abed or up, by night or day,
His teeth they chatter, chatter still.
Now think, ye farmers all, I pray,
Of Goody Blake and Harry Gill!

1798.

XVI.

PRELUDE,

PREFIXED TO THE VOLUME ENTITLED "POEMS CHIEFLY
OF EARLY AND LATE YEARS."

In desultory walk through orchard grounds,
Or some deep chestnut grove, oft have I paused
The while a Thrush, urged rather than restrained
By gusts of vernal storm, attuned his song
To his own genial instincts ; and was heard
(Though not without some plaintive tones between)
To utter, above showers of blossom swept
From tossing boughs, the promise of a calm,
Which the unsheltered traveller might receive
With thankful spirit. The descant, and the wind
That seemed to play with it in love or scorn,
Encouraged and endeared the strain of words
That haply flowed from me, by fits of silence
Impelled to livelier pace. But now, my Book!
Charged with those lays, and others of like mood,
Or loftier pitch if higher rose the theme,
Go, single, yet aspiring to be joined
With thy Forerunners that through many a year
Have faithfully prepared each other's way, —
Go forth upon a mission best fulfilled
When and wherever, in this changeful world,
Power hath been given to please for higher ends
Than pleasure only ; gladdening to prepare

For wholesome sadness, troubling to refine,
Calming to raise; and, by a sapient Art
Diffused through all the mysteries of our Being,
Softening the toils and pains that have not ceased
To cast their shadows on our mother Earth
Since the primeval doom.   Such is the grace
Which, though unsued for, fails not to descend
With heavenly inspiration; such the aim
That Reason dictates; and, as even the wish
Has virtue in it, why should hope to me
Be wanting, that sometimes, where fancied ills
Harass the mind and strip from off the bowers
Of private life their natural pleasantness,
A Voice — devoted to the love whose seeds
Are sown in every human breast, to beauty
Lodged within compass of the humblest sight,
To cheerful intercourse with wood and field,
And sympathy with man's substantial griefs —
Will not be heard in vain?   And in those days
When unforeseen distress spreads far and wide
Among a People mournfully cast down,
Or into anger roused by venal words
In recklessness flung out to overturn
The judgment, and divert the general heart
From mutual good, some strain of thine, my
          Book!
Caught at propitious intervals, may win
Listeners who not unwillingly admit
Kindly emotion tending to console
And reconcile; and both with young and old

Exalt the sense of thoughtful gratitude
For benefits that still survive, by faith
In progress, under laws divine, maintained.

 RYDAL MOUNT, *March* 26, 1842.

XVII.

TO A CHILD.

WRITTEN IN HER ALBUM.

SMALL service is true service while it lasts :
Of humblest Friends, bright Creature ! scorn not
   one :
The Daisy, by the shadow that it casts,
Protects the lingering dew-drop from the Sun.

       1834.

XVIII.

LINES

**WRITTEN IN THE ALBUM OF THE COUNTESS OF LONSDALE
NOV. 5, 1834.**

LADY ! a Pen (perhaps with thy regard,
Among the Favored, favored not the least)
Left, 'mid the Records of this Book inscribed,
Deliberate traces, registers of thought

And feeling, suited to the place and time
That gave them birth :— months passed, and still
      this hand,
That had not been too timid to imprint
Words which the virtues of thy Lord inspired,
Was yet not bold enough to write of thee.
And why that scrupulous reserve?   In sooth,
The blameless cause lay in the Theme itself.
Flowers are there many that delight to strive
With the sharp wind, and seem to court the shower,
Yet are by nature careless of the sun
Whether he shine on them or not; and some,
Where'er he moves along the unclouded sky,
Turn a broad front full on his fluttering beams:
Others do rather from their notice shrink,
Loving the dewy shade, — a humble band,
Modest and sweet, a progeny of earth,
Congenial with thy mind and character,
High-born Augusta !
              Witness Towers, and Groves!
And thou, wild Stream, that giv'st the honored
      name
Of Lowther to this ancient Line, bear witness
From thy most secret haunts; and ye Parterres,
Which She is pleased and proud to call her cwn,
Witness how oft upon my noble Friend
Mute offerings, tribute from an inward sense
Of admiration and respectful love,
Have waited, till the affections could no more
Endure that silence, and broke out in song

Snatches of music taken up and dropped,
Like those self-solacing, those under notes
Trilled by the redbreast, when autumnal leaves
Are thin upon the bough. Mine, only mine,
The pleasure was, and no one heard the praise,
Checked, in the moment of its issue, checked
And reprehended, by a fancied blush
From the pure qualities that called it forth.

Thus Virtue lives debarred from Virtue's meed;
Thus, Lady, is retiredness a veil,
That, while it only spreads a softening charm
O'er features looked at by discerning eyes,
Hides half their beauty from the common gaze;
And thus, even on the exposed and breezy hill
Of lofty station, female goodness walks,
When side by side with lunar gentleness,
As in a cloister. Yet the grateful Poor
(Such the immunities of low estate,
Plain Nature's enviable privilege,
Her sacred recompense for my wants)
Open their hearts before Thee, pouring out
All that they think and feel, with tears of joy,
And benedictions not unheard in heaven:
And friend in the ear of friend, where speech is free
To follow truth, is eloquent as they.

Then let the Book receive in these prompt lines
A just memorial; and thine eyes consent
To read that they, who mark thy course, behold

A life declining with the golden light
Of summer, in the season of sere leaves ;
See cheerfulness undamped by stealing Time ;
See studied kindness flow with easy stream,
Illustrated with inborn courtesy ;
And an habitual disregard of self
Balanced by vigilance for others' weal.

And shall the Verse not tell of lighter gifts
With these ennobling attributes conjoined
And blended, in peculiar harmony,
By youth's surviving spirit?   What agile grace !
A nymph-like liberty, in nymph-like form,
Beheld with wonder ; whether floor or path
Thou tread ; or sweep, borne on the managed
      steed,
Fleet as the shadows, over down or field,
Driven by strong winds at play among the clouds.

Yet one word more, — one farewell word, — a
      wish
Which came, but it has passed into a prayer, —
That, as thy sun in brightness is declining,
So — at an hour yet distant for *their* sakes
Whose tender love, here faltering on the way
Of a diviner love, will be forgiven, —
So may it set in peace, to rise again
For everlasting glory won by faith.

XIX.

GRACE DARLING.

AMONG the dwellers in the silent fields
The natural heart is touched, and public way
And crowded street resound with ballad strains,
Inspired by ONE whose very name bespeaks
Favor divine, exalting human love ;
Whom, since her birth on bleak Northumbria's
        coast,
Known unto few, but prized as far as known,
A single Act endears to high and low
Through the whole land ; — to Manhood, moved
        in spite
Of the world's freezing cares; to generous Youth;
To Infancy, that lisps her praise ; to Age
Whose eye reflects it, glistening through a tear
Of tremulous admiration.   Such true fáme
Awaits her *now ;* but, verily, good deeds
Do no imperishable record find,
Save in the rolls of heaven, where hers may live
A theme for angels, when they celebrate
The high-souled virtues which forgetful earth
Has witnessed.   O that winds and waves could
        speak
Of things which their united power called forth
From the pure depths of her humanity !
A Maiden gentle, yet, at duty's call,

Firm and unflinching as the Lighthouse reared
On the Island-rock, her lonely dwelling-place ;
Or like the invincible Rock itself, that braves,
Age after age, the hostile elements,
As when it guarded holy Cuthbert's cell.

All night the storm had raged, nor ceased, nor
paused,
When, as day broke, the Maid, through misty air,
Espies far off a Wreck, amid the surf,
Beating on one of those disastrous isles, —
Half of a Vessel, half, — no more ; the rest
Had vanished, swallowed up with all that there
Had for the common safety striven in vain,
Or thither thronged for refuge.   With quick glance
Daughter and Sire through optic-glass discern,
Clinging about the remnant of this Ship,
Creatures — how precious in the Maiden's sight !
For whom, belike, the old Man grieves still more
Than for their fellow-sufferers ingulfed
Where every parting agony is hushed,
And hope and fear mix not in further strife.
" But courage, Father ! let us out to sea, —
A few may yet be saved."   The Daughter's words,
Her earnest tone, and look beaming with faith,
Dispel the Father's doubts : nor do they lack
The noble-minded Mother's helping hand
To launch the boat ; and with her blessing cheered,
And inwardly sustained by silent prayer,
Together they put forth, Father and Child !

Each grasps an oar, and struggling on they go, —
Rivals in effort ; and, alike intent
Here to elude and there surmount, they watch
The billows lengthening, mutually crossed
And shattered, and regathering their might ;
As if the tumult by the Almighty's will
Were, in the conscious sea, roused and prolonged,
That woman's fortitude — so tried, so proved —
May brighten more and more !

              True to the mark,
They stem the current of that perilous gorge,
Their arms still strengthening with the strength-
      ening heart,
Though danger, as the Wreck is neared, becomes
More imminent.   Not unseen do they approach ;
And rapture, with varieties of fear
Incessantly conflicting, thrills the frames
Of those who, in that dauntless energy,
Foretaste deliverance ; but the least perturbed
Can scarcely trust his eyes, when he perceives
That of the pair, — tossed on the waves to bring
Hope to the hopeless, to the dying, life —
One is a Woman, a poor earthly sister,
Or, be the Visitant other than she seems,
A guardian Spirit sent from pitying Heaven,
In woman's shape.   But why prolong the tale,
Casting weak words amid a host of thoughts
Armed to repel them ?   Every hazard faced
And difficulty mastered, with resolve

That no one breathing should be left to perish,
'This last remainder of the crew are all
Placed in the little boat, then o'er the deep
Are safely borne, landed upon the beach,
And, in fulfilment of God's mercy, lodged
Within the sheltering Lighthouse. — Shout, ye
     Waves!
Send forth a song of triumph.   Waves and Winds,
Exult in this deliverance wrought through faith
In Him whose Providence your rage hath served!
Ye screaming Sea-mews, in the concert join!
And would that some immortal Voice — a Voice
Fitly attuned to all that gratitude
Breathes out from floor or couch, through pallid lips
Of the survivors — to the clouds might bear, —
Blended with praise of that parental love,
Beneath whose watchful eye the Maiden grew
Pious and pure, modest and yet so brave,
Though young so wise, though meek so resolute, —
Might carry to the clouds and to the stars,
Yea, to celestial Choirs, GRACE DARLING'S name!

                          1842.

XX.

THE RUSSIAN FUGITIVE.

PART I.

ENOUGH of rose-bud lips, and eyes
  Like harebells bathed in dew,
Of cheek that with carnation vies,
  And veins of violet hue ;
Earth wants not beauty that may scorn
  A likening to frail flowers ;
Yea, to the stars, if they were born
  For seasons and for hours.

Through Moscow's gates, with gold unbarred,
  Stepped one at dead of night,
Whom such high beauty could not guard
  From meditated blight ;
By stealth she passed, and fled as fast
  As doth the hunted fawn,
Nor stopped, till in the dappling east
  Appeared unwelcome dawn.

Seven days she lurked in brake and field,
  Seven nights her course renewed,
Sustained by what her scrip might yield,
  Or berries of the wood ;
At length, in darkness travelling on,
  When lowly doors were shut,
The haven of her hope she won,
  Her Foster-mother's hut.

"To put your love to dangerous proof
  I come," said she, "from far;
For I have left my Father's roof,
  In terror of the Czar."
No answer did the Matron give,
  No second look she cast,
But hung upon the Fugitive,
  Embracing and embraced.

She led the Lady to a seat
  Beside the glimmering fire,
Bathed duteously her way-worn feet,
  Prevented each desire: —
The cricket chirped, the house-dog dozed,
  And on that simple bed,
Where she in childhood had reposed,
  Now rests her weary head.

When she, whose couch had been the sod,
  Whose curtain, pine or thorn,
Had breathed a sigh of thanks to God,
  Who comforts the forlorn;
While over her the Matron bent,
  Sleep sealed her eyes, and stole
Feeling from limbs with travel spent,
  And trouble from the soul.

Refreshed, the Wanderer rose at morn,
  And soon again was dight
In those unworthy vestments worn
  Through long and perilous flight;

And "O beloved Nurse!" she said,
  " My thanks with silent tears
Have unto Heaven and you been paid:
  Now listen to my fears!

" Have you forgot " — and here she smiled —
  " The babbling flatteries
You lavished on me when a child
  Disporting round your knees?
I was your lambkin, and your bird,
  Your star, your gem, your flower :
Light words, that were more lightly heard
  In many a cloudless hour!

" The blossom you so fondly praised
  Is come to bitter fruit;
A mighty one upon me gazed;
  I spurned his lawless suit,
And must be hidden from his wrath:
  You, Foster-father dear
Will guide me in my forward path;
  I may not tarry here!

" I cannot bring to utter woe
  Your proved fidelity." —
" Dear Child, sweet Mistress, say not so!
  For you we both would die." —
" Nay, nay, I come with semblance feigned
  And check embrowned by art ·
Yet, being inwardly unstained,
  With courage will depart."

"But whither would you, could you, flee?
    A poor man's counsel take;
The Holy Virgin gives to me
    A thought for your dear sake;
Rest, shielded by our Lady's grace,
    And soon shall you be led
Forth to a safe abiding-place,
    Where never foot doth tread."

* * *

PART II.

THE dwelling of this faithful pair
    In a straggling village stood,
For one who breathed unquiet air
    A dangerous neighborhood;
But wide around lay forest ground
    With thickets rough and blind;
And pine-trees made a heavy shade
    Impervious to the wind.

And there, sequestered from the sight,
    Was spread a treacherous swamp,
On which the noonday sun shed light
    As from a lonely lamp;
And midway in the unsafe morass
    A single Island rose,
Of firm, dry ground with healthful grass
    Adorned, and shady boughs.

The Woodman knew, for such the craft
  This Russian vassal plied,
That never fowler's gun, nor shaft
  Of archer, there was tried;
A sanctuary seemed the spot
  From all intrusion free;
And there he planned an artful Cot
  For perfect secrecy.

With earnest pains, unchecked by dread
  Of Power's far-stretching hand,
The bold, good Man his labor sped
  At Nature's pure command;
Heart-soothed, and busy as a wren,
  While, in a hollow nook,
She moulds her sight-eluding den
  Above a murmuring brook.

His task accomplished to his mind,
  The twain, ere break of day
Creep forth, and through the forest wind
  Their solitary way;
Few words they speak, nor dare to slack
  Their pace from mile to mile,
Till they have crossed the quaking marsh,
  And reached the lonely Isle.

The sun above the pine-trees showed
  A bright and cheerful face,
And Ina looked for her abode,
  The promised hiding-place;

She sought in vain : the Woodman smiled ;
  No threshold could be seen,
Nor roof, nor window ; — all seemed wild
  As it had ever been.

Advancing, you might guess an hour,
  The front with such nice care
Is masked, " if house it be or bower,"
  But in they entered are ;
As shaggy as were wall and roof
  With branches intertwined,
So smooth was all within, air-proof,
  And delicately lined :

And hearth was there, and maple dish,
  And cups in seemly rows,
And couch, — all ready to a wish
  For nurture or repose ;
And Heaven doth to her virtue grant
  That there she may abide
In solitude, with every want
  By cautious love supplied.

No queen, before a shouting crowd,
  Led on in bridal state,
E'er struggled with a heart so proud,
  Entering her palace gate ;
Rejoiced to bid the world farewell,
  No saintly anchoress
E'er took possession of her cell
  With deeper thankfulness.

" Father of all, upon thy care
  And mercy am I thrown ;
Be thou my safeguard ! "—such her prayer
  When she was left alone,
Kneeling amid the wilderness
  When joy had passed away,
And smiles, fond efforts of distress
  To hide what they betray !

The prayer is heard, the Saints have seen,
  Diffused through form and face,
Resolves devotedly serene ;
  That monumental grace
Of Faith, which doth all passions tame
  That Reason *should* control ;
And shows in the untrembling frame
  A statue of the soul.

PART III.

'T is sung in ancient minstrelsy
  That Phœbus wont to wear
The leaves of any pleasant tree
  Around his golden hair ;
Till Daphne, desperate with pursuit
  Of his imperious love,
At her own prayer transformed, took root,
  A laurel in the grove.

Then did the penitent adorn
  His brow with laurel green;
And 'mid his bright locks never shorn
  No meaner leaf was seen;
And poets sage, through every age,
  About their temples wound
The bay; and conquerors thanked the Gods,
  With laurel chaplets crowned.

Into the mists of fabling Time
  So far runs back the praise
Of beauty, that disdains to climb
  Along forbidden ways;
That scorns temptation; power defies
  Where mutual love is not;
And to the tomb for rescue flies
  When life would be a blot.

To this fair Votaress, a fate
  More mild doth Heaven ordain
Upon her Island desolate;
  And words, not breathed in vain,
Might tell what intercourse she found
  Her silence to endear;
What birds she tamed, what flowers the ground
  Sent forth her peace to cheer.

To one mute Presence, above all
  Her soothed affections clung,
A picture on the cabin wall
  By Russian usage hung,—

The Mother-maid, whose countenance bright
  With love abridged the day ;
And, communed with by taper light,
  Chased spectral fears away.

And oft, as either Guardian came,
  The joy in that retreat
Might any common friendship shame,
  So high their hearts would beat ;
And to the lone Recluse, whate'er
  They brought, each visiting
Was like the crowding of the year
  With a new burst of spring.

But when she of her Parents thought,
  The pang was hard to bear ;
And, if with all things not enwrought,
  That trouble still is near.
Before her flight she had not dared
  Their constancy to prove ;
Too much the heroic Daughter feared
  The weakness of their love.

Dark is the past to them, and dark
  The future still must be,
Till pitying Saints conduct her bark
  Into a safer sea, —
Or gentle Nature close her eyes,
  And set her Spirit free
From the altar of this sacrifice,
  In vestal purity.

Yet, when above the forest-glooms
    The white swans southward passed,
High as the pitch of their swift plumes
    Her fancy rode the blast ;
And bore her toward the fields of France,
    Her Father's native land,
To mingle in the rustic dance,
    The happiest of the band !

Of those belovèd fields she oft
    Had heard her Father tell
In phrase that now with echoes soft
    Haunted her lonely cell ;
She saw the hereditary bowers,
    She heard the ancestral stream ;
The Kremlin and its haughty towers
    Forgotten like a dream !

PART IV.

THE ever-changing Moon had traced
    Twelve times her monthly round,
When through the unfrequented Waste
    Was heard a startling sound ;
A shout thrice sent from one who chased
    At speed a wounded deer,
Bounding through branches interlaced,
    And where the wood was clear.

The fainting creature took the marsh,
 And toward the Island fled,
While plovers screamed, with tumult harsh,
 Above his antlered head;
This Ina saw, and, pale with fear,
 Shrunk to her citadel;
The desperate deer rushed on, and near
 The tangled covert fell.

Across the marsh, the game in view,
 The Hunter followed fast,
Nor paused, till o'er the stag he blew
 A death-proclaiming blast;
Then, resting on her upright mind,
 Came forth the Maid. "In me
Behold," she said, "a stricken Hind
 Pursued by destiny!

"From your deportment, Sir! I deem
 That you have worn a sword,
And will not hold in light esteem
 A suffering woman's word;
There is my covert, there perchance
 I might have lain concealed,
My fortunes hid, my countenance
 Not even to you revealed.

"Tears might be shed, and I might pray,
 Crouching and terrified,
That what has been unveiled to-day
 You would in mystery hide;

But I will not defile with dust
  The knee that bends to adore
The God in heaven ;—attend, be just ;
  This ask I, and no more !

" I speak not of the winter's cold,
  For summer's heat exchanged,
While I have lodged in this rough hold,
  From social life estranged ;
Nor yet of trouble and alarms :
  High Heaven is my defence ;
And every season has soft arms
  For injured Innocence.

" From Moscow to the Wilderness
  It was my choice to come,
Lest virtue should be harborless,
  And honor want a home ;
And happy were I, if the Czar
  Retain his lawless will,
To end life here like this poor deer,
  Or a lamb on a green hill."

" Are you the Maid," the Stranger cried,
  " From Gallic parents sprung,
Whose vanishing was rumored wide,
  Sad theme for every tongue ?
Who foiled an Emperor's eager quest ?
  You, Lady, forced to wear
These rude habiliments, and rest
  Your head in this dark lair ! "

But wonder, pity, soon were quelled ;
    And in her face and mien
The soul's pure brightness he beheld
    Without a veil between :
He loved, he hoped, — a holy flame
    Kindled 'mid rapturous tears ;
The passion of a moment came
    As on the wings of years.

" Such bounty is no gift of chance,"
    Exclaimed he ; "righteous Heaven,
Preparing your deliverance,
    To me the charge hath given. -
The Czar full oft in words and deeds
    Is stormy and self-willed ;
But when the Lady Catherine pleads,
    His violence is stilled.

" Leave open to my wish the course,
    And I to her will go ;
From that humane and heavenly source
    Good, only good, can flow."
Faint sanction given, the Cavalier
    Was eager to depart,
Though question followed question, dear
    To the Maiden's filial heart.

Light was his step, — his hopes, more light,
    Kept pace with his desires ;
And the fifth morning gave him sight
    Of Moscow's glittering spires.

He sued: — heart-smitten by the wrong,
  To the lorn Fugitive
Thë Emperor sent a pledge as strong
  As sovereign power could give.

A more than mighty change! If e'er
  Amazement rose to pain,
And joy's excess produced a fear
  Of something void and vain,
'T was when the Parents, who had mourned
  So long the lost as dead,
Beheld their only Child returned,
  The household floor to tread.

Soon gratitude gave way to love
  Within the Maiden's breast:
Delivered and Deliverer move
  In bridal garments drest;
Meek Catherine had her own reward;
  The Czar bestowed a dower;
And universal Moscow shared
  The triumph of that hour.

Flowers strewed the ground; the nuptial feast
  Was held with costly state;
And there, 'mid many a noble guest,
  The Foster-parents sate;
Encouraged by the imperial eye,
  They shrank not into shade;
Great was their bliss, the honor high
  To them and nature paid!

1830.

INSCRIPTIONS.

I.

IN THE GROUNDS OF COLEORTON, THE SEAT OF SIR GEORGE
BEAUMONT, BART., LEICESTERSHIRE.

1808.

THE embowering rose, the acacia, and the pine
Will not unwillingly their place resign,
If but the Cedar thrive that near them stands,
Planted by Beaumont's and by Wordsworth's
    hands.
One wooed the silent Art with studious pains :
These groves have heard the other's pensive
    strains ;
Devoted thus, their spirits did unite
By interchange of knowledge and delight.
May Nature's kindliest powers sustain the Tree,
And Love protect it from all injury !
And when its potent branches, wide out-thrown,
Darken the brow of this memorial Stone,
Here may some Painter sit in future days,
Some future Poet meditate his lays ;
Not mindless of that distant age renowned

When Inspiration hovered o'er this ground,
The haunt of him who sang how spear and shield
In civil conflict met on Bosworth-field;
And of that famous Youth, full soon removed
From earth, perhaps by Shakespeare's self ap-
        proved,
Fletcher's Associate, Jonson's Friend beloved.

II.

IN A GARDEN OF THE SAME.

OFT is the medal faithful to its trust
When temples, columns, towers, are laid in dust;
And 't is a common ordinance of fate
That things obscure and small outlive the great:
Hence, when yon mansion and the flowery trim
Of this fair garden, and its alleys dim,
And all its stately trees, are passed away,
This little Niche, unconscious of decay,
Perchance may still survive.   And be it known
That it was scoped within the living stone, —
Not by the sluggish and ungrateful pains
Of laborer plodding for his daily gains,
But by an industry that wrought in love;
With help from female hands, that proudly strove
To aid the work, what time these walks and bowers
Were shaped to cheer dark Winter's lonely hours.

III.

WRITTEN AT THE REQUEST OF SIR GEORGE BEAUMONT,
BART., AND IN HIS NAME, FOR AN URN, PLACED BY HIM
AT THE TERMINATION OF A NEWLY PLANTED AVENUE,
IN THE SAME GROUNDS.

YE Lime-trees, ranged before this hallowed Urn,
Shoot forth with livelier power at Spring's return;
And be not slow a stately growth to rear
Of pillars, branching off from year to year,
Till they have learned to frame a darksome aisle;—
That may recall to mind that awful Pile
Where Reynolds, 'mid our country's noblest dead,
In the last sanctity of fame is laid.
— There, though by right the excelling Painter
　　　sleep
Where Death and Glory a joint sabbath keep,
Yet not the less his Spirit would hold dear
Self-hidden praise, and Friendship's private tear:
Hence, on my patrimonial grounds, have I
Raised this frail tribute to his memory;
From youth a zealous follower of the Art
That he professed; attached to him in heart;
Admiring, loving, and with grief and pride
Feeling what England lost when Reynolds died.

IV.

FOR A SEAT IN THE GROVES OF COLEORTON.

BENEATH yon eastern ridge, the craggy bound,
Rugged and high, of Charnwood's forest ground,
Stand yet, but, Stranger! hidden from thy view,
The ivied Ruins of forlorn GRACE DIEU;
Erst a religious House, which day and night
With hymns resounded, and the chanted rite:
And when those rites had ceased, the Spot gave
    birth
To honorable Men of various worth:
There, on the margin of a streamlet wild,
Did Francis Beaumont sport, an eager child;
There, under shadow of the neighboring rocks,
Sang youthful tales of shepherds and their flocks;
Unconscious prelude to heroic themes,
Heart-breaking tears, and melancholy dreams
Of slighted love, and scorn, and jealous rage,
With which his genius shook the buskined stage.
Communities are lost, and Empires die,
And things of holy use unhallowed lie;
They perish;—but the Intellect can raise,
From airy words alone, a Pile that ne'er decays.
1808.

V.

WRITTEN WITH A PENCIL UPON A STONE IN THE WALL
OF THE HOUSE (AN OUT-HOUSE), ON THE ISLAND AT
GRASMERE.

RUDE is this Edifice, and thou hast seen
Buildings, albeit rude, that have maintained
Proportions more harmonious, and approached
To closer fellowship with ideal grace.
But take it in good part : — alas! the poor
Vitruvius of our village had no help
From the great City; never, upon leaves
Of red Morocco folio saw displayed,
In long succession, pre-existing ghosts
Of Beauties yet unborn, — the rustic Lodge
Antique, and Cottage with verandah graced,
Nor lacking, for fit company, alcove,
Green-house, shell-grot, and moss-lined hermitage.
Thou seest a homely Pile, yet to these walls
The heifer comes in the snow-storm, and here
The new-dropped lamb finds shelter from the wind.
And hither does one Poet sometimes row
His pinnace, a small vagrant barge, up-piled
With plenteous store of heath and withered fern,
(A·lading which he with his sickle cuts,
Among the mountains,) and beneath this roof
He makes his summer couch, and here at noon
Spreads out his limbs, while, yet unshorn, the Sheep,
Panting beneath the burden of their wool,
Lie round him, even as if they were a part

Of his own Household: nor, while from his bed
He looks, through the open door-place, toward
          the lake
And to the stirring breezes, does he want
Creations lovely as the work of sleep, —
Fair sights, and visions of romantic joy!

VI.

WRITTEN WITH A SLATE PENCIL ON A STONE, ON THE SIDE
OF THE MOUNTAIN OF BLACK COMB.

STAY, bold Adventurer; rest awhile thy limbs
On this commodious Seat! for much remains
Of hard ascent before thou reach the top
Of this huge Eminence, — from blackness named
And to far-travelled storms of sea and land
A favorite spot of tournament and war!
But thee may no such boisterous visitants
Molest; may gentle breezes fan thy brow;
And neither cloud conceal, nor misty air
Bedim, the grand terraqueous spectacle,
From centre to circumference unveiled!
Know, if thou grudge not to prolong thy rest,
That on the summit whither thou art bound
A geographic Laborer pitched his tent,
With books supplied and instruments of art,
To measure height and distance; lonely task,
Week after week pursued! — To him was given

Full many a glimpse (but sparingly bestowed
On timid man) of Nature's processes
Upon the exalted hills.   He made report
That once, while there he plied his studious work
Within that canvas Dwelling, colors, lines,
And the whole surface of the out-spread map,
Became invisible : for all around
Had   darkness   fallen, — unthreatened, unpro-
    claimed, —
As if the golden day itself had been
Extinguished in a moment ; total gloom,
In which he sat alone, with unclosed eyes,
Upon the blinded mountain's silent top !

1813.

VII.

WRITTEN WITH A SLATE PENCIL UPON A STONE, THE LAR-
GEST OF A HEAP LYING NEAR A DESERTED QUARRY, UPON
ONE OF THE ISLANDS AT RYDAL.

STRANGER ! this hillock of misshapen stones
Is not a Ruin spared or made by time,
Nor, as perchance thou rashly deem'st, the Cairn
Of some old British Chief : 't is nothing more
Than the rude embryo of a little Dome
Or Pleasure-house, once destined to be built
Among the birch-trees of this rocky isle.
But, as it chanced, Sir William having learned

That from the shore a full-grown man might wade,
And make himself a freeman of this spot
At any hour he chose, the prudent Knight
Desisted, and the quarry and the mound
Are monuments of his unfinished task.
The block on which these lines are traced, perhaps,
Was once selected as the corner-stone
Of that intended Pile, which would have been
Some quaint odd plaything of elaborate skill,
So that, I guess, the linnet and the thrush,
And other little builders who dwell here,
Had wondered at the work.   But blame him not,
For old Sir William was a gentle Knight,
Bred in this vale, to which he appertained
With all his ancestry.   Then peace to him,
And for the outrage which he had devised,
Entire forgiveness ! — But if thou art one
On fire with thy impatience to become
An inmate of these mountains, — if, disturbed
By beautiful conceptions, thou hast hewn
Out of the quiet rock the elements
Of thy trim Mansion destined soon to blaze
In snow-white splendor, — think again ; and, taught
By old Sir William and his quarry, leave
Thy fragments to the bramble and the rose ;
There let the vernal slow-worm sun himself,
And let the redbreast hop from stone to stone.

1800.

VIII.

In these fair vales hath many a Tree
　　At Wordsworth's suit been spared;
And from the builder's hand this Stone,
For some rude beauty of its own,
　　Was rescued by the Bard:
So let it rest; and time will come
　　When here the tender-hearted
May heave a gentle sigh for him,
　　As one of the departed.

1830.

IX.

The massy Ways, carried across these heights
By Roman perseverance, are destroyed,
Or hidden under ground, like sleeping worms.
How venture then to hope that Time will spare
This humble Walk?　Yet on the mountain's side
A Poet's hand first shaped it; and the steps
Of that same Bard — repeated to and fro
At morn, at noon, and under moonlight skies
Through the vicissitudes of many a year —
Forbade the weeds to creep o'er its gray line.
No longer, scattering to the heedless winds
The vocal raptures of fresh poesy,
Shall he frequent these precincts; locked no more

In earnest converse with beloved Friends,
Here will he gather stores of ready bliss,
As from the beds and borders of a garden
Choice flowers are gathered!   But, if Power may
      spring
Out of a farewell yearning, — favored more
Than kindred wishes mated suitably
With vain regrets, — the Exile would consign
This Walk, his loved possession, to the care
Of those pure Minds that reverence the Muse.

                                        1826.

X.

INSCRIPTIONS SUPPOSED TO BE FOUND IN AND NEAR A HERMIT'S CELL.

1818.

I.

HOPES, what are they? — Beads of morning
Strung on slender blades of grass;
Or a spider's web adorning
In a strait and treacherous pass.

What are fears but voices airy,
Whispering harm where harm is not,
And deluding the unwary
Till the fatal bolt is shot?

What is glory? — in the socket
See how dying tapers fare!
What is pride? — a whizzing rocket
That would emulate a star.

What is friendship? — do not trust her,
Nor the vows which she has made;
Diamonds dart their brightest.lustre
From a palsy-shaken head.

What is truth? — a staff rejected;
Duty? — an unwelcome clog;
Joy? — a moon by fits reflected
In a swamp or watery bog;

Bright, as if through ether steering,
To the Traveller's eye it shone:
He hath hailed it reappearing, —
And as quickly it is gone;

Such is Joy, — as quickly hidden,
Or misshapen to the sight,
And by sullen weeds forbidden
To resume its native light.

What is youth? — a dancing billow,
(Winds behind, and rocks before!)
Age? — a drooping, tottering willow
On a flat and lazy shore.

What is peace? — when pain is over
And love ceases to rebel,
Let the last faint sight discover
That precedes the passing-knell!

XI.

INSCRIBED UPON A ROCK.

II.

PAUSE, Traveller! whosoe'er thou be
Whom chance may lead to this retreat,
Where silence yields reluctantly
Even to the fleecy straggler's bleat;

Give voice to what my hand shall trace,
And fear not lest an idle sound
Of words unsuited to the place
Disturb its solitude profound.

I saw this Rock, while vernal air
Blew softly o'er the russet heath,
Uphold a Monument as fair
As church or abbey furnisheth.

Unsullied did it meet the day,
Like marble, white, like ether, pure;
As if, beneath, some hero lay,
Honored with costliest sepulture.

My fancy kindled as I gazed;
And, ever as the sun shone forth,
The flattered structure glistened, blazed,
And seemed the proudest thing on earth.

But frost had reared the gorgeous Pile,
Unsound as those which Fortune builds,
To undermine with secret guile,
Sapped by the very beam that gilds.

And, while I gazed, with sudden shock
Fell the whole Fabric to the ground;
And naked left this dripping Rock,
With shapeless ruin spread around!

XII.

III.

Hast thou seen, with flash incessant,
Bubbles gliding under ice,
Bodied forth and evanescent,
No one knows by what device?

Such are thoughts! — A wind-swept meadow
Mimicking a troubled sea,
Such is life; and death a shadow
From the rock eternity!

XIII.

NEAR THE SPRING OF THE HERMITAGE.

IV.

TROUBLED long with warring notions
Long impatient of thy rod,
I resign my soul's emotions
Unto Thee, mysterious God!

What avails the kindly shelter
Yielded by this craggy rent,
If my spirit toss and welter
On the waves of discontent?

Parching Summer hath no warrant
To consume this crystal Well;
Rains, that make each rill a torrent,
Neither sully it nor swell.

Thus, dishonoring not her station,
Would my Life present to Thee,
Gracious God, the pure oblation
Of divine tranquillity!

XIV.

V.

NOT seldom, clad in radiant vest,
Deceitfully goes forth the Morn;

·Not seldom Evening in the west
Sinks smilingly forsworn.

The smoothest seas will sometimes prove,
To the confiding Bark, untrue;
And, if she trust the stars above,
They can be treacherous too.

The umbrageous Oak, in pomp outspread,
Full oft, when storms the welkin rend,
Draws lightning down upon the head
It promised to defend.

But Thou art true, incarnate Lord,
Who didst vouchsafe for man to die;
Thy smile is sure, thy plighted word
No change can falsify!

I bent before thy gracious throne,
And asked for peace on suppliant knee;
And peace was given, — nor peace alone,
But faith sublimed to ecstasy!

XV.

FOR THE SPOT WHERE THE HERMITAGE STOOD ON ST.
HERBERT'S ISLAND, DERWENT-WATER.

If thou in the dear love of some one Friend
Hast been so happy that thou know'st what thoughts

Will sometimes in the happiness of love
Make the heart sink, then wilt thou reverence
This quiet spot; and, Stranger! not unmoved
Wilt thou behold this shapeless heap of stones,
The desolate ruins of St. Herbert's Cell.
Here stood his threshold; here was spread the roof
That sheltered him, a self-secluded Man,
After long exercise in social cares
And offices humane, intent to adore
The Deity, with undistracted mind,
And meditate on everlasting things,
In utter solitude. — But he had left
A Fellow-laborer, whom the good Man loved
As his own soul.   And when, with eye upraised
To heaven, he knelt before the crucifix,
While o'er the Lake the cataract of Lodore
Pealed to his orisons, and when he paced
Along the beach of this small isle and thought
Of his Companion, he would pray that both
(Now that their earthly duties were fulfilled)
Might die in the same moment.   Nor in vain
So prayed he: — as our chronicles report,
Though here the Hermit numbered his last day
Far from St. Cuthbert his beloved Friend,
Those holy Men both died in the same hour.

1800.

XVI.

ON THE BANKS OF A ROCKY STREAM.

BEHOLD an emblem of our human mind,
Crowded with thoughts that need a settled home,
Yet, like to eddying balls of foam
Within this whirlpool, they each other chase
Round and round, and neither find
An outlet nor a resting-place!
Stranger, if such disquietude be thine,
Fall on thy knees and sue for help divine.

SELECTIONS FROM CHAUCER.

MODERNIZED.

I.

THE PRIORESS' TALE.

"Call up him who left half told
The story of Cambuscan bold."

In the following Poem no further deviation from the original has been made than was necessary for the fluent reading and instant understanding of the Author: so much, however, is the language altered since Chaucer's time, especially in pronunciation, that much was removed, and its place supplied with as little incongruity as possible. The ancient accent has been retained in a few conjunctions, as *alsò* and *alwày*, from a conviction that such sprinklings of antiquity would be admitted, by persons of taste, to have a graceful ac cordance with the subject. The fierce bigotry of the Prioress forms a fine back-ground for her tender-hearted sympathies with the Mother and Child; and the mode in which the story is told amply atones for the extravagance of the miracle.

I.

"O LORD, our Lord! how wondrously," quoth she,
"Thy name in this large world is spread abroad !
For not alone by men of dignity
Thy worship is performed and precious laud ;

But by the mouths of children, gracious God !
Thy goodness is set forth ; they when they lie
Upon the breast thy name do glorify.

II.

Wherefore in praise, the worthiest that I may,
Jesu ! of thee, and the white Lily-flower
Which did thee bear, and is a Maid for aye,
To tell a story I will use my power ;
Not that I may increase her honor's dower,
For she herself is honor, and the root
Of goodness, next her Son, our soul's best boot.

III.

O Mother Maid ! O Maid and Mother free !
O bush unburnt ! burning in Moses' sight !
That down didst ravish from the Deity,
Through humbleness, the spirit that did alight
Upon thy heart, whence, through that glory's might,
Conceivèd was the Father's sapience,
Help me to tell it in thy reverence !

IV.

Lady ! thy goodness, thy magnificence,
Thy virtue, and thy great humility,
Surpass all science and all utterance ;
For sometimes, Lady ! ere men pray to thee
Thou goest before in thy benignity,
The light to us vouchsafing to our prayer,
To be our guide unto thy Son so dear.

v.

My knowledge is so weak, O blissful Queen !
To tell abroad thy mighty worthiness,
That I the weight of it may not sustain ;
But as a child of twelve months old or less,
That laboreth his language to express,
Even so fare I; and therefore, I thee pray,
Guide thou my song which I of thee shall say.

vi.

There was in Asia, in a mighty town,
'Mong Christian folk, a street where Jews might be,
Assigned to them and given them for their own
By a great Lord, for gain and usury,
Hateful to Christ and to his company ;
And through this street who list might ride and wend;
Free was it, and unbarred at either end.

vii.

A little school of Christian people stood
Down at the further end, in which there were
A nest of children come of Christian blood,
That learnèd in that school from year to year
Such sort of doctrine as men usèd there,
That is to say, to sing and read alsò,
As little children in their childhood do.

viii.

Among these children was a Widow's son,
A little scholar, scarcely seven years old,
Who day by day unto this school hath gone,

And eke, when he the image did behold
Of Jesu's Mother, as he had been told,
This Child was wont to kneel adown and say
Ave Marie, as he goeth by the way.

IX.

This Widow thus her little Son hath taught
Our blissful Lady, Jesu's Mother dear,
To worship aye, and he forgat it not;
For simple infant hath a ready ear.
Sweet is the holiness of youth: and hence,
Calling to mind this matter when I may,
Saint Nicholas in my presence standeth aye,
For he so young to Christ did reverence.

X.

This little Child, while in the school he sat
His Primer conning with an earnest cheer,
The whilst the rest their anthem-book repeat
The *Alma Redemptoris* did he hear;
And as he durst he drew him near and near,
And hearkened to the words and to the note,
Till the first verse he learned it all by rote.

XI.

This Latin knew he nothing what it said,
For he too tender was of age to know;
But to his comrade he repaired, and prayed
That he the meaning of this song would show,
And unto him declare why men sing so;
This oftentimes, that he might be at ease,
This child did him beseech on his bare knees.

XII.

His Schoolfellow, who elder was than he,
Answered him thus: 'This song, I have heard say,
Was fashioned for our blissful Lady free;
Her to salute, and also her to pray
To be our help upon our dying day:
If there is more in this, I know it not;
Song do I learn,—small grammar I have got.'

XIII.

' And is this song fashioned in reverence
Of Jesu's Mother?' said this Innocent;
' Now, certès, I will use my diligence
To con it all ere Christmas-tide be spent;
Although I for my Primer shall be shent,
And shall be beaten three times in an hour,
Our Lady I will praise with all my power.'

XIV.

His Schoolfellow, whom he had so besought,
As they went homeward, taught him privily,
And then he sang it well and fearlessly,
From word to word according to the note:
Twice in a day it passèd through his throat;
Homeward and schoolward whensoe'er he went,
On Jesu's Mother fixed was his intent.

XV.

Through all the Jewry (this before said I)
This little Child, as he came to and fro,
Full merrily then would he sing and cry,

O Alma Redemptoris! high and low:
The sweetness of Christ's Mother piercèd so
His heart, that her to praise, to her to pray,
He cannot stop his singing by the way.

XVI

The Serpent, Satan, our first foe, that hath
His wasp's nest in Jew's heart, upswelled. 'O woe,
O Hebrew people!' said he in his wrath,
' Is it an honest thing?   Shall this be so?
That such a Boy where'er he lists shall go
In your despite, and sing his hymns and saws,
Which is against the reverence of our laws!'

XVII.

From that day forward have the Jews conspired
Out of the world this Innocent to chase;
And to this end a Homicide they hired,
That in an alley had a privy place,
And, as the Child 'gan to the school to pace,
This cruel Jew him seized, and held him fast
And cut his throat, and in a pit him cast.

XVIII.

I say that him into a pit they threw,
A loathsome pit, whence noisome scents exhale;
O cursed folk! away, ye Herods new!
What may your ill intentions you avail?
Murder will out; certès it will not fail;
Know, that the honor of high God may spread,
The blood cries out on your accursèd deed.

XIX.

O Martyr 'stablished in virginity!
Now mayst thou sing aye before the throne,
Following the Lamb celestial," quoth she,
" Of which the great Evangelist, Saint John,
In Patmos wrote, who saith of them that go
Before the Lamb singing continually,
That never fleshly woman they did know.

XX.

Now this poor widow waiteth all that night
After her little Child, and he came not ;
For which, by earliest glimpse of morning light,
With face all pale with dread and busy thought,
She at the School and elsewhere him hath sought,
Until thus far she learned, that he had been
In the Jews' street, and there he last was seen.

XXI.

With Mother's pity in her breast inclosed
She goeth, as she were half out of her mind,
To every place wherein she hath supposed
By likelihood her little Son to find ;
And ever on Christ's Mother meek and kind
She cried, till to the Jewry she was brought,
And him among the accursèd Jews she sought.

XXII.

She asketh, and she piteously doth pray
To every Jew that dwelleth in that place,
To tell her if her child had passed that way ;

They all said, Nay; but Jesu of his grace
Gave to her thought, that in a little space
She for her Son in that same spot did cry
Where he was cast into a pit hard by.

XXIII.

O thou great God that dost perform thy laud
By mouths of Innocents, lo ! here thy might;
This gem of chastity, this emerald,
And eke of martyrdom this ruby bright,
There, where with mangled throat he lay upright,
The *Alma Redemptoris* 'gan to sing,
So loud, that with his voice the place did ring.

XXIV.

The Christian folk that through the Jewry went
Come to the spot in wonder at the thing;
And hastily they for the Provost sent;
Immediately he came, not tarrying,
And praiseth Christ that is our Heavenly King,
And eke his Mother, honor of Mankind:
Which done, he bade that they the Jews should
        bind.

XXV.

This Child with piteous lamentation then
Was taken up, singing his song alwày;
And with procession great and pomp of men
To the next Abbey him they bare away;
His Mother swooning by the body lay:
And scarcely could the people that were near
Remove this second Rachel from the bier.

XXVI.

Torment and shameful death to every one
This Provost doth for those bad Jews prepare
That of this murder wist, and that anon:
Such wickedness his judgments cannot spare;
Who will do evil, evil shall he bear;
Them therefore with wild horses did he draw,
And after that he hung them by the law.

XXVII.

Upon his bier this Innocent doth lie
Before the altar while the Mass doth last:
The Abbot with his convent's company
Then sped themselves to bury him full fast;
And, when they holy water on him cast,
Yet spake this Child when sprinkled was the water,
And sang, *O Alma Redemptoris Mater!*

XXVIII.

This Abbot, for he was a holy man,
As all Monks are, or surely ought to be,
In supplication to the Child began,
Thus saying: 'O dear Child! I summon thee,
In virtue of the holy Trinity,
Tell me the cause why thou dost sing this hymn,
Since that thy throat is cut, as it doth seem.'

XXIX.

' My throat is cut unto the bone, I trow,'
Said this young Child, 'and by the law of kind,
I should have died, yea many hours ago,

But Jesus Christ, as in the books ye find,
Will that his glory last, and be in mind;
And, for the worship of his Mother dear,
Yet may I sing, *O Alma!* loud and clear.

XXX.

' This well of mercy, Jesu's Mother sweet,
After my knowledge I have lived alwày;
And in the hour when I my death did meet,
To me she came, and thus to me did say,
"Thou in thy dying sing this holy lay,"
As ye have heard; and soon as I had sung,
Methought she laid a grain upon my tongue.

XXXI.

' Wherefore I sing, nor can from song refrain,
In honor of that blissful Maiden free,
Till from my tongue off-taken is the grain.
And after that thus said she unto me:
"My little Child, then will I come for thee
Soon as the grain from off thy tongue they take:
Be not dismayed, I will not thee forsake!"'

XXXII.

This holy Monk, this Abbot, him mean I,
Touched then his tongue, and took away the grain;
And he gave up the ghost full peacefully;
And, when the Abbot had this wonder seen,
His salt tears trickled down like showers of rain;
And on his face he dropped upon the ground,
And still he lay as if he had been bound.

XXXIII.

Eke the whole Convent on the pavement lay,
Weeping and praising Jesu's Mother dear;
And after that they rose, and took their way,
And lifted up this Martyr from the bier,
And in a tomb of precious marble clear
Inclosed his uncorrupted body sweet.—
Where'er he be, God grant us him to meet!

XXXIV.

Young Hew of Lincoln! in like sort laid low
By cursed Jews,—thing well and widely known,
For it was done a little while ago,—
Pray also thou for us, while here we tarry,
Weak, sinful folk, that God, with pitying eye,
In mercy would his mercy multiply
On us, for reverence of his Mother Mary!"

II.

THE CUCKOO AND THE NIGHTINGALE.

I.

The God of Love,—*ah benedicite!*
How mighty and how great a Lord is he!
For he of low hearts can make high, of high
He can make low, and unto death bring nigh;
And hard hearts he can make them kind and free.

II.

Within a little time, as hath been found,
He can make sick folk whole and fresh and sound:
Them who are whole in body and in mind,
He can make sick,—bind can he and unbind
All that he will have bound, or have unbound.

III.

To tell his might my wit may not suffice;
Foolish men he can make them out of wise;—
For he may do all that he will devise;
Loose livers he can make abate their vice,
And proud hearts can make tremble in a trice.

IV.

In brief, the whole of what he will, he may;
Against him dare not any wight say nay;
To humble or afflict whome'er he will,
To gladden or to grieve, he hath like skill;
But most his might he sheds on the eve of May.

V.

For every true heart, gentle heart and free,
That with him is, or thinketh so to be,
Now against May shall have some stirring,—
      whether
To joy, or be it to some mourning; never
At other time, methinks, in like degree.

VI.

For now when they may hear the small birds' song,
And see the budding leaves the branches throng,

This unto their remembrance doth bring
All kinds of pleasure mixed with sorrowing;
And longing of sweet thoughts that ever long.

VII.

And of that longing heaviness doth come,
Whence oft great sickness grows of heart and home;
Sick are they all for lack of their desire;
And thus in May their hearts are set on fire,
So that they burn forth in great martyrdom.

VIII.

In sooth, I speak from feeling, what though now
Old am I, and to genial pleasure slow;
Yet have I felt of sickness through the May,
Both hot and cold, and heart-aches every day,—
How hard, alas! to bear, I only know.

IX.

Such shaking doth the fever in me keep
Through all this May, that I have little sleep;
And also 't is not likely unto me,
That any living heart should sleepy be
In which Love's dart its fiery point doth steep.

X.

But tossing lately on a sleepless bed,
I of a token thought which Lovers heed;
How among them it was a common tale,
That it was good to hear the Nightingale
Ere the vile Cuckoo's note be utterèd.

XI.

And then I thought anon, as it was day,
I gladly would go somewhere to essay
If I perchance a Nightingale might hear;
For yet had I heard none, of all that year,
And it was then the third night of the May.

XII.

And soon as I a glimpse of day espied,
No longer would I in my bed abide,
But straightway to a wood that was hard by
Forth did I go, alone and fearlessly,
And held the pathway down by a brook-side;

XIII.

Till to a lawn I came, all white and green,
I in so fair a one had never been.
The ground was green, with daisy powdered over;
Tall were the flowers, the grove a lofty cover,
All green and white; and nothing else was seen.

XIV.

There sat I down among the fair, fresh flowers,
And saw the birds come tripping from their bowers,
Where they had rested them all night; and they
Who were so joyful at the light of day,
Began to honor May with all their powers.

XV.

Well did they know that service all by rote,
And there was many and many a lovely note,

Some, singing loud, as if they had complained;
Some with their notes another manner feigned;
And some did sing all out with the full throat.

XVI.

They pruned themselves, and made themselves
    right gay,
Dancing and leaping light upon the spray;
And ever two and two together were,
The same as they had chosen for the year,
Upon Saint Valentine's returning day.

XVII.

Meanwhile the stream, whose bank I sat upon,
Was making such a noise as it ran on
Accordant to the sweet Birds' harmony;
Methought that it was the best melody
Which ever to man's ear a passage won.

XVIII.

And for delight, but how I never wot,
I in a slumber and a swoon was caught,
Not all asleep and yet not waking wholly;
And as I lay, the Cuckoo, bird unholy,
Broke silence, or I heard him in my thought.

XIX.

And that was right upon a tree fast by,
And who was then ill satisfied but I?
Now, God, quoth I, that died upon the rood,
From thee and thy base throat keep all that's good,
Full little joy have I now of thy cry.

XX.

And, as I with the Cuckoo thus 'gan chide,
In the next bush that was me fast beside,
I heard the lusty Nightingale so sing,
That her clear voice made a loud rioting,
Echoing through all the greenwood wide.

XXI.

Ah ! good sweet Nightingale ! for my heart's cheer
Hence hast thou stayed a little while too long ;
For we have had the sorry Cuckoo here,
And she hath been before thee with her song ;
Evil light on her ! she hath done me wrong.

XXII.

But hear you now a wondrous thing, I pray ;
As long as in that swooning-fit I lay,
Methought I wist right well what these birds meant,
And had good knowing both of their intent,
And of their speech, and all that they would say.

XXIII.

The Nightingale thus in my hearing spake : —
Good Cuckoo, seek some other bush or brake,
And, prithee, let us that can sing dwell here ;
For every wight eschews thy song to hear,
Such uncouth singing verily dost thou make.

XXIV.

What ! quoth she then, what is 't that ails thee now ?
It seems to me I sing as well as thou ;

For mine 's a song that is both true and plain, —
Although I cannot quaver so in vain
As thou dost in thy throat, I wot not how.

XXV.

All men may understanding have of me,
But, Nightingale, so may they not of thee;
For thou hast many a foolish and quaint cry: —
Thou sayst OSEE, OSEE, then how may I
Have knowledge, I thee pray, what this may be?

XXVI.

Ah, fool! quoth she, wist thou not what it is?
Oft as I say OSEE, OSEE, I wis,
Then mean I, that I should be wonderous fain
That shamefully they one and all were slain,
Whoever against Love mean aught amiss.

XXVII.

And also would I that they all were dead,
Who do not think in love their life to lead;
For who is loth the God of Love to obey
Is only fit to die, I dare well say,
And for that cause OSEE I cry; take heed!

XXVIII.

Ay, quoth the Cuckoo, that is a quaint law,
That all must love or die; but I withdraw,
And take my leave of all such company,
For my intent it neither is to die,
Nor ever while I live Love's yoke to draw.

XXIX.

For lovers, of all folk that be alive,
The most disquiet have, and least do thrive;
Most feeling have of sorrow, woe, and care,
And the least welfare cometh to their share;
What need is there against the truth to strive?

XXX

What! quoth she, thou art all out of thy mind,
That in thy churlishness a cause canst find
To speak of Love's true Servants in this mood;
For in this world no service is so good
To every wight that gentle is of kind.

XXXI.

For thereof comes all goodness and all worth;
All gentiless and honor thence come forth;
Thence worship comes, content, and true heart's
        pleasure,
And full-assured trust, joy without measure,
And jollity, fresh cheerfulness, and mirth;

XXXII.

And bounty, lowliness, and courtesy,
And seemliness, and faithful company,
And dread of shame that will not do amiss;
For he that faithfully Love's servant is,
Rather than be disgraced, would chuse to die.

XXXIII

And that the very truth it is which I
Now say, — in such belief I 'll live and die;

And, Cuckoo, do thou so, by my advice.
Then, quoth she, let me never hope for bliss,
If with that counsel I do e'er comply.

XXXIV.

Good Nightingale! thou speakest wondrous fair,
Yet, for all that, the truth is found elsewhere;
For Love in young folk is but rage, I wis,
And Love in old folk a great dotage is;
Who most it useth, him 't will most impair.

XXXV.

For thereof come all contraries to gladness;
Thence sickness comes, and overwhelming sadness,
Mistrust and jealousy, despite, debate,
Dishonor, shame, envy importunate,
Pride, anger, mischief, poverty, and madness.

XXXVI.

Loving is aye an office of despair,
And one thing is therein which is not fair;
For whoso gets of love a little bliss,
Unless it always stay with him, I wis
He may full soon go with an old man's hair.

XXXVII.

And therefore, Nightingale! do thou keep nigh:
For trust me well, in spite of thy quaint cry,
If long time from thy mate thou be, or far,
Thou 'lt be as others that forsaken are:
Then shalt thou raise a clamor as do

XXXVIII.

Fie, quoth she, on thy name, Bird ill beseen!
The God of Love afflict thee with all teen.
For thou art worse than mad a thousand-fold;
For many a one hath virtues manifold,
Who had been naught, if Love had never been.

XXXIX.

For evermore his servants Love amendeth,
And he from every blemish them defendeth;
And maketh them to burn, as in a fire,
In loyalty, and worshipful desire,
And, when it likes him, joy enough them sendeth.

XL.

Thou Nightingale! the Cuckoo said, be still,
For Love no reason hath but his own will;—
For to th' untrue he oft gives ease and joy;
True lovers doth so bitterly annoy,
He lets them perish through that grievous ill.

XLI.

With such a master would I never be;*
For he, in sooth, is blind, and may not see,
And knows not when he hurts and when he heals;
Within this court full seldom Truth avails,
So diverse in his wilfulness is he.

* From a manuscript in the Bodleian MS are also stanzas 44
and 45, which are necessary to complete the sense.

XLII.

Then of the Nightingale did I take note
How from her inmost heart a sigh she brought,
And said, Alas that ever I was born !
Not one word have I now, I am so forlorn ; —
And with that word, she into tears burst out.

XLIII.

Alas, alas ! my very heart will break,
Quoth she, to hear this churlish bird thus speak
Of Love, and of his holy services ;
Now, God of Love ! thou help me in some wise,
That vengeance on this Cuckoo I may wreak.

XLIV.

And so methought I started up anon,
And to the brook I ran and got a stone,
Which at the Cuckoo hardily I cast,
And he for dread did fly away full fast ;
And glad, in sooth, was I when he was gone.

XLV.

And as he flew, the Cuckoo, ever and aye,
Kept crying, " Farewell ! — farewell, Popinjay !"
As if in scornful mockery of me ;
And on I hunted him from tree to tree,
Till he was far, all out of sight, away.

XLVI.

Then straightway came the Nightingale to me,
And said, Forsooth, my friend, do I thank thee,

That thou wert near to rescue me ; and now
Unto the God of Love I make a vow,
That all this May I will thy songstress be.

XLVII.

Well satisfied, I thanked her, and she said,
By this mishap no longer be dismayed,
Though thou the Cuckoo heard, ere thou heard'st me
Yet if I live it shall amended be,
When next May comes, if I am not afraid.

XLVIII.

And one thing will I counsel thee alsó :
The Cuckoo trust not thou, nor his Love's saw ;
All that he said is an outrageous lie.
Nay, nothing shall me bring thereto, quoth I,
For Love, and it hath done me mighty woe.

XLIX.

Yea, hath it ? use, quoth she, this medicine ;
This May-time, every day before thou dine,
Go look on the fresh daisy ; then say I,
Although for pain thou mayst be like to die,
Thou wilt be eased, and less wilt droop and pine.

L.

And mind always that thou be good and true,
And I will sing one song, of many new,
For love of thee, as loud as I may cry ;
And then did she begin this song full high,
" Beshrew all them that are in love untrue."

LI.

And soon as she had sung it to an end,
Now farewell, quoth she, for I hence must wend;
And, God of Love, that can right well and may,
Send unto thee as mickle joy this day,
As ever he to Lover yet did send.

LII.

Thus takes the Nightingale her leave of me;
I pray to God with her always to be,
And joy of love to send her evermore;
And shield us from the Cuckoo and her lore,
For there is not so false a bird as she.

LIII.

Forth then she flew, the gentle Nightingale,
To all the Birds that lodged within that dale,
And gathered each and all into one place,
And them besought to hear her doleful case;
And thus it was that she began her tale.

LIV.

The Cuckoo, — 't is not well that I should hide
How she and I did each the other chide,
And without ceasing, since it was daylight;
And now I pray you all to do me right
Of that false Bird, whom Love cannot abide.

LV.

Then spake one Bird, and full assent all gave.
This matter asketh counsel good as grave,

For birds we are, — all here together brought;
And, in good sooth, the Cuckoo here is not;
And therefore we a Parliament will have.

LVI.

And thereat shall the Eagle be our Lord,
And other Peers whose names are on record;
A summons to the Cuckoo shall be sent,
And judgment there be given; or, that intent
Failing, we finally shall make accord.

LVII.

And all this shall be done, without a nay,
The morrow after Saint Valentine's day,
Under a maple that is well beseen,
Before the chamber-window of the Queen,
At Woodstock, on the meadow green and gay.

LVIII.

She thankèd them; and then her leave she took,
And flew into a hawthorn by that brook;
And there she sat and sung, upon that tree,
" For term of life Love shall have hold of me," —
So loudly, that I with that song awoke.

———————

Unlearned Book and rude, as well I know,
For beauty thou hast none, nor eloquence,
Who did on thee the hardiness bestow
To appear before my Lady? but a sense
Thou surely hast of her benevolence,

Whereof her hourly bearing proof doth give;
For of all good she is the best alive.

Alas, poor Book! for thy unworthiness,
To show to her some pleasant meanings writ
In winning words, since through her gentiless,
Thee she accepts as for her service fit!
Oh! it repents me I have neither wit
Nor leisure unto thee more worth to give;
For of all good she is the best alive.

Beseech her meekly with all lowliness,
Though I be far from her I reverence,
To think upon my truth and stedfastness,
And to abridge my sorrow's violence,
Caused by the wish, as knows your sapience,
She of her liking proof to me would give;
For of all good she is the best alive.

L'ENVOY.

Pleasure's Aurora, Day of gladsomeness!
Luna by night, with heavenly influence
Illumined! root of beauty and goodnesse,
Write, and allay, by your beneficence,
My sighs breathed forth in silence, — comfort give!
Since of all good you are the best alive.

EXPLICIT.

III.

TROILUS AND CRESIDA.

Next morning Troilus began to clear
His eyes from sleep, at the first break of day,
And unto Pandarus, his own Brother dear,
For love of God, full piteously did say,
We must the Palace see of Cresida;
For since we yet may have no other feast,
Let us behold her Palace at the least!

And therewithal to cover his intent,
A cause he found into the Town to go,
And they right forth to Cresid's Palace went;
But, Lord, this simple Troilus was woe,
Him thought his sorrowful heart would break in two;
For when he saw her doors fast bolted all,
Wellnigh for sorrow down he 'gan to fall.

Therewith when this true Lover 'gan behold
How shut was every window of the place,
Like frost he thought his heart was icy cold;
For which, with changèd, pale, and deadly face,
Without word uttered, forth he 'gan to pace;
And on his purpose bent so fast to ride,
That no wight his continuance espied.

Then said he thus: O Palace desolate!
O house of houses, once so richly dight!

O Palace empty and disconsolate!
Thou lamp of which extinguished is the light!
O Palace whilom day that now art night!
Thou ought'st to fall and I to die; since she
Is gone who held us both in sovereignty.

O of all houses once the crownèd boast!
Palace illumined with the sun of bliss!
O ring of which the ruby now is lost!
O cause of woe, that cause has been of bliss!
Yet, since I may no better, would I kiss
Thy cold doors; but I dare not for this rout;
Farewell, thou shrine of which the Saint is out!

Therewith he cast on Pandarus an eye,
With changèd face, and piteous to behold;
And when he might his time aright espy,
Aye as he rode, to Pandarus he told
Both his new sorrow and his joys of old,
So piteously, and with so dead a hue,
That every wight might on his sorrow rue.

Forth from the spot he rideth up and down,
And everything to his rememberànce
Came, as he rode by places of the town
Where he had felt such perfect pleasure once.
Lo, yonder saw I mine own Lady dance,
And in that Temple she with her bright eyes,
My Lady dear, first bound me captive-wise.

And yonder with joy-smitten heart have I
Heard my own Cresid's laugh; and once at play
I yonder saw her eke full blissfully;
And yonder once she unto me 'gan say,
Now, my sweet Troilus, love me well, I pray!
And there so graciously did me behold,
That hers unto the death my heart I hold.

And at the corner of that selfsame house
Heard I my most beloved Lady dear,
So womanly, with voice melodious
Singing so well, so goodly, and so clear,
That in my soul methinks I yet do hear
The blissful sound; and in that very place
My Lady first me took unto her grace.

O blissful God of Love! then thus he cried,
When I the process have in memory,
How thou hast wearied me on every side,
Men thence a book might make, a history;
What need to seek a conquest over me,
Since I am wholly at thy will? what joy
Hast thou thy own liege subjects to destroy?

Dread Lord! so fearful when provoked, thine ire
Well hast thou wreaked on me by pain and grief;
Now mercy, Lord! thou know'st well I desire
Thy grace above all pleasures first and chief;
And live and die I will in thy belief;

For which I ask for guerdon but one boon,
That Cresida again thou send me soon.

Constrain her heart as quickly to return,
As thou dost mine with longing her to see,
Then know I well that she would not sojourn.
Now, blissful Lord, so cruel do not be
Unto the blood of Troy, I pray to thee,
As Juno was unto the Theban blood,
From whence to Thebes came griefs in multitude.

And after this he to the gate did go
Whence Cresid rode, as if in haste she was;
And up and down there went, and to and fro,
And to himself full oft he said, Alas!
From hence my hope, and solace forth did pass.
O would the blissful God now for his joy,
I might her see again coming to Troy!

And up to yonder hill was I her guide;
Alas! and there I took of her my leave;
Yonder I saw her to her Father ride,
For very grief of which my heart shall cleave;—
And hither home I came when it was eve;
And here I dwell, an outcast from all joy,
And shall, unless I see her soon in Troy.

And of himself did he imagine oft,
That he was blighted, pale, and waxen less

Than he was wont; and that in whispers soft
Men said, What may it be, can no one guess
Why Troilus hath all this heaviness?
All which he of himself conceited wholly
Out of his weakness and his melancholy.

Another time he took into his head,
That every wight, who in the way passed by,
Had of him ruth, and fancied that they said,
I am right sorry Troilus will die:
And thus a day or two drove wearily;
As ye have heard; such life 'gan he to lead
As one that standeth betwixt hope and dread.

For which it pleased him in his songs to show
The occasion of his woe, as best he might;
And made a fitting song, of words but few,
Somewhat his woful heart to make more light;
And when he was removed from all men's sight,
With a soft night voice, he of his Lady dear,
That absent was, 'gan sing, as ye may hear:—

O star, of which I lost have all the light,
With a sore heart well ought I to bewail,
That ever dark in torment, night by night,
Toward my death with wind I steer and sail;
For which upon the tenth night if thou fail
With thy bright beams to guide me but one hour,
My ship and me Charybdis will devour.

As soon as he this song had thus sung through,
He fell again into his sorrows old ;
And every night, as was his wont to do,
Troilus stood the bright moon to behold ;
And all his trouble to the moon he told,
And said : I wis, when thou art horned anew,
I shall be glad if all the world be true.

Thy horns were old as now upon that morrow,
When hence did journey my bright Lady dear,
That cause is of my torment and my sorrow;
For which, O gentle Luna, bright and clear,
For love of God, run fast above thy sphere;
For when thy horns begin once more to spring,
Then shall she come, that with her bliss may bring.

The day is more, and longer every night,
Than they were wont to be, — for he thought so ;
And that the sun did take his course not right,
By longer way than he was wont to go ;
And said, I am in constant dread, I trow,
That Phaëton his son is yet alive,
His too fond father's car amiss to drive.

Upon the walls fast also would he walk,
To the end that he the Grecian host might see;
And ever thus he to himself would talk . —
Lo ! yonder is my own bright Lady free ;
Or yonder is it that the tents must be ;

And thence does come this air which is so sweet,
That in my soul I feel the joy of it.

And certainly this wind, that more and more
By moments thus increaseth in my face,
Is of my Lady's sighs heavy and sore ;
I prove it thus : for in no other space
Of all this town, save only in this place,
Feel I a wind, that soundeth so like pain ;
It saith, Alas ! why severed are we twain?

A weary while in pain he tosseth thus,
Till fully passed and gone was the ninth night ;
And ever at his side stood Pandarus,
Who busily made use of all his might
To comfort him, and make his heart more light ;
Giving him always hope, that she the morrow
Of the tenth day will come, and end his sorrow.

POEMS REFERRING TO THE PERIOD OF OLD AGE.

I.

THE OLD CUMBERLAND BEGGAR.

The class of Beggars, to which the old man here described belongs, will probably soon be extinct. It consisted of poor, and, mostly, old and infirm persons, who confined themselves to a stated round in their neighborhood, and had certain fixed days on which, at different houses, they regularly received alms, sometimes in money, but mostly in provisions.

I saw an aged Beggar in my walk;
And he was seated, by the highway-side,
On a low structure of rude masonry
Built at the foot of a huge hill, that they
Who lead their horses down the steep, rough road
May thence remount at ease. The aged man
Had placed his staff across a broad, smooth stone
That overlays the pile; and, from a bag
All white with flour, the dole of village dames,
He drew his scraps and fragments, one by one;
And scanned them with a fixed and serious look
Of idle computation. In the sun,

Upon the second step of that small pile,
Surrounded by those wild, unpeopled hills,
He sat, and ate his food in solitude :
And ever, scattered from his palsied hand,
That, still attempting to prevent the waste,
Was baffled still, the crumbs in little showers
Fell on the ground ; and the small mountain birds,
Not venturing yet to peck their destined meal,
Approached within the length of half his staff.

　　Him from my childhood have I known ; and then
He was so old, he seems not older now ;
He travels on, a solitary man,
So helpless in appearance, that for him
The sauntering horseman throws not with a slack
And careless hand his alms upon the ground,
But stops, — that he may safely lodge the coin
Within the old man's hat ; nor quits him so,
But still, when he has given his horse the rein,
Watches the aged Beggar with a look
Sidelong, and half-reverted.　She who tends
The toll-gate, when in summer at her door
She turns her wheel, if on the road she sees
The aged Beggar coming, quits her work,
And lifts the latch for him that he may pass.
The post-boy, when his rattling wheels o'ertake
The aged Beggar in the woody lane,
Shouts to him from behind ; and if, thus warned,
The old man does not change his course, the boy
Turns with less noisy wheels to the road-side,

And passes gently by, without a curse
Upon his lips, or anger at his heart.

He travels on, a solitary man ;
His age has no companion.   On the ground
His eyes are turned, and, as he moves along,
They move along the ground ; and, evermore,
Instead of common and habitual sight
Of fields with rural works, of hill and dale,
And the blue sky, one little span of earth
Is all his prospect.   Thus, from day to day,
Bow-bent, his eyes forever on the ground,
He plies his weary journey ; seeing still,
And seldom knowing that he sees, some straw,
Some scattered leaf, or marks which, in one track,
The nails of cart or chariot-wheel have left
Impressed on the white road, — in the same line,
At distance still the same.   Poor Traveller !
His staff trails with him ; scarcely do his feet
Disturb the summer dust ; he is so still
In look and motion, that the cottage curs,
Ere he has passed the door, will turn away,
Weary of barking at him.   Boys and girls,
The vacant and the busy, maids and youths,
And urchins newly breeched, — all pass him by :
Him even the slow-paced wagon leaves behind.

But deem not this man useless.   Statesmen ! ye
Who are so restless in your wisdom, ye
Who have a broom still ready in your hands

To rid the world of nuisances ; ye proud,
Heart-swoln, while in your pride ye contemplate
Your talents, power, or wisdom, deem him not
A burden of the earth ! 'T is nature's law
That none, the meanest of created things,
Of forms created the most vile and brute,
The dullest or most noxious, should exist
Divorced from good, — a spirit and pulse of good,
A life and soul, to every mood of being
Inseparably linked.   Then be assured
That least of all can aught — that ever owned
The heaven-regarding eye and front sublime
Which man is born to — sink, howe'er depressed,
So low as to be scorned without a sin ;
Without offence to God, cast out of view ;
Like the dried remnants of a garden-flower
Whose seeds are shed, or as an implement
Worn out and worthless. While from door to door
This old man creeps, the villagers in him
Behold a record which together binds
Past deeds and offices of charity,
Else unremembered, and so keeps alive
The kindly mood in hearts which lapse of years,
And that half-wisdom half-experience gives,
Make slow to feel, and by sure steps resign
To selfishness and cold, oblivious cares.
Among the farms and solitary huts,
Hamlets and thinly scattered villages,
Where'er the aged Beggar takes his rounds,
The mild necessity of use compels

To acts of love; and habit does the work
Of reason; yet prepares that after-joy
Which reason cherishes.　And thus the soul,
By that sweet taste of pleasure unpursued,
Doth find herself insensibly disposed
To virtue and true goodness.
　　　　　　　　　　　　Some there are,
By their good works exalted, lofty minds
And meditative, authors of delight
And happiness, which to the end of time
Will live, and spread, and kindle : even such minds
In childhood, from this solitary Being,
Or from like wanderer, haply have received
(A thing more precious far than all that books
Or the solicitudes of love can do !)
That first mild touch of sympathy and thought,
In which they found their kindred with a world
Where want and sorrow were.　The easy man
Who sits at his own door, and, like the pear
That overhangs his head from the green wall,
Feeds in the sunshine; the robust and young,
The prosperous and unthinking, they who live
Sheltered, and flourish in a little grove
Of their own kindred ; — all behold in him
A silent monitor, which on their minds
Must needs impress a transitory thought
Of self-congratulation, to the heart
Of each recalling his peculiar boons,
His charters and exemptions; and, perchance,
Though he to no one give the fortitude

And circumspection needful to preserve
His present blessings, and to husband up
The respite of the season, he at least,
And 't is no vulgar service, makes them felt.

      Yet further.—— Many, I believe, there are,
Who live a life of virtuous decency,
Men who can hear the Decalogue, and feel
No self-reproach; who of the moral law
Established in the land where they abide
Are strict observers; and not negligent
In acts of love to those with whom they dwell,
Their kindred, and the children of their blood.
Praise be to such, and to their slumbers peace!
— But of the poor man ask, the abject poor;
Go, and demand of him, if there be here,
In this cold abstinence from evil deeds,
And these inevitable charities,
Wherewith to satisfy the human soul?
No, — man is dear to man; the poorest poor
Long for some moments in a weary life
When they can know and feel that they have been,
Themselves, the fathers and the dealers-out
Of some small blessings; have been kind to such
As needed kindness, for this single cause,
That we have all of us one human heart.
— Such pleasure is to one kind Being known,
My neighbor, when with punctual care, each week,
Duly as Friday comes, though pressed herself
By her own wants, she from her store of meal

Takes one unsparing handful for the scrip
Of this old Mendicant, and, from her door
Returning with exhilarated heart,
Sits by her fire, and builds her hope in heaven.

Then let him pass, a blessing on his head!
And while, in that vast solitude to which
The tide of things has borne him, he appears
To breathe and live but for himself alone,
Unblamed, uninjured, let him bear about
The good which the benignant law of Heaven
Has hung around him: and, while life is his,
Still let him prompt the unlettered villagers
To tender offices and pensive thoughts.
— Then let him pass, a blessing on his head!
And, long as he can wander, let him breathe
The freshness of the valleys ; let his blood
Struggle with frosty air and winter snows ;
And let the chartered wind that sweeps the heath
Beat his gray locks against his withered face.
Reverence the hope whose vital anxiousness
Gives the last human interest to his heart.
May never HOUSE, misnamed of INDUSTRY,
Make him a captive! — for that pent-up din,
Those life-consuming sounds that clog the air,
Be his the natural silence of old age !
Let him be free of mountain solitudes ;
And have around him, whether heard or not,
The pleasant melody of woodland birds.
Few are his pleasures : if his eyes have now
Been doomed so long to settle upon earth,

That not without some effort they behold
The countenance of the horizontal sun,
Rising or setting, let the light at least
Find a free entrance to their languid orbs.
And let him, *where* and *when* he will, sit down
Beneath the trees, or on a grassy bank
Of highway-side, and with the little birds,
Share his chance-gathered meal ; and, finally,
As in the eye of Nature he has lived,
So in the eye of Nature let him die !

1798.

II.

THE FARMER OF TILSBURY VALE.

'T is not for the unfeeling, the falsely refined,
The squeamish in taste, and the narrow of mind,
And the small critic wielding his delicate pen,
That I sing of old Adam, the pride of old men.

He dwells in the centre of London's wide Town ;
His staff is a sceptre, his gray hairs a crown ;
And his bright eyes look brighter, set off by the
  streak
Of the unfaded rose that still blooms on his cheek.

'Mid the dews, in the sunshine of morn, — 'mid
  the joy
Of the fields, he collected that bloom, when a boy ;

That countenauce there fashioned, which, spite of
    a stain,
That his life hath received, to the last will remain.

A Farmer he was; and his house far and near
Was the boast of the country for excellent cheer:
How oft have I heard in sweet Tilsbury Vale
Of the silver-rimmed horn whence he dealt his
    mild ale!

Yet Adam was far as the farthest from ruin,
His fields seemed to know what their master was
    doing;
And turnips, and corn-land, and meadow, and lea,
All caught the infection, — as generous as he.

Yet Adam prized little the feast and the bowl, —
The fields better suited the ease of his soul:
He strayed through the fields like an indolent
    wight, —
The quiet of nature was Adam's delight.

For Adam was simple in thought; and the poor,
Familiar with him, made an inn of his door:
He gave them the best that he had; or, to say
What less may mislead you, they took it away.

Thus thirty smooth years did he thrive on his
    farm:
The Genius of Plenty preserved him from harm.

At length, what to most is a season of sorrow,
His means are run out, — he must beg, or must
    borrow.

To the neighbors he went, — all were free with
    their money;
For his hive had so long been replenished with
    honey,
That they dreamt not of dearth; — he continued
    his rounds,
Knocked here, and knocked there, pounds still
    adding to pounds.

He paid what he could with his ill-gotten pelf,
And something, it might be, reserved for himself:
Then, (what is too true,) without hinting a word,
Turned his back on the country, — and off like a
    bird.

You lift up your eyes! — but I guess that you frame
A judgment too harsh of the sin and the shame;
In him it was scarcely a business of art,
For this he did all in the *ease* of his heart.

To London — a sad emigration I ween —
With his gray hairs he went, from the brook and
    the green:
And there, with small wealth but his legs and his
    hands,
As lonely he stood as a crow on the sands.

All trades, as need was, did old Adam assume, —
Served as stable-boy, errand-boy, porter, and groom;
But nature is gracious, necessity kind,
And, in spite of the shame that may lurk in his
    mind,

He seems ten birthdays younger, is green and is
    stout;
Twice as fast as before does his blood run about;
You would say that each hair of his beard was alive,
And his fingers are busy as bees in a hive.

For he 's not like an old man that leisurely goes
About work that he knows, in a track that he knows;
But often his mind is compelled to demur,
And you guess that the more then his body must
    stir.

In the throng of the town like a stranger is he,
Like one whose own country 's far over the sea;
And Nature, while through the great city he hies,
Full ten times a day takes his heart by surprise.

This gives him the fancy of one that is young,
More of soul in his face than of words on his tongue;
Like a maiden of twenty he trembles and sighs,
And tears of fifteen will come into his eyes.

What 's a tempest to him, or the dry parching heats?
Yet he watches the clouds that pass over the streets;

With a look of such earnestness often will stand,
You might think he 'd twelve reapers at work in
    the Strand.

Where proud Covent Garden, in desolate hours
Of snow and hoar-frost, spreads her fruits and her
        flowers,
Old Adam will smile at the pains that have made
Poor Winter look fine in such strange masquerade.

'Mid coaches and chariots, a wagon of straw,
Like a magnet, the heart of old Adam can draw;
With a thousand soft pictures his memory will teem,
And his hearing is touched with the sounds of a
    dream.

Up the Haymarket hill he oft whistles his way,
Thrusts his hands in a wagon, and smells at the hay;
He thinks of the fields he so often hath mown,
And is happy as if the rich freight were his own.

But chiefly to Smithfield he loves to repair, —
If you pass by at morning, you 'll meet with him there.
The breath of the cows you may see him inhale,
And his heart all the while is in Tilsbury Vale.

Now farewell, old Adam! when low thou art laid,
May one blade of grass spring over thy head;
And I hope that thy grave, wheresoever it be,
Will hear the wind sigh through the leaves of a tree.

1803.

III.

THE SMALL CELANDINE.

THERE is a Flower, the lesser Celandine,
That shrinks, like many more, from cold and rain;
And, the first moment that the sun may shine,
Bright as the sun himself, 't is out again!

When hailstones have been falling, swarm on
       swarm,
Or blasts the green field and the trees distressed,
Oft have I seen it muffled up from harm,
In close self-shelter, like a thing at rest.

But lately, one rough day, this Flower I passed
And recognized it, though an altered form,
Now standing forth an offering to the blast,
And buffeted at will by rain and storm.

I stopped, and said with inly muttered voice,
" It doth not love the shower, nor seek the cold:
This neither is its courage nor its choice,
But its necessity in being old.

" The sunshine may not cheer it, nor the dew;
It cannot help itself in its decay;
Stiff in its members, withered, changed of hue."
And, in my spleen, I smiled that it was gray.

To be a Prodigal's Favorite, — then, worse truth,
A Miser's Pensioner, — behold our lot!
O Man, that from thy fair and shining youth
Age might but take the things Youth needed not!

1804.

IV.

THE TWO THIEVES;

OR, THE LAST STAGE OF AVARICE.

O now that the genius of Bewick were mine,
And the skill which he learned on the banks of
      the Tyne !
Then the Muses might deal with me just as they
      chose,
For I 'd take my last leave both of verse and of
      prose.

What feats would I work with my magical hand !
Book-learning and books should be banished the
      land :
And, for hunger and thirst and such troublesome
      calls,
Every ale-house should then have a feast on its
      walls.

The traveller would hang his wet clothes on a chair;
Let them smoke, let them burn, not a straw would
      he care !

For the Prodigal Son, Joseph's Dream and his
    Sheaves,
O, what would they be to my tale of Two Thieves?

The one, yet unbreeched, is not three birthdays old,
His Grandsire that age more than thirty times told;
There are ninety good seasons of fair and foul
    weather
Between them, and both go a pilfering together.

With chips is the carpenter strewing his floor?
Is a cart-load of turf at an old woman's door?
Old Daniel his hand to the treasure will slide!
And his Grandson 's as busy at work by his side.

Old Daniel begins; he stops short, — and his eye,
Through the lost look of dotage, is cunning and sly:
'T is a look which at this time is hardly his own,
But tells a plain tale of the days that are flown.

He once had a heart which was moved by the wires
Of manifold pleasures and many desires:
And what if he cherished his purse?   'T was no
    more
Than treading a path trod by thousands before.

'T was a path trod by thousands; but Daniel is one
Who went something farther than others have gone;
And now with old Daniel you see how it fares,
You see to what end he has brought his gray hairs.

The pair sally forth hand in hand : ere the sun
Has peered o'er the beeches, their work is begun :
And yet, into whatever sin they may fall,
This child but half knows it, and that not at all.

They hunt through the streets with deliberate tread,
And each, in his turn, becomes leader or led ;
And, wherever they carry their plots and their wiles,
Every face in the village is dimpled with smiles.

Neither checked by the rich nor the needy, they
      roam ;
For the gray-headed Sire has a daughter at home,
Who will gladly repair all the damage that 's done ;
And three, were it asked, would be rendered for one.

Old Man ! whom so oft I with pity have eyed,
I love thee, and love the sweet Boy at thy side :
Long yet mayst thou live ! for a teacher we see
That lifts up the veil of our nature in thee.

1800.

V.

ANIMAL TRANQUILLITY AND DECAY.

      The little hedgerow birds,
That peck along the road, regard him not.
He travels on, and in his face, his step,

His gait, is one expression : every limb,
His look and bending figure, all bespeak
A man who does not move with pain, but moves
With thought. — He is insensibly subdued
To settled quiet : he is one by whom
All effort seems forgotten ; one to whom
Long patience hath such mild composure given,
That patience now doth seem a thing of which
He hath no need.   He is by nature led
To peace so perfect, that the young behold
With envy what the Old Man hardly feel.

1798.

EPITAPHS AND ELEGIAC PIECES.

EPITAPHS

I.

WEEP not, beloved Friends! nor let the air
For me with sighs be troubled.   Not from life
Have I been taken ; this is genuine life
And this alone, — the life which now I live
In peace eternal ; where desire and joy
Together move in fellowship without end.—
Francesco Ceni willed that, after death,
His tombstone thus should speak for him. And
     surely
Small cause there is for that fond wish of ours
Long to continue in this world ; a world
That keeps not faith, nor yet can point a hope
To good, whereof itself is destitute.

II.

PERHAPS some needful service of the State
Drew TITUS from the depth of studious bowers,

And doomed him to contend in faithless courts,
Where gold determines between right and wrong.
Yet did at length his loyalty of heart,
And his pure native genius, lead him back
To wait upon the bright and gracious Muses,
Whom he had early loved.   And not in vain
Such course he held !   Bologna's learned schools
Were gladdened by the Sage's voice, and hung
With fondness on those sweet Nestorian strains.
There pleasure crowned his days; and all his
          thoughts
A roseate fragrance breathed.* — O human life,
That never art secure from dolorous change !
Behold a high injunction suddenly
To Arno's side hath brought him, and he charmed
A Tuscan audience : but full soon was called
To the perpetual silence of the grave.
Mourn, Italy, the loss of him who stood
A Champion steadfast and invincible,
To quell the rage of literary War !

O THOU who movest onward with a mind
Intent upon thy way, pause, though in haste !
'T will be no fruitless moment.   I was born
Within Savona's walls, of gentle blood.

       * Ivi vivea giocondo e i suoi pensieri
          Erano tutti rose.
The Translator had not skill to come nearer to his original.

On Tiber's banks my youth was dedicate
To sacred studies ; and the Roman Shepherd
Gave to my charge Urbino's numerous flock.
Well did I watch, much labored, nor had power
To escape from many and strange indignities ;
Was smitten by the great ones of the world,
But did not fall ; for Virtue braves all shocks,
Upon herself resting immovably.
Me did a kindlier fortune then invite
To serve the glorious Henry, King of France,
And in his hands I saw a high reward
Stretched out for my acceptance, — but Death
     came.
Now, Reader, learn from this my fate, how false,
How treacherous to her promise, is the world ;
And trust in God, — to whose eternal doom
Must bend the sceptred Potentates of earth.

IV.

THERE never breathed a man who, when his life
Was closing, might not of that life relate
Toils long and hard. — The warrior will report
Of wounds, and bright swords flashing in the field,
And blast of trumpets.   He who hath been doomed
To bow his forehead in the courts of kings,
Will tell of fraud and never-ceasing hate,
Envy and heart-inquietude, derived
From intricate cabals of treacherous friends.

I, who on shipboard lived from earliest youth,
Could represent the countenance horrible
Of the vexed waters, and the indignant rage
Of Auster and Boötes.   Fifty years
Over the well-steered galleys did I rule :—
From huge Pelorus to the Atlantic pillars,
Rises no mountain to mine eyes unknown ;
And the broad gulfs I traversed oft and oft.
Of every cloud which in the heavens might stir
I knew the force ; and hence the rough sea's pride
Availed not to my Vessel's overthrow.
What noble pomp and frequent have not I
On regal decks beheld ! yet in the end
I learned that one poor moment can suffice
To equalize the lofty and the low.
We sail the sea of life, — a *Calm* one finds,
And one a *Tempest*, — and, the voyage o'er,
Death is the quiet haven of us all.
If more of my condition ye would know,
Savona was my birthplace, and I sprang
Of noble parents : seventy years and three
Lived I, — then yielded to a slow disease.

v.

TRUE is it that Ambrosio Salinero,
With an untoward fate, was long involved
In odious litigation ; and full long,
Fate harder still ! had he to endure assaults

Of racking malady.   And true it is,
That not the less a frank, courageous heart
And buoyant spirit triumphed over pain ;
And he was strong to follow in the steps
Of the fair Muses.   Not a covert path
Leads to the dear Parnassian forest's shade,
That might from him be hidden ; not a track
Mounts to pellucid Hippocrene, but he
Had traced its windings. — This Savona knows,
Yet no sepulchral honors to her Son
She paid, for in our age the heart is ruled
Only by gold.   And now a simple stone
Inscribed with this memorial here is raised
By his bereft, his lonely Chiabrera.
Think not, O Passenger who read'st the lines!
That an exceeding love hath dazzled me ;
No, — he was one whose memory ought to spread
Where'er Permessus bears an honored name,
And live as long as its pure stream shall flow.

VI.

Destined to war from very infancy
Was I, Roberto Dati, and I took
In Malta the white symbol of the Cross :
Nor in life's vigorous season did I shun
Hazard or toil ; among the sands was seen
Of Lybia ; and not seldom on the banks
Of wide Hungarian Danube, 't was my lot

To hear the sanguinary trumpet sounded.
So lived I, and repined not at such fate:
This only grieves me, for it seems a wrong,
That, stripped of arms, I to my end am brought
On the soft down of my paternal home.
Yet haply Arno shall be spared all cause
To blush for me.   Thou, loiter not nor halt
In thy appointed way, and bear in mind
How fleeting and how frail is human life!

VII.

O FLOWER of all that springs from gentle blood,
And all that generous nurture breeds to make
Youth amiable !   O friend so true of soul
To fair Aglaia ! by what envy moved,
Lelius! has death cut short thy brilliant day
In its sweet opening? and what dire mishap
Has from Savona torn her best delight?
For thee she mourns, nor e'er will cease to mourn;
And, should the outpourings of her eyes suffice not
For her heart's grief, she will entreat Sebeto
Not to withhold his bounteous aid, Sebeto,
Who saw thee, on his margin, yield to death,
In the chaste arms of thy belovèd Love!
What profit riches ? what does youth avail?
Dust are our hopes ; — I, weeping bitterly,
Penned these sad lines, nor can forbear to pray
That every gentle Spirit hither led
May read them not without some bitter tears.

VIII.

Not without heavy grief of heart did he
On whom the duty fell (for at that time
The father sojourned in a distant land)
Deposit in the hollow of this tomb
A brother's Child, most tenderly beloved!
Francesco was the name the Youth had borne,
Pozzobonnelli his illustrious house;
And when beneath this stone the Corse was laid,
The eyes of all Savona streamed with tears.
Alas! the twentieth April of his life
Had scarcely flowered: and at this early time,
By genuine virtue he inspired a hope
That greatly cheered his country: to his kin
He promised comfort; and the flattering thoughts
His friends had in their fondness entertained,*
He suffered not to languish or decay.
Now is there not good reason to break forth
Into a passionate lament? — O Soul!
Short while a Pilgrim in our nether world,
Do thou enjoy the calm empyreal air;
And round this earthly tomb let roses rise,
An everlasting spring! in memory
Of that delightful fragrance which was once
From thy mild manners quietly exhaled.

* In justice to the Author, I subjoin the original: —

——— e degli amici
Non lasciava languire i bei pensieri.

IX.

PAUSE, courteous Spirit ! — Balbi supplicates
That thou, with no reluctant voice, for him
Here laid in mortal darkness, wouldst prefer
A prayer to the Redeemer of the world.
This to the dead by sacred right belongs ;
All else is nothing. — Did occasion suit
To tell his worth, the marble of this tomb
Would ill suffice : for Plato's lore sublime,
And all the wisdom of the Stagirite,
Enriched and beautified his studious mind :
With Archimedes also he conversed
As with a chosen friend ; nor did he leave
Those laureate wreaths ungathered which the
        Nymphs
Twine near their loved Permessus. — Finally,
Himself above each lower thought uplifting,
His ears he closed to listen to the songs
Which Sion's Kings did consecrate of old ;
And his Permessus found on Lebanon.
A blessed man ! who of protracted days
Made not, as thousands do, a vulgar sleep ;
But truly did *he* live his life.   Urbino,
Take pride in him ! — O Passenger, farewell !

I.

By a blest Husband guided, Mary came
From nearest kindred, Vernon her new name;
She came, though meek of soul, in seemly pride
Of happiness and hope, a youthful Bride.
O dread reverse! if aught *be* so, which proves
That God will chasten whom he dearly loves.
Faith bore her up through pains in mercy given,
And troubles that were each a step to Heaven:
Two Babes were laid in earth before she died;
A third now slumbers at the Mother's side;
Its Sister-twin survives, whose smiles afford
A trembling solace to her widowed Lord.

Reader! if to thy bosom cling the pain
Of recent sorrow combated in vain;
Or if thy cherished grief have failed to thwart
Time still intent on his insidious part,
Lulling the mourner's best good thoughts asleep,
Pilfering regrets we would, but cannot, keep;
Bear with him, — judge *him* gently who makes
      known
His bitter loss by this memorial Stone;
And pray that in his faithful breast the grace
Of resignation find a hallowed place.

II.

Six months to six years added he remained
Upon this sinful earth, by sin unstained:
O blessed Lord! whose mercy then removed
A Child whom every eye that looked on loved;
Support us, teach us calmly to resign
What we possessed, and now is wholly thine!

III.

CENOTAPH.

In affectionate remembrance of Frances Fermor, whose remains are deposited in the church of Claines, near Worcester,
this stone is erected by her sister, Dame Margaret, wife of Sir
George Beaumont, Bart., who, feeling not less than the love
of a brother for the deceased, commends this memorial to
the care of his heirs and successors in the possession of this
place.

   By vain affections unenthralled,
   Though resolute when duty called
   To meet the world's broad eye,
   Pure as the holiest cloistered nun
   That ever feared the tempting sun,
   Did Fermor live and die.

   This Tablet, hallowed by her name,
   One heart-relieving tear may claim;
   But if the pensive gloom

Of fond regret be still thy choice,
Exalt thy spirit, hear the voice
Of Jesus from her tomb!

"I AM THE WAY, THE TRUTH, AND THE LIFE."

IV.

EPITAPH

IN THE CHAPEL-YARD OF LANGDALE, WESTMORELAND.

By playful smiles, (alas! too oft
A sad heart's sunshine,) by a soft
And gentle nature, and a free
Yet modest hand of charity,
Through life was Owen Lloyd endeared
To young and old; and how revered
Had been that pious spirit, a tide
Of humble mourners testified,
When, after pains dispensed to prove
The measure of God's chastening love,
Here, brought from far, his corse found rest,—
Fulfilment of his own request;—
Urged less for this Yew's shade, though he
Planted with such fond hope the tree,
Less for the love of stream and rock,
Dear as they were, than that his Flock,
When they no more their Pastor's voice
Could hear to guide them in their choice

Through good and evil, help might have,
Admonished, from his silent grave,
Of righteousness, of sins forgiven,
For peace on earth and bliss in heaven.

---

v.

ADDRESS TO THE SCHOLARS OF THE VILLAGE SCHOOL OF ——.

1798.

I COME, ye little noisy Crew,
Not long your pastime to prevent;
I heard the blessing which to you
Our common Friend and Father sent.
I kissed his cheek before he died;
And when his breath was fled,
I raised, while kneeling by his side,
His hand: — it dropped like lead.
Your hands, dear Little-ones, do all
That can be done, will never fall
Like his till they are dead.
By night or day, blow foul or fair,
Ne'er will the best of all your train
Play with the locks of his white hair,
Or stand between his knees again.

Here did he sit confined for hours;
But he could see the woods and plains,

Could hear the wind and mark the showers
Come streaming down the streaming panes.
Now stretched beneath his grass-green mound
He rests a prisoner of the ground.
He loved the breathing air,
He loved the sun, but if it rise
Or set, to him where now he lies,
Brings not a moment's care.
Alas ! what idle words ; but take
The Dirge which, for our Master's sake
And yours, love prompted me to make.
The rhymes so homely in attire
With learned ears may ill agree,
But, chanted by your Orphan Choir,
Will make a touching melody.

DIRGE.

Mourn, Shepherd, near thy old gray stone ;
Thou Angler, by the silent flood ;
And mourn when thou art all alone,
Thou Woodman, in the distant wood !

Thou one blind Sailor, rich in joy
Though blind, thy tunes in sadness hum ;
And mourn, thou poor half-witted Boy !
Born deaf, and living deaf and dumb.

Thou drooping sick Man, bless the Guide
Who checked or turned thy headstrong youth,

As he before had sanctified
Thy infancy with heavenly truth.

Ye Striplings, light of heart and gay,
Bold settlers on some foreign shore,
Give, when your thoughts are turned this way,
A sigh to him whom we deplore.

For us who here in funeral strain
With one accord our voices raise,
Let sorrow overcharged with pain
Be lost in thankfulness and praise.

And when our hearts shall feel a sting
From ill we meet or good we miss,
May touches of his memory bring
Fond healing, like a mother's kiss.

BY THE SIDE OF THE GRAVE SOME YEARS AFTER.

LONG time his pulse hath ceased to beat;
But benefits, his gift, we trace,—
Expressed in every eye we meet
Round this dear Vale, his native place.

To stately Hall and Cottage rude
Flowed from his life what still they hold,
Light pleasures, every day renewed,
And blessings half a century old.

O true of heart, of spirit gay,
Thy faults, where not already gone
From memory, prolong their stay
For charity's sweet sake alone.

Such solace find we for our loss;
And what beyond this thought we crave
Comes in the promise from the Cross,
Shining upon thy happy grave.*

VI.

ELEGIAC STANZAS,

**SUGGESTED BY A PICTURE OF PEELE CASTLE, IN A STORM,
PAINTED BY SIR GEORGE BEAUMONT.**

I WAS thy neighbor once, thou rugged Pile!
Four summer weeks I dwelt in sight of thee:
I saw thee every day; and all the while
Thy Form was sleeping on a glassy sea.

So pure the sky, so quiet was the air!
So like, so very like, was day to day!
Whene'er I looked, thy Image still was there;
It trembled, but it never passed away.

* See, upon the subject of the three foregoing pieces, the
Fountain, &c., in the fourth volume of the Author's Poems.

How perfect was the calm! it seemed no sleep;
No mood, which season takes away, or brings:
I could have fancied that the mighty Deep
Was even the gentlest of all gentle Things.

Ah! THEN, if mine had been the Painter's hand,
To express what then I saw; and add the gleam,
The light that never was, on sea or land,
The consecration, and the Poet's dream;

I would have planted thee, thou hoary Pile,
Amid a world how different from this!
Beside a sea that could not cease to smile;
On tranquil land, beneath a sky of bliss.

Thou shouldst have seemed a treasure-house di-
         vine
Of peaceful years; a chronicle of heaven; —
Of all the sunbeams that did ever shine,
The very sweetest had to thee been given.

A Picture had it been of lasting ease,
Elysian quiet, without toil or strife;
No motion but the moving tide, a breeze,
Or merely silent Nature's breathing life.

Such, in the fond illusion of my heart,
Such Picture would I at that time have made:
And seen the soul of truth in every part,
A steadfast peace that might not be betrayed.

So once it would have been, — 't is so no more;
I have submitted to a new control;
A power is gone, which nothing can restore;
A deep distress hath humanized my soul.

Not for a moment could I now behold
A smiling sea, and be what I have been:
The feeling of my loss will ne'er be old;
This, which I know, I speak with mind serene.

Then, Beaumont, Friend! who would have been
    the Friend,
If he had lived, of him whom I deplore,
This work of thine I blame not, but commend;
This sea in anger, and that dismal shore.

O 't is a passionate Work! — yet wise and well,
Well chosen is the spirit that is here;
That Hulk which labors in the deadly swell,
This rueful sky, this pageantry of fear!

And this huge Castle, standing here sublime,
I love to see the look with which it braves,
Cased in the unfeeling armor of old time,
The lightning, the fierce wind, and trampling waves.

Farewell, farewell the heart that lives alone,
Housed in a dream, at distance from the Kind!
Such happiness, wherever it be known,
Is to be pitied; for 't is surely blind.

But welcome fortitude, and patient cheer,
And frequent sights of what is to be borne !
Such sights, or worse, as are before me here. —
Not without hope we suffer and we mourn.

1805

VII.

TO THE DAISY.

SWEET Flower ! belike one day to have
A place upon thy Poet's grave,
I welcome thee once more :
But he, who was on land, at sea,
My Brother, too, in loving thee,
Although he loved more silently,
Sleeps by his native shore.

Ah ! hopeful, hopeful was the day
When to that Ship he bent his way,
To govern and to guide :
His wish was gained : a little time
Would bring him back, in manhood's prime
And free for life, these hills to climb,
With all his wants supplied.

And full of hope day followed day
While that stout Ship at anchor lay
Beside the shores of Wight ;
The May had then made all things green,

And, floating there, in pomp serene,
That Ship was goodly to be seen,
IIis pride and his delight!

Yet then, when called ashore, he sought
The tender peace of rural thought:
In more than happy mood
To your abodes, bright daisy Flowers!
He then would steal at leisure hours,
And loved you glittering in your bowers,
A starry multitude.

But hark the word! — the ship is gone ; —
Returns from her long course ; — anon
Sets sail; — in season due,
Once more on English earth they stand :
But, when a third time from the land
They parted, sorrow was at hand
For him and for his crew.

Ill-fated Vessel! — ghastly shock !
— At length delivered from the rock,
The deep she hath regained ;
And through the stormy night they steer,
Laboring for life, in hope and fear,
To reach a safer shore, — how near,
Yet not to be attained !

"Silence!" the brave Commander cried ;
To that calm word a shriek replied,

It was the last death-shriek.
— A few (my soul oft sees that sight)
Survive upon the tall mast's height;
But one dear remnant of the night, —
For him in vain I seek.

Six weeks beneath the moving sea
He lay in slumber quietly;
Unforced by wind or wave
To quit the ship for which he died,
(All claims of duty satisfied;)
And there they found him at her side,
And bore him to the grave.

Vain service! yet not vainly done
For this, if other end were none,
That he, who had been cast
Upon a way of life unmeet
For such a gentle Soul and sweet,
Should find an undisturbed retreat
Near what he loved, at last —

The neighborhood of grove and field
To him a resting-place should yield,
A meek man and a brave!
The birds shall sing and ocean make
A mournful murmur for *his* sake;
And thou, sweet flower, shalt sleep and wake
Upon his senseless grave.

1805.

VIII.

ELEGIAC VERSES,

IN MEMORY OF MY BROTHER, JOHN WORDSWORTH,

Commander of the E. I. Company's ship, the Earl of Abergavenny, in which he perished by a calamitous shipwreck, Feb. 6th, 1805. Composed near the mountain track, that leads from Grasmere through Grisdale Hawes, where it descends towards Patterdale.

1805.

I.

THE Sheep-boy whistled loud, and lo !
That instant, startled by the shock,
The Buzzard mounted from the rock
Deliberate and slow :
Lord of the air, he took his flight ;
O, could he on that woful night
Have lent his wing, my Brother dear,
For one poor moment's space, to thee,
And all who struggled with the Sea,
When safety was so near !

II.

Thus in the weakness of my heart
I spoke, (but let that pang be still,)
When, rising from the rock at will,
I saw the bird depart.
And let me calmly bless the Power

That meets me in this unknown flower,
Affecting type of him I mourn!
With calmness suffer and believe,
And grieve, and know that I must grieve,
Not cheerless, though forlorn.

III.

Here did we stop; and here looked round
While each into himself descends,
For that last thought of parting Friends
That is not to be found.
Hidden was Grasmere Vale from sight,
Our home and his, his heart's delight,
His quiet heart's selected home.
But time before him melts away,
And he hath feeling of a day
Of blessedness to come.

IV.

Full soon in sorrow did I weep,
Taught that the mutual hope was dust,
In sorrow, but for higher trust,
How miserably deep!
All vanished in a single word,
A breath, a sound, and scarcely heard.
Sea,—ship,—drowned,—shipwreck,—so it came,
The meek, the brave, the good, was gone;
He who had been our living John
Was nothing but a name.

v.

That was indeed a parting ! O,
Glad am I, glad that it is past !
For there were some on whom it cast
Unutterable woe.
But they as well as I have gains ; —
From many a humble source, to pains
Like these, there comes a mild release ;
Even here I feel it, even this Plant
Is in its beauty ministrant
To comfort and to peace.

vi.

He would have loved thy modest grace,
Meek Flower !   To him I would have said,
" It grows upon its native bed
Beside our Parting-place ;
There, cleaving to the ground, it lies,
With multitude of purple eyes,
Spangling a cushion green like moss ;
But we will see it, joyful tide !
Some day, to see it in its pride,
The mountain we will cross."

vii.

— Brother and friend, if verse of mine
Have power to make thy virtues known,
Here let a monumental Stone
Stand, sacred as a Shrine ;
And to the few who pass this way,

Traveller or Shepherd, let it say,
Long as these mighty rocks endure, —
O, do not thou too fondly brood,
Although deserving of all good,
On any earthly hope, however pure ! *

IX.

SONNET.

WHY should we weep or mourn, Angelic Boy,
For such thou wert ere from our sight removed,
Holy, and ever dutiful, — beloved
From day to day with never-ceasing joy,
And hopes as dear as could the heart employ
In aught to earth pertaining?   Death has proved
His might, nor less his mercy, as behoved, —
Death, conscious that he only could destroy
The bodily frame.·   That beauty is laid low
To moulder in a far-off field of Rome ;
But Heaven is now, blest Child, thy Spirit's home:
When such divine communion, which we know,
Is felt, thy Roman burial-place will be
Surely a sweet remembrancer of thee.

1846.

* The plant alluded to is the Moss Campion (Silene acaulis
of Linnæus).   See note at the end of the volume.   See, among
the Poems on the "Naming of Places," No. VI.

X.

LINES

Composed at Grasmere, during a walk one Evening, after a
stormy day, the Author having just read in a Newspaper
that the dissolution of Mr. Fox was hourly expected.

Loud is the Vale! the Voice is up
With which she speaks when storms are gone,
A mighty unison of streams!
Of all her Voices, one!

Loud is the Vale;—this inland Depth
In peace is roaring like the Sea;
Yon star upon the mountain-top
Is listening quietly.

Sad was I, even to pain depressed,
Importunate and heavy load!*
The Comforter hath found me here,
Upon this lonely road;

And many thousands now are sad,—
Wait the fulfilment of their fear;
For he must die who is their stay,
Their glory disappear.

A Power is passing from the earth
To breathless Nature's dark abyss;

* Importuna e grave salma.   MICHAEL ANGELO.

But when the great and good depart
What is it more than this, —

That man, who is from God sent forth,
Doth yet again to God return ?—
Such ebb and flow must ever be,
Then wherefore should we mourn ?

1806.

XI.

INVOCATION TO THE EARTH.

FEBRUARY, 1816.

I.

" Rest, rest, perturbèd Earth!
O rest, thou doleful Mother of Mankind!"
A Spirit sang in tones more plaintive than the wind,
" From regions where no evil thing has birth
I come, — thy stains to wash away,
Thy cherished fetters to unbind,
And open thy sad eyes upon a milder day.
The Heavens are thronged with martyrs that have
    risen
      From out thy noisome prison ;
      The penal caverns groan
With tens of thousands rent from off the tree
Of hopeful life, — by battle's whirlwind blow
Into the deserts of Eternity.
Unpitied havoc ! Victims unlamented !

But not on high, where madness is resented,
And murder causes some sad tears to flow,
Though, from the widely-sweeping blow,
The choirs of Angels spread, triumphantly aug-
mented.

II.

" False Parent of mankind !
Obdurate, proud, and blind,
I sprinkle thee with soft celestial dews,
Thy lost, maternal heart to re-infuse !
Scattering this far-fetched moisture from my wings,
Upon the act a blessing I implore,
Of which the rivers in their secret springs,
The rivers stained so oft with human gore,
Are conscious ; — may the like return no more !
May Discord, — for a Seraph's care
Shall be attended with a bolder prayer, —
May she, who once disturbed the seats of bliss
These mortal spheres above,
Be chained for ever to the black abyss !
And thou, O rescued Earth, by peace and love,
And merciful desires, thy sanctity approve ! "

The Spirit ended his mysterious rite,
And the pure vision closed in darkness infinite.

XII.

LINES

WRITTEN ON A BLANK LEAF IN A COPY OF THE AUTHOR'S
POEM "THE EXCURSION," UPON HEARING OF THE DEATH
OF THE LATE VICAR OF KENDAL.

To public notice, with reluctance strong,
Did I deliver this unfinished Song;
Yet for one happy issue; — and I look
With self-congratulation on the Book
Which pious, learned MURFITT saw and read; —
Upon my thoughts his saintly Spirit fed;
He conned the new-born Lay with grateful
      heart, —
Foreboding not how soon he must depart;
Unweeting that to him the joy was given
Which good men take with them from earth to
      heaven.

XIII.

ELEGIAC STANZAS.

(ADDRESSED TO SIR G. H. B. UPON THE DEATH OF HIS
SISTER-IN-LAW.)

1824.

O FOR a dirge! But why complain?
Ask rather a triumphal strain
When FERMOR's race is run ;

A garland of immortal boughs
To twine around the Christian's brows,
Whose glorious work is done.

We pay a high and holy debt;
No tears of passionate regret
Shall stain this votive lay;
Ill-worthy, Beaumont! were the grief
That flings itself on wild relief
When Saints have passed away.

Sad doom, at Sorrow's shrine to kneel,
For ever covetous to feel,
And impotent to bear!
Such once was hers, — to think and think
On severed love, and only sink
From anguish to despair!

But nature to its inmost part
Faith had refined; and to her heart
A peaceful cradle given:
Calm as the dew-drop's, free to rest
Within a breeze-fanned rose's breast
Till it exhales to Heaven.

Was ever Spirit that could bend
So graciously? — that could descend,
Another's need to suit,
So promptly from her lofty throne? —
In works of love, in these alone,
How restless, how minute!

Pale was her hue; yet mortal cheek
Ne'er kindled with a livelier streak
When aught had suffered wrong, —
When aught that breathes had felt a wound;
Such look the Oppressor might confound,
However proud and strong.

But hushed be every thought that springs
From out the bitterness of things;
Her quiet is secure;
No thorns can pierce her tender feet,
Whose life was, like the violet, sweet,
As climbing jasmine, pure, —

As snowdrop on an infant's grave,
Or lily heaving with the wave
That feeds it and defends;
As Vesper, ere the star hath kissed
The mountain-top, or breathed the mist
That from the vale ascends.

Thou takest not away, O Death!
Thou strikest, — absence perisheth,
Indifference is no more;
The future brightens on our sight;
For on the past hath fallen a light
That tempts us to adore.

XIV.

ELEGIAC MUSINGS.

IN THE GROUNDS OF COLEORTON HALL, THE SEAT OF THE LATE SIR G. H. BEAUMONT, BART.

In these grounds stands the Parish Church, wherein is a mural monument bearing an Inscription, which, in deference to the earnest request of the deceased, is confined to name, dates, and these words: — " Enter not into judgment with thy servant, O Lord! "

WITH copious eulogy in prose or rhyme
Graven on the tomb, we struggle against Time,
Alas, how feebly! but our feelings rise
And still we struggle when a good man dies.
Such offering BEAUMONT dreaded and forbade,
A spirit meek in self-abasement clad.
Yet *here* at least, though few have numbered days
That shunned so modestly the light of praise,
His graceful manners, and the temperate ray
Of that arch fancy which would round him play,
Brightening a converse never known to swerve
From courtesy and delicate reserve ;
That sense, the bland philosophy of life,
Which checked discussion ere it warmed to strife ;
Those rare accomplishments, and varied powers,
Might have their record among sylvan bowers.
Oh, fled for ever! vanished like a blast
That shook the leaves in myriads as it passed ; —
Gone from this world of earth, air, sea, and sky,

From all its spirit-moving imagery,
Intensely studied with a painter's eye,
A poet's heart; and, for congenial view,
Portrayed with happiest pencil, not untrue
To common recognitions while the line
Flowed in a course of sympathy divine;—
Oh! severed, too abruptly, from delights
That all the seasons shared with equal rights;—
Rapt in the grace of undismantled age,
From soul-felt music, and the treasured page
Lit by that evening lamp which loved to shed
Its mellow lustre round thy honored head;
While Friends beheld thee give, with eye, voice,
        mien,
More than theatric force to Shakespeare's scene;—
If thou hast heard me,—if thy Spirit know
Aught of these bowers, and whence their pleasures
        flow;
If things in our remembrance held so dear,
And thoughts and projects fondly cherished here,
To thy exalted nature only seem
Time's vanities, light fragments of earth's dream,—
Rebuke us not!—The mandate is obeyed
That said, "Let praise be mute where I am laid";
The holier deprecation, given in trust
To the cold marble, waits upon thy dust;
Yet have we found how slowly genuine grief
From *silent* admiration wins relief.
Too long abashed, thy Name is like a rose
That doth "within itself its sweetness close";

A drooping daisy changed into a cup
In which her bright-eyed beauty is shut up.
Within these groves, where still are flitting by
Shades of the Past, oft noticed with a sigh,
Shall stand a votive Tablet, haply free,
When towers and temples fall, to speak of Thee!
If sculptured emblems of our mortal doom
Recall not there the wisdom of the Tomb,
Green ivy, risen from out the cheerful earth,
Will fringe the lettered stone; and herbs spring forth,
Whose fragrance, by soft dews and rain unbound,
Shall penetrate the heart without a wound;
While truth and love their purposes fulfil,
Commemorating genius, talent, skill,
That could not lie concealed where thou **wert**
      known;
Thy virtues *He* must judge, and He alone,
The God upon whose mercy they are thrown.

                                  Nov., 1830.

XV.

WRITTEN AFTER THE DEATH OF CHARLES LAMB.

To a good Man of most dear memory
This Stone is sacred.   Here he lies apart
From the great city where he first drew breath,
Was reared and taught; and humbly earned his
      bread,

To the strict labors of the merchant's desk
By duty chained.   Not seldom did those tasks
Tease, and the thought of time so spent depress,
His spirit, but the recompense was high ;
Firm Independence, Bounty's rightful sire ;
Affections, warm as sunshine, free as air ;
And when the precious hours of leisure came,
Knowledge and wisdom, gained from converse sweet
With books, or while he ranged the crowded streets
With a keen eye, and overflowing heart :
So genius triumphed over seeming wrong,
And poured out truth in works by thoughtful love
Inspired, — works potent over smiles and tears.
And as round mountain-tops the lightning plays,
Thus innocently sported, breaking forth
As from a cloud of some grave sympathy,
Humor and wild instinctive wit, and all
The vivid flashes of his spoken words.
From the most gentle creature nursed in fields
Had been derived the name he bore, — a name,
Wherever Christian altars have been raised,
Hallowed to meekness and to innocence ;
And if in him meekness at times gave way,
Provoked out of herself by troubles strange,
Many and strange, that hung about his life,
Still, at the centre of his being, lodged
A soul by resignation sanctified :
And if too often, self-reproached, he felt
That innocence belongs not to our kind,
A power that never ceased to abide in him,

Charity, 'mid the multitude of sins
That she can cover, left not his exposed
To an unforgiving judgment from just Heaven.
O, he was good, if e'er a good Man lived!

    *   *   *   *   *

From a reflecting mind and sorrowing heart
Those simple lines flowed, with an earnest wish,
Though but a doubting hope, that they might serve
Fitly to guard the precious dust of him
Whose virtues called them forth. That aim is
      missed;
For much that truth most urgently required
Had from a faltering pen been asked in vain:
Yet, haply, on the printed page received,
The imperfect record, there, may stand unblamed
As long as verse of mine shall breathe the air
Of memory, or see the light of love.

    Thou wert a scorner of the fields, my Friend,
But more in show than truth; and from the fields,
And from the mountains, to thy rural grave
Transported, my soothed spirit hovers o'er
Its green, untrodden turf, and blowing flowers;
And, taking up a voice, shall speak (though still
Awed by the theme's peculiar sanctity
Which words less free presumed not even to touch)
Of that fraternal love, whose heaven-lit lamp
From infancy, through manhood, to the last
Of threescore years, and to thy latest hour,
Burnt on with ever-strengthening light, enshrined
Within thy bosom.

"Wonderful" hath been
The love established between man and man,
"Passing the love of women"; and between
Man and his helpmate in fast wedlock joined
Through God, is raised a spirit and soul of love
Without whose blissful influence Paradise
Had been no Paradise; and earth were now
A waste where creatures bearing human form,
Direst of savage beasts, would roam in fear,
Joyless and comfortless.   Our days glide on;
And let him grieve who cannot choose but grieve
That he hath been an Elm without his Vine,
And her bright dower of clustering charities,
That, round his trunk and branches, might have
      clung,
Enriching and adorning.   Unto thee,
Not so enriched, not so adorned, to thee
Was given (say rather thou of later birth
Wert given to her) a Sister, — 't is a word
Timidly uttered, for she *lives*, the meek,
The self-restraining, and the ever kind;
In whom thy reason and intelligent heart
Found — for all interests, hopes, and tender cares,
All softening, humanizing, hallowing powers,
Whether withheld, or for her sake unsought —
More than sufficient recompense !
                 Her love
(What weakness prompts the voice to tell it here?)
Was as the love of mothers; and when years,
Lifting the boy to man's estate, had called

The long protected to assume the part
Of a protector, the first filial tie
Was undissolved; and, in or out of sight,
Remained imperishably interwoven
With life itself.   Thus, 'mid a shifting world,
Did they together testify of time
And season's difference, — a double tree
With two collateral stems sprung from one root;
Such were they, — such through life they *might*
        have been
In union, in partition only such;
Otherwise wrought the will of the Most High;
Yet, through all visitations and all trials,
Still they were faithful; like two vessels launched
From the same beach, one ocean to explore,
With mutual help, and sailing — to their league
True, as inexorable winds, or bars
Floating or fixed of polar ice, allow.

But turn we rather, let my spirit turn
With thine, O silent and invisible Friend!
To those dear intervals, nor rare nor brief,
When, reunited, and by choice withdrawn
From miscellaneous converse, ye were taught
That the remembrance of foregone distress,
And the worse fear of future ill, (which oft
Doth hang around it, as a sickly child
Upon its mother,) may be both alike
Disarmed of power to unsettle present good,
So prized, and things inward and outward held

In such an even balance, that the heart
Acknowledges God's grace, his mercy feels,
And in its depth of gratitude is still.

O gift divine of quiet sequestration !
The hermit, exercised in prayer and praise,
And feeding daily on the hope of heaven,
Is happy in his vow, and fondly cleaves
To life-long singleness ; but happier far
Was to your souls, and, to the thoughts of others,
A thousand times more beautiful appeared,
Your *dual* loneliness.   The sacred tie
Is broken ; yet why grieve ? for Time but holds
His moiety in trust, till Joy shall lead
To the blest world where parting is unknown.

1835.

XVI.

EXTEMPORE EFFUSION UPON THE DEATH OF JAMES HOGG.

WHEN first, descending from the moorlands,
I saw the stream of Yarrow glide
Along a bare and open valley,
The Ettrick Shepherd was my guide.

When last along its banks I wandered,
Through groves that had begun to shed

Their golden leaves upon the pathways,
My steps the Border-minstrel led.

The mighty Minstrel breathes no longer,
'Mid mouldering ruins low he lies ;
And death upon the braes of Yarrow
Has closed the Shepherd-poet's eyes ;

Nor has the rolling year twice measured,
From sign to sign, its steadfast course,
Since every mortal power of Coleridge
Was frozen at its marvellous source ;

The rapt one, of the godlike forehead,
The heaven-eyed creature sleeps in earth :
And Lamb, the frolic and the gentle,
Has vanished from his lonely hearth.

Like clouds that rake the mountain-summits,
Or waves that own no curbing hand,
How fast has brother followed brother,
From sunshine to the sunless land !

Yet I, whose lids from infant slumber
Were earlier raised, remain to hear
A timid voice, that asks in whispers,
" Who next will drop and disappear ? "

Our haughty life is crowned with darkness,
Like London with its own black wreath,

On which, with thee, O Crabbe! forth-looking,
I gazed from Hampstead's breezy heath.

As if but yesterday departed,
Thou too art gone before ; but why,
O'er ripe fruit, seasonably gathered,
Should frail survivors heave a sigh ?

Mourn rather for that holy Spirit,
Sweet as the spring, as ocean deep ;
For her who, ere her summer faded,
Has sunk into a breathless sleep.

No more of old romantic sorrows,
For slaughtered youth or love-lorn maid !
With sharper grief is Yarrow smitten,
And Ettrick mourns with her their Poet dead.*

Nov., 1835.

XVII.

INSCRIPTION

FOR A MONUMENT IN CROSTHWAITE CHURCH, IN THE
VALE OF KESWICK.

YE vales and hills whose beauty hither drew
The poet's steps, and fixed him here, on you,
His eyes have closed !   And ye, loved books, no
    more

* See Note.

Shall Southey feed upon your precious lore,
To works that ne'er shall forfeit their renown
Adding immortal labors of his own, —
Whether he traced historic truth, with zeal
For the State's guidance, or the Church's weal,
Or Fancy, disciplined by studious art,
Informed his pen, or wisdom of the heart,
Or judgments sanctioned in the Patriot's mind
By reverence for the rights of all mankind.
Wide were his aims, yet in no human breast
Could private feelings meet for holier rest.
His joys, his griefs, have vanished like a cloud
From Skiddaw's top; but he to heaven was vowed
Through his industrious life, and Christian faith
Calmed in his soul the fear of change and death.

ODE.

INTIMATIONS OF IMMORTALITY FROM RECOL-LECTIONS OF EARLY CHILDHOOD.

The Child is father of the Man;
And I could wish my days to be
Bound each to each by natural piety.
See Vol. I. p. 187.

I.

THERE was a time when meadow, grove, and stream
The earth, and every common sight,
    To me did seem
    Apparelled in celestial light,
The glory and the freshness of a dream.
It is not now as it hath been of yore; —
    Turn wheresoe'er I may,
    By night or day,
The things which I have seen I now can see no
    more.

II.

The Rainbow comes and goes,
And lovely is the Rose ;
The Moon doth with delight

Look round her when the heavens are bare ;
    Waters on a starry night
    Are beautiful and fair ;
The sunshine is a glorious birth ;
But yet I know, where'er I go,
That there hath passed away a glory from the earth.

III.

Now, while the birds thus sing a joyous song,
    And while the young lambs bound
    As to the tabor's sound,
To me alone there came a thought of grief:
A timely utterance gave that thought relief,
    And I again am strong :
The cataracts blow their trumpets from the steep ;
No more shall grief of mine the season wrong ;
I hear the echoes through the mountains throng,
The winds come to me from the fields of sleep,
    And all the earth is gay ;
    Land and sea
    Give themselves up to jollity,
    And with the heart of May
Doth every beast keep holiday ; —
    Thou Child of Joy,
Shout round me, let me hear thy shouts, thou hap-
py Shepherd-boy !

IV.

Ye blessed Creatures, I have heard the call
    Ye to each other make ; I see

The heavens laugh with you in your jubilee;
My heart is at your festival,
My head hath its coronal,
The fulness of your bliss, I feel, I feel it all.
O evil day! if I were sullen
While Earth herself is adorning,
This sweet May-morning,
And the Children are culling
On every side,
In a thousand valleys far and wide,
Fresh flowers; while the sun shines warm,
And the Babe leaps up on his Mother's arm: —
I hear, I hear, with joy I hear!
—But there 's a Tree, of many, one,
A single Field which I have looked upon,
Both of them speak of something that is gone:
The pansy at my feet
Doth the same tale repeat:
Whither is fled the visionary gleam?
Where is it now, the glory and the dream?

V.

Our birth is but a sleep and a forgetting:
The Soul that rises with us, our life's Star,
Hath had elsewherè its setting,
And cometh from afar:
Not in entire forgetfulness,
And not in utter nakedness,
But trailing clouds of glory, do we come
From God, who is our home:

Heaven lies about us in our infancy !
Shades of the prison-house begin to close
      Upon the growing Boy,
But he beholds the light, and whence it flows,
      He sees it in his joy ;
The Youth, who daily farther from the east
      Must travel, still is Nature's Priest,
      And by the vision splendid
      Is on his way attended ;
At length the Man perceives it die away,
And fade into the light of common day.

VI.

Earth fills her lap with pleasures of her own ;
Yearnings she hath in her own natural kind,
And, even with something of a Mother's mind,
      And no unworthy aim,
      The homely Nurse doth all she can
To make her Foster-child, her Inmate Man,
      Forget the glories he hath known,
And that imperial palace whence he came.

VII.

Behold the Child among his new-born blisses,
A six years' Darling of a pigmy size !
See, where 'mid work of his own hand he lies,
Fretted by sallies of his mother's kisses,
With light upon him from his father's eyes !
See, at his feet, some little plan or chart,
Some fragment from his dream of human life,

Shaped by himself with newly-learned art;
    A wedding or a festival,
    A mourning or a funeral;
      And this hath now his heart,
      And unto this he frames his song:
      Then will he fit his tongue
To dialogues of business, love, or strife;
    But it will not be long
    Ere this be thrown aside,
    And with new joy and pride
The little Actor cons another part;
Filling from time to time his " humorous stage "
With all the Persons, down to palsied Age,
That Life brings with her in her equipage;
    As if his whole vocation
    Were endless imitation.

VIII.

Thou, whose exterior semblance doth belie
    Thy Soul's immensity;
Thou best Philosopher, who yet dost keep
Thy heritage, thou Eye among the blind,
That, deaf and silent, read'st the eternal deep,
Haunted for ever by the eternal mind, —
    Mighty Prophet! Seer blest !
    On whom those truths do rest,
Which we are toiling all our lives to find,
In darkness lost, the darkness of the grave;
Thou, over whom thy Immortality
Broods like the Day, a Master o'er a Slave,

A Presence which is not to be put by;
Thou little Child, yet glorious in the might
Of heaven-born freedom on thy being's height,
Why with such earnest pains dost thou provoke
The years to bring the inevitable yoke,
Thus blindly with thy blessedness at strife?
Full soon thy Soul shall have her earthly freight,
And custom lie upon thee with a weight,
Heavy as frost, and deep almost as life!

IX.

O joy! that in our embers
Is something that doth live,
That Nature yet remembers
What was so fugitive!
The thought of our past years in me doth breed
Perpetual benediction: not indeed
For that which is most worthy to be blest;
Delight and liberty, the simple creed
Of Childhood, whether busy or at rest,
With new-fledged hope still fluttering in his
breast:—
Not for these I raise
The song of thanks and praise;
But for those obstinate questionings
Of sense and outward things,
Fallings from us, vanishings;
Blank misgivings of a Creature
Moving about in worlds not realized,
High instincts before which our mortal Nature

Did tremble like a guilty thing surprised :
    But for those first affections,
    Those shadowy recollections,
    Which, be they what they may,
Are yet the fountain light of all our day,
Are yet a master light of all our seeing ;
    Uphold us, cherish, and have power to make
Our noisy years seem moments in the being
Of the eternal Silence : truths that wake,
    To perish never ;
Which neither listlessness, nor mad endeavor,
    Nor Man nor Boy,
Nor all that is at enmity with joy,
Can utterly abolish or destroy !
    Hence in a season of calm weather
    Though inland far we be,
Our souls have sight of that immortal sea
    Which brought us hither,
    Can in a moment travel thither,
And see the Children sport upon the shore,
And hear the mighty waters rolling evermore.

x.

Then sing, ye Birds, sing, sing a joyous song !
    And let the young Lambs bound
    As to the tabor's sound !
We in thought will join your throng,
    Ye that pipe and ye that play,
    Ye that through your hearts to-day
    Feel the gladness of the May !
What though the radiance which was once so bright

Be now for ever taken from my sight,
     Though nothing can bring back the hour
Of splendor in the grass, of glory in the flower;
     We will grieve not, rather find
     Strength in what remains behind;
     In the primal sympathy
     Which, having been, must ever be;
     In the soothing thoughts that spring
     Out of human suffering;
     In the faith that looks through death,
In years that bring the philosophic mind.

XI.

And O ye Fountains, Meadows, Hills, and Groves,
Forebode not any severing of our loves!
Yet in my heart of hearts I feel your might;
I only have relinquished one delight
To live beneath your more habitual sway.
I love the Brooks which down their channels fret,
Even more than when I tripped lightly as they;
The innocent brightness of a new-born Day
     Is lovely yet;
The Clouds that gather round the setting sun
Do take a sober coloring from an eye
That hath kept watch o'er man's mortality;
Another race hath been, and other palms are won.
Thanks to the human heart by which we live,
Thanks to its tenderness, its joys, and fears,
To me the meanest flower that blows can give
Thoughts that do often lie too deep for tears.

1803 – 6

NOTES.

Page 36.

" The Horn of Egremont Castle."

This story is a Cumberland tradition. I have heard it also related of the Hall of Hutton John, an ancient residence of the Hudlestons, in a sequestered valley upon the river Dacor.

Page 56.

" The Russian Fugitive."

Peter Henry Bruce, having given in his entertaining Memoirs the substance of this Tale, affirms that, besides the concurring reports of others, he had the story from the lady's own mouth.

The Lady Catherine, mentioned towards the close, is the famous Catherine, then bearing that name as the acknowledged wife of Peter the Great.

Page 126.

" The Farmer of Tilsbury Vale."

With this picture, which was taken from real life, compare the imaginative one of " The Reverie of Poor Susan," Vol. II., p. 132; and see (to make up the deficiencies of this class) " The Excursion," passim.

Page 159.

" Moss Campion (Silene acaulis)."

This most beautiful plant is scarce in England, though it is found in great abundance upon the mountains of Scotland.

The first specimen I ever saw of it, in its native bed, was singularly fine, the turf or cushion being at least eight inches in diameter, and the root proportionably thick. I have only met with it in two places among our mountains, in both of which I have since sought for it in vain.

Botanists will not, I hope, take it ill, if I caution them against carrying off, inconsiderately, rare and beautiful plants. This has often been done, particularly from Ingleborough and other mountains in Yorkshire, till the species have totally disappeared, to the great regret of lovers of nature living near the places where they grew.

Page 169.

" From the most gentle creature nursed in fields."

This way of indicating the name of my lamented friend has been found fault with; perhaps rightly so; but I may say in justification of the double sense of the word, that similar allusions are not uncommon in epitaphs. One of the best in our language in verse, I ever read, was upon a person who bore the name of Palmer; and the course of the thought, throughout, turned upon the Life of the Departed, considered as a pilgrimage. Nor can I think that the objection in the present case will have much force with any one who remembers Charles Lamb's beautiful sonnet addressed to his own name, and ending,

"No deed of mine shall shame thee, gentle name!"

Page 175.

Walter Scott	.	.	.	died 21st Sept., 1832.
S. T. Coleridge	.	.	.	" 25th July, 1834.
Charles Lamb	.	.	.	" 27th Dec., 1834.
George Crabbe	.	.	.	" 3d Feb , 1832.
Felicia Hemans	.	.	.	" 16th May, 1835.

APPENDIX, PREFACES,

ETC., ETC.

MUCH the greatest part of the foregoing Poems has been so long before the Public that no prefatory matter, explanatory of any portion of them, or of the arrangement which has been adopted, appears to be required; and had it not been for the observations contained in those Prefaces upon the principles of Poetry in general, they would not have been reprinted even as an Appendix in this Edition.

PREFACE

TO THE SECOND EDITION OF SEVERAL OF THE FOREGOING
POEMS, PUBLISHED, WITH AN ADDITIONAL VOLUME,
UNDER THE TITLE OF "LYRICAL BALLADS."

Note.—In succeeding Editions, when the Collection was much enlarged and diversified, this Preface was transferred to the end of the Volumes, as having little of a special application to their contents.

THE first Volume of these Poems has already been submitted to general perusal. It was published as an experiment, which, I hoped, might be of some use, to ascertain how far, by fitting to metrical arrangement a selection of the real language of men in a state of vivid sensation, that sort of pleasure and that quantity of pleasure may be imparted, which a Poet may rationally endeavor to impart.

I had formed no very inaccurate estimate of the probable effect of those Poems: I flattered myself that they who should be pleased with them would read them with more than common pleasure; and, on the other hand, I was well aware, that by those who should dislike them they would be read with more than common dislike. The result has differed from my expectation in this only, that a greater number have been pleased than I ventured to hope I should please.

Several of my Friends are anxious for the success of these Poems, from a belief, that, if the views with which they were composed were indeed realized, a class of Poetry would be produced, well adapted to interest mankind permanently, and not unimportant in the quality, and in the multiplicity of its moral relations : and on this account they have advised me to prefix a systematic defence of the theory upon which the Poems were written.   But I was unwilling to undertake the task, knowing that on this occasion the Reader would look coldly upon my arguments, since I might be suspected of having been principally influenced by the selfish and foolish hope of *reasoning* him into an approbation of these particular Poems : and I was still more unwilling to undertake the task, because adequately to display the opinions, and fully to enforce the arguments, would require a space wholly disproportionate to a preface. For, to treat the subject with the clearness and coherence of which it is susceptible, it would be necessary to give a full account of the present state of the public taste in this country, and to determine how far this taste is healthy or depraved; which, again, could not be determined, without pointing out in what manner language and the human mind act and react on each other, and without retracing the revolutions, not of liter‑ ature alone, but likewise of society itself. I have therefore altogether declined to enter regularly upon this defence; yet I am sensible that there would be something like impropriety in abruptly obtruding upon the Public, without a few words of introduction, Poems so materially different from those upon which general approbation is at present bestowed.

It is supposed, that by the act of writing in verse an Author makes a formal engagement that he will gratify certain known habits of association; that he not only thus apprises the Reader that certain classes of ideas and expressions will be found in his book, but that others will be carefully excluded. This exponent or symbol held forth by metrical language must in different eras of literature have excited very different expectations: for example, in the age of Catullus, Terence, and Lucretius, and that of Statius or Claudian; and in our own country, in the age of Shakespeare and Beaumont and Fletcher, and that of Donne and Cowley, or Dryden, or Pope. I will not take upon me to determine the exact import of the promise which, by the act of writing in verse, an Author, in the present day, makes to his reader; but it will undoubtedly appear to many persons that I have not fulfilled the terms of an engagement thus voluntarily contracted.

They who have been accustomed to the gaudiness and inane phraseology of many modern writers, if they persist in reading this book to its conclusion, will, no doubt, frequently have to struggle with feelings of strangeness and awkwardness : they will look round for poetry, and will be induced to inquire by what species of courtesy these attempts can be permitted to assume that title.   I hope, therefore, the reader will not censure me for attempting to state what I have proposed to myself to perform ; and also (as far as the limits of a preface will permit) to explain some of the chief reasons which have determined me in the choice of my purpose : that at least he may be spared any unpleasant feeling of disappointment, and that I myself may be protected from one of the most dishonorable accusations which can be brought against an Author ; namely, that of an indolence which prevents him from endeavoring to ascertain what is his duty, or, when his duty is ascertained, prevents him from performing it.

The principal object, then, proposed in these Poems, was to choose incidents and situations from common life, and to relate or describe them, throughout, as far as was possible, in a selection of language really used by men, and, at the same time, to throw over them a certain coloring of imagination, whereby ordinary things should be presented to the mind in an unusual aspect ; and, further, and above all, to make these incidents and situations interesting by tracing in them, truly though not ostentatiously, the primary laws of our nature: chiefly, as far as regards the manner in which we associate ideas in a state of excitement. Humble and rustic life was generally chosen, because in that condition the essential passions of the heart find a better soil in which they can attain their maturity, are less under restraint, and speak a plainer and more emphatic language; because in that condition of life our elementary feelings coexist in a state of greater simplicity, and, consequently, may be more accurately contemplated, and more forcibly communicated; because the manners of rural life germinate from those elementary feelings, and, from the necessary character of rural occupations, are more easily comprehended, and are more durable; and, lastly, because in that condition the passions of men are incorporated with the beautiful and permanent forms of nature. The language, too, of these men has been adopted, (purified indeed from what appear to be its real defects, from all lasting and rational causes of dislike or disgust,) because such men hourly communicate with the best objects from which the best part of language is originally derived; and because, from their rank in society and the sameness and narrow circle of their intercourse, being less under the influence of social vanity, they convey their feelings and notions in simple and unelaborated expressions. Accordingly, such a language, arising out of repeated experience and regular feelings, is a more permanent, and a far more philosophical language, than that which is frequently substituted for it by Poets, who think that they are conferring honor upon themselves and their art, in proportion as they separate themselves from the sympathies of men, and indulge in arbitrary and capricious habits of expression, in order to furnish food for fickle tastes, and fickle appetites, of their own creation.*

I cannot, however, be insensible to the present outcry against the triviality and meanness, both of thought and language, which some of my contemporaries have occasionally introduced into their metrical compositions ; and I acknowledge that this defect, where it exists, is more dishonorable to the Writer's own character than false refinement or arbitrary innovation, though I should contend, at the same time, that it is far less pernicious in the sum of its consequences.   From such verses the Poems in these volumes will be found distinguished at least by one mark of difference, that each of them has a worthy *purpose*.   Not that I always began to write with a distinct purpose formally conceived ; but habits of meditation have, I trust, so prompted and regulated my feel-

* It is worth while here to observe, that the affecting parts of Chaucer are almost always expressed in language pure and universally intelligible even to this day.

ings, that my descriptions of such objects as
strongly excite those feelings will be found to carry along with them a *purpose*.   If this opinion be
erroneous, I can have little right to the name of a
Poet.   For all good poetry is the spontaneous
overflow of powerful feelings : and though this be
true, Poems to which any value can be attached
were never produced on any variety of subjects
but by a man who, being possessed of more than
usual organic sensibility, had also thought long and
deeply.   For our continued influxes of feeling are
modified and directed by our thoughts, which are
indeed the representatives of all our past feelings;
and as, by contemplating the relation of these general representatives to each other, we discover
what is really important to men, so, by the repeti-
tion and continuance of this act, our feelings will
be connected with important subjects, till at length,
if we be originally possessed of much sensibility,
such habits of mind will be produced, that, by
obeying blindly and mechanically the impulses of
those habits, we shall describe objects, and utter
sentiments, of such a nature, and in such connection with each other, that the understanding of the
Reader must necessarily be in some degree enlightened, and his affections strengthened and purified.

It has been said that each of these Poems has a
purpose.   Another circumstance must be mentioned which distinguishes these Poems from the

popular Poetry of the day; it is this, that the feeling therein developed gives importance to the action and situation, and not the action and situation to the feeling.

A sense of false modesty shall not prevent me from asserting, that the Reader's attention is pointed to this mark of distinction, far less for the sake of these particular Poems than from the general importance of the subject. The subject is indeed important! For the human mind is capable of being excited without the application of gross and violent stimulants; and he must have a very faint perception of its beauty and dignity who does not know this, and who does not further know, that one being is elevated above another in proportion as he possesses this capability. It has therefore appeared to me, that to endeavor to produce or enlarge this capability is one of the best services in which, at any period, a Writer can be engaged; but this service, excellent at all times, is especially so at the present day. For a multitude of causes, unknown to former times, are now acting with a combined force to blunt the discriminating powers of the mind, and, unfitting it for all voluntary exertion, to reduce it to a state of almost savage torpor. The most effective of these causes are the great national events which are daily taking place, and the increasing accumulation of men in cities, where the uniformity of their occupations produces a craving for extraordinary incident, which the rapid communication of intelligence hourly gratifies. To this tendency of life and manners the literature and theatrical exhibitions of the country have conformed themselves. The invaluable works of our elder writers, I had almost said the works of Shakespeare and Milton, are driven into neglect by frantic novels, sickly and stupid German Tragedies, and deluges of idle and extravagant stories in verse. When I think upon this degrading thirst after outrageous stimulation, I am almost ashamed to have spoken of the feeble endeavor made in these volumes to counteract it; and, reflecting upon the magnitude of the general evil, I should be oppressed with no dishonorable melancholy, had I not a deep impression of certain inherent and indestructible qualities of the human mind, and likewise of certain powers in the great and permanent objects that act upon it, which are equally inherent and indestructible; and were there not added to this impression a belief, that the time is approaching when the evil will be systematically opposed, by men of greater powers, and with far more distinguished success.

Having dwelt thus long on the subjects and aim of these Poems, I shall request the Reader's permission to apprise him of a few circumstances relating to their *style*, in order, among other reasons, that he may not censure me for not having performed what I never attempted. The Reader will find that personifications of abstract ideas rarely occur in these volumes; and are utterly rejected, as an ordinary device to elevate the style, and raise it above prose. My purpose was to imitate, and, as far as is possible, to adopt the very language of men; and assuredly such personifications do not make any natural or regular part of that language. They are, indeed, a figure of speech occasionally prompted by passion, and I have made use of them as such; but have endeavored utterly to reject them as a mechanical device of style, or as a family language which Writers in metre seem to lay claim to by prescription. I have wished to keep the Reader in the company of flesh and blood, persuaded that by so doing I shall interest him. Others who pursue a different track will interest him likewise; I do not interfere with their claim, but wish to prefer a claim of my own. There will also be found in these volumes little of what is usually called poetic diction; as much pains has been taken to avoid it as is ordinarily taken to produce it; this has been done for the reason already alleged, to bring my language near to the language of men; and further, because the pleasure which I have proposed to myself to impart, is of a kind very different from that which is supposed by many persons to be the proper object of poetry. Without being culpably particular, I do not know how to give my Reader a more exact notion of the style in which it was my wish and intention to write, than by informing him that I have at all times endeavored to look steadily at my subject; consequently, there is, I hope, in these Poems, little falsehood of description, and my ideas are expressed in language fitted to their respective importance. Something must have been gained by this practice, as it is friendly to one property of all good poetry, namely, good sense: but it has necessarily cut me off from a large portion of phrases and figures of speech which from father to son have long been regarded as the common inheritance of Poets. I have also thought it expedient to restrict myself still further, having abstained from the use of many expressions, in themselves proper and beautiful, but which have been foolishly repeated by bad Poets, till such feelings of disgust are connected with them as it is scarcely possible by any art of association to overpower.

If in a poem there should be found a series of lines, or even a single line, in which the language, though naturally arranged, and according to the strict laws of metre, does not differ from that of prose, there is a numerous class of critics, who, when they stumble upon these prosaisms, as they call them, imagine that they have made a notable discovery, and exult over the Poet as over a man ignorant of his own profession. Now these men would establish a canon of criticism which the

Reader will conclude he must utterly reject, if he wishes to be pleased with these volumes.   And it would be a most easy task to prove to him, that not only the language of a large portion of every good poem, even of the most elevated character, must necessarily, except with reference to the metre, in no respect differ from that of good prose, but likewise that some of the most interesting parts of the best poems will be found to be strictly the language of prose when prose is well written. The truth of this assertion might be demonstrated by innumerable passages from almost all the poetical writings, even of Milton himself.   To illustrate the subject in a general manner, I will here adduce a short composition of Gray, who was at the head of those who, by their reasonings, have attempted to widen the space of separation betwixt Prose and Metrical composition, and was more than any other man curiously elaborate in the structure of his own poetic diction.

> " In vain to me the smiling mornings shine,
> And reddening Phœbus lifts his golden fire:
> The birds in vain their amorous descant join,
> Or cheerful fields resume their green attire.
> These ears, alas! for other notes repine;
> *A different object do these eyes require;*
> *My lonely anguish melts no heart but mine;*
> *And in my breast the imperfect joys expire;*
> Yet morning smiles the busy race to cheer,
> And new-born pleasure brings to happier men;
> The fields to all their wonted tribute bear;
> To warm their little loves the birds complain.
> *I fruitless mourn to him that cannot hear,*
> *And weep the more because I weep in vain.*"

It will easily be perceived, that the only part of this Sonnet which is of any value is the lines printed in Italics; it is equally obvious, that, except in the rhyme, and in the use of the single word "fruitless" for fruitlessly, which is so far a defect, the language of these lines does in no respect differ from that of prose.

By the foregoing quotation it has been shown that the language of Prose may yet be well adapted to Poetry; and it was previously asserted, that a large portion of the language of every good poem can in no respect differ from that of good Prose. We will go further. It may be safely affirmed, that there neither is, nor can be, any *essential* difference between the language of prose and metrical composition. We are fond of tracing the resemblance between Poetry and Painting, and, accordingly, we call them Sisters: but where shall we find bonds of connection sufficiently strict to typify the affinity betwixt metrical and prose composition? They both speak by and to the same organs; the bodies in which both of them are clothed may be said to be of the same substance, their affections are kindred, and almost identical, not necessarily differing even in degree; Poetry * sheds no tears "such as Angels weep,"

---

* I here use the word "Poetry" (though against my own judgment) as opposed to the word Prose, and synonymous with metrical composition. But much confusion has been introduced into criticism by this contradistinction of Poetry

but natural and human tears ; she can boast of no
celestial ichor that distinguishes her vital juices
from those of Prose ; the same human blood cir-
culates through the veins of them both.

If it be affirmed that rhyme and metrical arrangement of themselves constitute a distinction
which overturns what has just been said on the
strict affinity of metrical language with that of
prose, and paves the way for other artificial distinctions which the mind voluntarily admits, I answer that the language of such Poetry as is here
recommended is, as far as is possible, a selection
of the language really spoken by men; that this
selection, wherever it is made with true taste and
feeling, will of itself form a distinction far greater
than would at first be imagined, and will entirely
separate the composition from the vulgarity and
meanness of ordinary life; and if metre be superadded thereto, I believe that a dissimilitude will
be produced altogether sufficient for the gratification of a rational mind. What other distinction
would we have? Whence is it to come? And
where is it to exist? Not, surely, where the
Poet speaks through the mouths of his characters :
it cannot be necessary here, either for elevation of

and Prose, instead of the more philosophical one of Poetry
and Matter of Fact, or Science. The only strict antithesis to
Prose is Metre; nor is this, in truth, a *strict* antithesis, because
lines and passages of metre so naturally occur in writing
prose, that it would be scarcely possible to avoid them, even
were it desirable.

style, or any of its supposed ornaments: for, if the Poet's subject be judiciously chosen, it will naturally, and upon fit occasion, lead him to passions, the language of which, if selected truly and judiciously, must necessarily be dignified and variegated, and alive with metaphors and figures. I forbear to speak of an incongruity which would shock the intelligent Reader, should the Poet interweave any foreign splendor of his own with that which the passion naturally suggests: it is sufficient to say that such addition is unnecessary. And, surely, it is more probable that those passages, which with propriety abound with metaphors and figures, will have their due effect, if, upon other occasions where the passions are of a milder character, the style also be subdued and temperate.

But, as the pleasure which I hope to give by the Poems now presented to the Reader must depend entirely on just notions upon this subject, and as it is in itself of high importance to our taste and moral feelings, I cannot content myself with these detached remarks. And if, in what I am about to say, it shall appear to some that my labor is unnecessary, and that I am like a man fighting a battle without enemies, such persons may be reminded, that, whatever be the language outwardly holden by men, a practical faith in the opinions which I am wishing to establish is almost unknown. If my conclusions are admitted, and carried as far as they must be carried if admitted at all, our judgments concerning the works of the greatest Poets, both ancient and modern, will be far different from what they are at present, both when we praise and when we censure; and our moral feelings influencing and influenced by these judgments will, I believe, be corrected and purified.

Taking up the subject, then, upon general grounds, let me ask, What is meant by the word Poet? What is a Poet? To whom does he address himself? And what language is to be expected from him?—He is a man speaking to men: a man, it is true, endowed with more lively sensibility, more enthusiasm and tenderness, who has a greater knowledge of human nature and a more comprehensive soul, than are supposed to be common among mankind; a man pleased with his own passions and volitions, and who rejoices more than other men in the spirit of life that is in him; delighting to contemplate similar volitions and passions as manifested in the goings-on of the Universe, and habitually impelled to create them where he does not find them. To these qualities he has added a disposition to be affected more than other men by absent things as if they were present; an ability of conjuring up in himself passions, which are indeed far from being the same as those produced by real events, yet (especially in those parts of the general sympathy which are pleasing and delightful) do more nearly resemble the passions produced by real events, than anything which, from the motions of their own minds merely, other men are accustomed to feel in themselves : — whence, and from practice, he has acquired a greater readiness and power in expressing what he thinks and feels, and especially those thoughts and feelings which, by his own choice, or from the structure of his own mind, arise in him without immediate external excitement.

But whatever portion of this faculty we may suppose even the greatest Poet to possess, there cannot be a doubt that the language which it will suggest to him must often, in liveliness and truth, fall short of that which is uttered by men in real life, under the actual pressure of those passions, certain shadows of which the Poet thus produces, or feels to be produced, in himself.

However exalted a notion we would wish to cherish of the character of a Poet, it is obvious, that, while he describes and imitates passions, his employment is in some degree mechanical, compared with the freedom and power of real and substantial action and suffering. So that it will be the wish of the Poet to bring his feelings near to those of the persons whose feelings he describes, nay, for short spaces of time, perhaps, to let himself slip into an entire delusion, and even confound and identify his own feelings with theirs; modifying only the language which is thus suggested to

him by a consideration that he describes for a particular purpose, that of giving pleasure. Here,
then, he will apply the principle of selection which
has been already insisted upon. He will depend
upon this for removing what would otherwise be
painful or disgusting in the passion ; he will feel
that there is no necessity to trick out or to elevate
nature : and, the more industriously he applies
this principle, the deeper will be his faith that no
words, which *his* fancy or imagination can suggest,
will be to be compared with those which are the
emanations of reality and truth.

But it may be said by those who do not object
to the general spirit of these remarks, that, as it is
impossible for the Poet to produce upon all occasions language as exquisitely fitted for the passion
as that which the real passion itself suggests, it is
proper that he should consider himself as in the
situation of a translator, who does not scruple to
substitute excellences of another kind for those
which are unattainable by him ; and endeavors
occasionally to surpass his original, in order to make
some amends for the general inferiority to which
he feels that he must submit. But this would be
to encourage idleness and unmanly despair. Further, it is the language of men who speak of what
they do not understand ; who talk of Poetry as of
a matter of amusement and idle pleasure ; who
will converse with us as gravely about a *taste* for
Poetry, as they express it, as if it were a thing as

indifferent as a taste for rope-dancing, or Frontiniac, or Sherry. Aristotle, I have been told, has said, that Poetry is the most philosophic of all writing. It is so : its object is truth, not individual and local, but general, and operative ; not standing upon external testimony, but carried alive into the heart by passion ; truth which is its own testimony, which gives competence and confidence to the tribunal to which it appeals, and receives them from the same tribunal. Poetry is the image of man and nature. The obstacles which stand in the way of the fidelity of the Biographer and Historian, and of their consequent utility, are incalculably greater than those which are to be encountered by the Poet who comprehends the dignity of his art. The Poet writes under one restriction only, namely, the necessity of giving immediate pleasure to a human Being possessed of that information which may be expected from him, not as a lawyer, a physician, a mariner, an astronomer, or a natural philosopher, but as a Man. Except this one restriction, there is no object standing between the Poet and the image of things ; between this, and the Biographer and Historian, there are a thousand.

Nor let this necessity of producing immediate pleasure be considered as a degradation of the Poet's art. It is far otherwise. It is an acknowledgment of the beauty of the universe, an acknowledgment the more sincere, because not formal, but indirect; it is a task light and easy to him who looks at the world in the spirit of love: further, it is a homage paid to the native and naked dignity of man, to the grand elementary principle of pleasure, by which he knows, and feels, and lives, and moves. We have no sympathy but what is propagated by pleasure: I would not be misunderstood; but wherever we sympathize with pain, it will be found that the sympathy is produced and carried on by subtle combinations with pleasure. We have no knowledge, that is, no general principles drawn from the contemplation of particular facts, but what has been built up by pleasure, and exists in us by pleasure alone. The Man of science, the Chemist and Mathematician, whatever difficulties and disgusts they may have had to struggle with, know and feel this. However painful may be the objects with which the Anatomist's knowledge is connected, he feels that his knowledge is pleasure; and where he has no pleasure, he has no knowledge. What then does the Poet? He considers man and the objects that surround him as acting and reacting upon each other, so as to produce an infinite complexity of pain and pleasure; he considers man in his own nature and in his ordinary life as contemplating this with a certain quantity of immediate knowledge, with certain convictions, intuitions, and deductions, which from habit acquire the quality of intuitions; he considers him as looking upon this complex scene of ideas and sensations, and finding everywhere objects that immediately excite in him sympathies which, from the necessities of his nature, are accompanied by an overbalance of enjoyment.

To this knowledge which all men carry about with them, and to these sympathies, in which, without any other discipline than that of our daily life, we are fitted to take delight, the Poet principally directs his attention.   He considers man and nature as essentially adapted to each other, and the mind of man as naturally the mirror of the fairest and most interesting properties of nature. And thus the Poet, prompted by this feeling of pleasure, which accompanies him through the whole course of his studies, converses with general nature, with affections akin to those which, through labor and length of time, the Man of science has raised up in himself, by conversing with those particular parts of nature which are the objects of his studies.   The knowledge both of the Poet and the Man of science is pleasure ; but the knowledge of the one cleaves to us as a necessary part of our existence, our natural and unalienable inheritance ; the other is a personal and individual acquisition, slow to come to us, and by no habitual and direct sympathy connecting us with our fellow-beings.   The Man of science seeks truth as a remote and unknown benefactor ; he cherishes and loves it in his solitude : the Poet, singing a song in which all human beings join with him, rejoices in the presence of truth as our visible friend and hourly companion. Poetry is the breath and finer spirit of all knowledge; it is the impassioned expression which is in the countenance of all Science. Emphatically may it be said of the Poet, as Shakespeare hath said of man, " that he looks before and after." He is the rock of defence for human nature; an upholder and preserver, carrying everywhere with him relationship and love. In spite of difference of soil and climate, of language and manners, of laws and customs, — in spite of things silently gone out of mind, and things violently destroyed, — the Poet binds together by passion and knowledge the vast empire of human society, as it is spread over the whole earth, and over all time. The objects of the Poet's thoughts are everywhere; though the eyes and senses of man are, it is true, his favorite guides, yet he will follow wheresoever he can find an atmosphere of sensation in which to move his wings. Poetry is the first and last of all knowledge, — it is as immortal as the heart of man. If the labors of Men of science should ever create any material revolution, direct or indirect, in our condition, and in the impressions which we habitually receive, the Poet will sleep then no more than at present; he will be ready to follow the steps of the Man of science, not only in those general indirect effects, but he will be at his side, carrying sensation into the midst of the objects of the science itself. The remotest discoveries of the Chemist, the Botanist, or Mineralogist, will be as proper objects of the Poet's art as any upon which it can be employed, if the time should ever come when these things shall be familiar to us, and the relations under which they are contemplated by the followers of these respective sciences shall be manifestly and palpably material to us as enjoying and suffering beings. If the time should ever come when what is now called science, thus familiarized to men, shall be ready to put on, as it were, a form of flesh and blood, the Poet will lend his divine spirit to aid the transfiguration, and will welcome the being thus produced, as a dear and genuine inmate of the household of man. — It is not, then, to be supposed that any one, who holds that sublime notion of Poetry which I have attempted to convey, will break in upon the sanctity and truth of his pictures by transitory and accidental ornaments, and endeavor to excite admiration of himself by arts, the necessity of which must manifestly depend upon the assumed meanness of his subject.

What has been thus far said applies to Poetry in general; but especially to those parts of composition where the Poet speaks through the mouths of his characters; and upon this point it appears to authorize the conclusion, that there are few persons of good sense, who would not allow

that the dramatic parts of composition are defec-
tive, in proportion as they deviate from the real
language of nature, and are colored by a diction of
the Poet's own, either peculiar to him as an individual Poet or belonging simply to Poets in general; to a body of men who, from the circumstance
of their compositions being in metre, it is expected
will employ a particular language.

It is not, then, in the dramatic parts of composition that we look for this distinction of language; but still it may be proper and necessary
where the Poet speaks to us in his own person
and character.   To this I answer by referring the
Reader to the description before given of a Poet.
Among the qualities there enumerated as principally conducing to form a Poet, is implied nothing differing in kind from other men, but only in
degree.   The sum of what was said is, that the
Poet is chiefly distinguished from other men by a
greater promptness to think and feel without immediate external excitement, and a greater power
in expressing such thoughts and feelings as are
produced in him in that manner.   But these passions and thoughts and feelings are the general
passions and thoughts and feelings of men.   And
with what are they connected?   Undoubtedly
with our moral sentiments and animal sensations,
and with the causes which excite these; with the
operations of the elements, and the appearances
of the visible universe; with storm and sunshine,

with the revolutions of the seasons, with cold and
heat, with loss of friends and kindred, with inju-
ries and resentments, gratitude and hope, with
fear and sorrow. These, and the like, are the
sensations and objects which the Poet describes,
as they are the sensations of other men, and the
objects which interest them. The Poet thinks
and feels in the spirit of human passions. How,
then, can his language differ in any material degree from that of all other men who feel vividly
and see clearly? It might be *proved* that it is impossible. But supposing that this were not the
case, the Poet might then be allowed to use a peculiar language when expressing his feelings for
his own gratification, or that of men like himself.
But Poets do not write for Poets alone, but for
men. Unless, therefore, we are advocates for that
admiration which subsists upon ignorance, and that
pleasure which arises from hearing what we do
not understand, the Poet must descend from this
supposed height; and, in order to excite rational
sympathy, he must express himself as other men
express themselves. To this it may be added,
that while he is only selecting from the real language of men, or, which amounts to the same
thing, composing accurately in the spirit of such
selection, he is treading upon safe ground, and we
know what we are to expect from him. Our feelings are the same with respect to metre; for, as
it may be proper to remind the Reader, the dis-

tinction of metre is regular and uniform, and not, like that which is produced by what is usually called POETIC DICTION, arbitrary, and subject to infinite caprices upon which no calculation whatever can be made. In the one case, the Reader is utterly at the mercy of the Poet, respecting what imagery or diction he may choose to connect with the passion; whereas, in the other, the metre obeys certain laws, to which the Poet and Reader both willingly submit, because they are certain, and because no interference is made by them with the passion, but such as the concurring testimony of ages has shown to heighten and improve the pleasure which coexists with it.

It will now be proper to answer an obvious question, namely, Why, professing these opinions, have I written in verse? To this, in addition to such answer as is included in what has been already said, I reply, in the first place, Because, however I may have restricted myself, there is still left open to me what confessedly constitutes the most valuable object of all writing, whether in prose or verse; the great and universal passions of men, the most general and interesting of their occupations, and the entire world of nature before me, to supply endless combinations of forms and imagery. Now, supposing for a moment that whatever is interesting in these objects may be as vividly described in prose, why should I be condemned for attempting to superadd to such description the charm which, by the consent of all nations, is acknowledged to exist in metrical language ? To this, by such as are yet unconvinced, it may be answered, that a very small part of the pleasure given by Poetry depends upon the metre, and that it is injudicious to write in metre, unless it be accompanied with the other artificial distinctions of style with which metre is usually accompanied, and that, by such deviation, more will be lost from the shock which will thereby be given to the Reader's associations than will be counterbalanced by any pleasure which he can derive from the general power of numbers. In answer to those who still contend for the necessity of accompanying metre with certain appropriate colors of style in order to the accomplishment of its appropriate end, and who also, in my opinion, greatly underrate the power of metre in itself, it might perhaps, as far as relates to these Volumes, have been almost sufficient to observe, that poems are extant, written upon more humble subjects, and in a still more naked and simple style, which have continued to give pleasure from generation to generation. Now, if nakedness and simplicity be a defect, the fact here mentioned affords a strong presumption that poems somewhat less naked and simple are capable of affording pleasure at the present day ; and what I wished *chiefly* to attempt, at present, was to justify myself for having written under the impression of this belief.

But various causes might be pointed out why, when the style is manly, and the subject of some importance, words metrically arranged will long continue to impart such a pleasure to mankind as he who proves the extent of that pleasure will be desirous to impart. The end of Poetry is to produce excitement in coexistence with an overbalance of pleasure; but, by the supposition, excitement is an unusual and irregular state of the mind; ideas and feelings do not, in that state, succeed each other in accustomed order. If the words, however, by which this excitement is produced be in themselves powerful, or the images and feelings have an undue proportion of pain connected with them, there is some danger that the excitement may be carried beyond its proper bounds. Now the co-presence of something regular, something to which the mind has been accustomed in various moods and in a less excited state, cannot but have great efficacy in tempering and restraining the passion by an intertexture of ordinary feeling, and of feeling not strictly and necessarily connected with the passion. This is unquestionably true; and hence, though the opinion will at first appear paradoxical, from the tendency of metre to divest language, in a certain degree, of its reality, and thus to throw a sort of half-consciousness of unsubstantial existence over the whole composition, there can be little doubt but that more pathetic situations and sentiments, that is, those which have a greater proportion of pain connected with them, may be endured in metrical composition, especially in rhyme, than in prose. The metre of the old ballads is very artless; yet they contain many passages which would illustrate this opinion; and I hope, if the following Poems be attentively perused, similar instances will be found in them. This opinion may be further illustrated by appealing to the Reader's own experience of the reluctance with which he comes to the reperusal of the distressful parts of Clarissa Harlowe, or the Gamester; while Shakespeare's writings, in the most pathetic scenes, never act upon us, as pathetic, beyond the bounds of pleasure, — an effect which, in a much greater degree than might at first be imagined, is to be ascribed to small, but continual and regular, impulses of pleasurable surprise from the metrical arrangement. — On the other hand, (what it must be allowed will much more frequently happen,) if the Poet's words should be incommensurate with the passion, and inadequate to raise the Reader to a height of desirable excitement, then (unless the Poet's choice of his metre has been grossly injudicious) in the feelings of pleasure which the Reader has been accustomed to connect with metre in general, and in the feeling, whether cheerful or melancholy, which he has been accustomed to connect with that particular movement of metre, there will be found something which will greatly contribute to impart passion to the words, and to effect the complex end which the Poet proposes to himself.

If I had undertaken a SYSTEMATIC defence of the theory here maintained, it would have been my duty to develop the various causes upon which the pleasure received from metrical language depends. Among the chief of these causes is to be reckoned a principle which must be well known to those who have made any of the Arts the object of accurate reflection ; namely, the pleasure which the mind derives from the perception of similitude in dissimilitude. This principle is the great spring of the activity of our minds, and their chief feeder. From this principle the direction of the sexual appetite, and all the passions connected with it, take their origin : it is the life of our ordinary conversation ; and upon the accuracy with which similitude in dissimilitude, and dissimilitude in similitude are perceived, depend our taste and our moral feelings. It would not be a useless employment to apply this principle to the consideration of metre, and to show that metre is hence enabled to afford much pleasure, and to point out in what manner that pleasure is produced. But my limits will not permit me to enter upon this subject, and I must content myself with a general summary.

I have said that poetry is the spontaneous overflow of powerful feelings : it takes its origin from emotion recollected in tranquillity : the emotion is contemplated till, by a species of reaction, the tranquillity gradually disappears, and an emotion, kindred to that which was before the subject of contemplation, is gradually produced, and does itself actually exist in the mind. In this mood successful composition generally begins, and in a mood similar to this it is carried on ; but the emotion, of whatever kind, and in whatever degree, from various causes, is qualified by various pleasures, so that in describing any passions whatsoever, which are voluntarily described, the mind will, upon the whole, be in a state of enjoyment. If Nature be thus cautious to preserve in a state of enjoyment a being so employed, the Poet ought to profit by the lesson held forth to him, and ought especially to take care, that, whatever passions he communicates to his Reader, those passions, if his Reader's mind be sound and vigorous, should always be accompanied with an overbalance of pleasure. Now the music of harmonious metrical language, the sense of difficulty overcome, and the blind association of pleasure which has been previously received from works of rhyme or metre of the same or similar construction, an indistinct perception perpetually renewed of language closely resembling that of real life, and yet, in the circumstance of metre, differing from it so widely, — all these imperceptibly make up a complex feeling of delight, which is of the most important use in tempering the painful feeling always found intermingled with powerful descriptions of the deeper passions. This effect is always produced in pathetic and impassioned poetry; while, in lighter compositions, the ease and gracefulness with which the Poet manages his numbers are themselves confessedly a principal source of the gratification of the Reader. All that is *necessary* to say, however, upon this subject, may be effected by affirming, what few persons will deny, that, of two descriptions, either of passions, manners, or characters, each of them equally well executed, the one in prose and the other in verse, the verse will be read a hundred times where the prose is read once.

Having thus explained a few of my reasons for writing in verse, and why I have chosen subjects from common life, and endeavored to bring my language near to the real language of men, if I have been too minute in pleading my own cause, I have at the same time been treating a subject of general interest; and for this reason a few words shall be added with reference solely to these particular poems, and to some defects which will probably be found in them. I am sensible that my associations must have sometimes been particular instead of general, and that, consequently, giving to things a false importance, I may have sometimes written upon unworthy subjects; but I am less apprehensive on this account, than that my language may frequently have suffered from those arbitrary connections of feelings and ideas with particular words and phrases, from which no man can altogether protect himself. Hence I have no doubt, that, in some instances, feelings, even of the ludicrous, may be given to my Readers by expressions which appeared to me tender and pathetic. Such faulty expressions, were I convinced they were faulty at present, and that they must necessarily continue to be so, I would willingly take all reasonable pains to correct. But it is dangerous to make these alterations on the simple authority of a few individuals, or even of certain classes of men ; for where the understanding of an Author is not convinced, or his feelings altered, this cannot be done without great injury to himself: for his own feelings are his stay and support ; and, if he set them aside in one instance, he may be induced to repeat this act till his mind shall lose all confidence in itself, and become utterly debilitated. To this it may be added, that the critic ought never to forget that he is himself exposed to the same errors as the Poet, and perhaps in a much greater degree : for there can be no presumption in saying of most readers, that it is not probable they will be so well acquainted with the various stages of meaning through which words have passed, or with the fickleness or stability of the relations of particular ideas to each other ; and, above all, since they are so much less interested in the subject, they may decide lightly and carelessly.

Long as the Reader has been detained, I hope he will permit me to caution him against a mode of false criticism which has been applied to Poetry, in which the language closely resembles that of life and nature. Such verses have been triumphed over in parodies, of which Dr. Johnson's stanza is a fair specimen : —

> "I put my hat upon my head
>   And walked into the Strand,
> And there I met another man
>   Whose hat was in his hand."

Immediately under these lines let us place one of the most justly admired stanzas of the *Babes in the Wood.*

> " These pretty Babes with hand in hand
>   Went wandering up and down;
> But never more they saw the Man
>   Approaching from the Town."

In both these stanzas the words, and the order of the words, in no respect differ from the most unimpassioned conversation. There are words in both, for example, " the Strand," and "the Town," connected with none but the most familiar ideas; yet the one stanza we admit as admirable, and the other as a fair example of the superlative contemptible. Whence arises this difference? Not from the metre, not from the language, not from the order of the words; but the *matter* expressed in Dr. Johnson's stanza is contemptible. The proper method of treating trivial and simple verses, to which Dr. Johnson's stanza would be a fair parallelism, is not to say, this is a bad kind of poetry, or, this is not poetry; but, this wants sense; it is neither interesting in itself, nor can *lead* to anything interesting; the images neither originate in that sane state of feeling which arises out of thought, nor can excite thought or feeling in the Reader. This is the only sensible manner of dealing with such verses. Why trouble yourself about the species till you have previously decided upon the genus? Why take pains to prove that an ape is not a Newton, when it is self-evident that he is not a man?

One request I must make of my reader, which is, that in judging these Poems he would decide by his own feelings genuinely, and not by reflection upon what will probably be the judgment of others. How common is it to hear a person say, I myself do not object to this style of composition, or this or that expression, but to such and such classes of people it will appear mean or ludicrous! This mode of criticism, so destructive of all sound, unadulterated judgment, is almost universal: let the Reader then abide, independently, by his own feelings, and, if he finds himself affected, let him not suffer such conjectures to interfere with his pleasure.

If an Author, by any single composition, has impressed us with respect for his talents, it is useful to consider this as affording a presumption, that, on other occasions where we have been displeased, he, nevertheless, may not have written ill or absurdly ; and further, to give him so much credit for this one composition as may induce us to review what has displeased us with more care than we should otherwise have bestowed upon it. This is not only an act of justice, but, in our decisions upon poetry especially, may conduce, in a high degree, to the improvement of our own taste : for an *accurate* taste in poetry, and in all the other arts, as Sir Joshua Reynolds has observed, is an *acquired* talent, which can only be produced by thought and long-continued intercourse with the best models of composition. This is mentioned, not with so ridiculous a purpose as to prevent the most inexperienced Reader from judging for himself, (I have already said that I wish him to judge for himself,) but merely to temper the rashness of decision, and to suggest, that, if Poetry be a subject on which much time has not been bestowed, the judgment may be erroneous ; and that in many cases it necessarily will be so.

Nothing would, I know, have so effectually contributed to further the end which I have in view, as to have shown of what kind the pleasure is, and how that pleasure is produced, which is confessedly produced by metrical composition essentially

different from that which I have here endeavored
to recommend: for the Reader will say that he
has been pleased by such composition ; and what
more can be done for him ? The power of any
art is limited; and he will suspect, that, if it be
proposed to furnish him with new friends, that can
be only upon condition of his abandoning his old
friends. Besides, as I have said, the Reader is
himself conscious of the pleasure which he has
received from such composition, composition to
which he has peculiarly attached the endearing
name of Poetry ; and all men feel an habitual
gratitude, and something of an honorable bigotry,
for the objects which have long continued to
please them : we not only wish to be pleased,
but to be pleased in that particular way in which
we have been accustomed to be pleased. There
is in these feelings enough to resist a host of arguments ; and I should be the less able to combat
them successfully, as I am willing to allow, that,
in order entirely to enjoy the Poetry which I am
recommending, it would be necessary to give up
much of what is ordinarily enjoyed. But, would
my limits have permitted me to point out how this
pleasure is produced, many obstacles might have
been removed, and the Reader assisted in perceiving that the powers of language are not so limited
as he may suppose ; and that it is possible for poetry to give other enjoyments, of a purer, more
lasting, and more exquisite nature. This part of

the subject has not been altogether neglected, but it has not been so much my present aim to prove that the interest excited by some other kinds of poetry is less vivid, and less worthy of the nobler powers of the mind, as to offer reasons for presuming, that, if my purpose were fulfilled, a species of poetry would be produced, which is genuine poetry; in its nature well adapted to interest mankind permanently, and likewise important in the multiplicity and quality of its moral relations.

From what has been said, and from a perusal of the Poems, the Reader will be able clearly to perceive the object which I had in view: he will determine how far it has been attained; and, what is a much more important question, whether it be worth attaining: and upon the decision of these two questions will rest my claim to the approbation of the Public.

APPENDIX.

See page 214, — " by what is usually called POETIC DIC-
TION."

PERHAPS, as I have no right to expect that attentive perusal without which, confined, as I have
been, to the narrow limits of a preface, my meaning cannot be thoroughly understood, I am anxious to give an exact notion of the sense in which
the phrase Poetic Diction has been used ; and for
this purpose a few words shall here be added,
concerning the origin and characteristics of the
phraseology which I have condemned under that
name.

The earliest Poets of all nations generally wrote
from passion excited by real events ; they wrote
naturally, and as men : feeling powerfully as they
did, their language was daring, and figurative.
In succeeding times, Poets, and men ambitious of
the fame of Poets, perceiving the influence of such
language, and desirous of producing the same effect without being animated by the same passion,
set themselves to a mechanical adoption of these
figures of speech and made use of them, some-

times with propriety, but much more frequently applied them to feelings and thoughts with which they had no natural connection whatsoever. A language was thus insensibly produced, differing materially from the real language of men in *any situation*. The Reader or Hearer of this distorted language found himself in a perturbed and unusual state of mind : when affected by the genuine language of passion, he had been in a perturbed and unusual state of mind also : in both cases he was willing that his common judgment and understanding should be laid asleep, and he had no instinctive and infallible perception of the true to make him reject the false ; the one served as a passport for the other. The emotion was in both cases delightful, and no wonder if he confounded the one with the other, and believed them both to be produced by the same, or similar causes. Besides, the Poet spake to him in the character of a man to be looked up to, a man of genius and authority. Thus, and from a variety of other causes, this distorted language was received with admiration ; and Poets, it is probable, who had before contented themselves for the most part with misapplying only expressions which at first had been dictated by real passion, carried the abuse still further, and introduced phrases composed apparently in the spirit of the original figurative language of passion, yet altogether of their own invention, and characterized by various degrees of wanton deviaation from good sense and nature.

It is indeed true, that the language of the earliest Poets was felt to differ materially from ordinary language, because it was the language of extraordinary occasions; but it was really spoken by men, language which the Poet himself had uttered when he had been affected by the events which he described, or which he had heard uttered by those around him. To this language it is probable that metre of some sort or other was early superadded. This separated the genuine language of Poetry still further from common life, so that whoever read or heard the poems of these earliest Poets felt himself moved in a way in which he had not been accustomed to be moved in real life, and by causes manifestly different from those which acted upon him in real life. This was the great temptation to all the corruptions which have followed: under the protection of this feeling, succeeding Poets constructed a phraseology which had one thing, it is true, in common with the genuine language of poetry, namely, that it was not heard in ordinary conversation; that it was unusual. But the first Poets, as I have said, spake a language which, though unusual, was still the language of men. This circumstance, however, was disregarded by their successors: they found that they could please by easier means: they became proud of modes of expression which they themselves had invented, and which were uttered only by themselves. In process of time metre became a symbol or promise of this unusual language, and whoever took upon him to write in metre, according as he possessed more or less of true poetic genius, introduced less or more of this adulterated phraseology into his compositions, and the true and the ralse were inseparably interwoven, until, the taste of men becoming gradually preverted, this language was received as a natural language; and at length, by the influence of books upon men, did to a certain degree really become so.   Abuses of this kind were imported from one nation to another, and with the progress of refinement this diction became daily more and more corrupt, thrusting out of sight the plain humanities of nature by a motley masquerade of tricks, quaintnesses, hieroglyphics, and enigmas.

It would not be uninteresting to point out the causes of the pleasure given by this extravagant and absurd diction.   It depends upon a great variety of causes, but upon none, perhaps, more than its influence in impressing a notion of the peculiarity and exaltation of the Poet's character, and in flattering the Reader's self-love by bringing him nearer to a sympathy with that character; an effect which is accomplished by unsettling ordinary habits of thinking, and thus assisting the Reader to approach to that perturbed and dizzy state of mind in which if he does not find himself, he imagines that he is *balked* of a peculiar enjoyment which poetry can and ought to bestow.

The sonnet quoted from Gray, in the Preface, except the lines printed in Italics, consists of little else but this diction, though not of the worst kind; and indeed, if one may be permitted to say so, it is far too common in the best writers both ancient and modern. Perhaps in no way, by positive example, could more easily be given a notion of what I mean by the phrase *poetic diction*, than by referring to a comparison between the metrical paraphrase which we have of passages in the Old and New Testament, and those passages as they exist in our common Translation. See Pope's "Messiah" throughout; Prior's "Did sweeter sounds adorn my flowing tongue," &c., &c. "Though I speak with the tongues of men and of angels," &c., &c. 1st Corinthians, chap. xiii. By way of immediate example, take the following of Dr. Johnson: —

> "Turn on the prudent Ant thy heedless eyes,
> Observe her labors, Sluggard, and be wise;
> No stern command, no monitory voice,
> Prescribes her duties, or directs her choice;
> Yet, timely provident, she hastes away
> To snatch the blessings of a plenteous day;
> When fruitful Summer loads the teeming plain,
> She crops the harvest, and she stores the grain.
> How long shall sloth usurp thy useless hours,
> Unnerve thy vigor, and enchain thy powers?
> While artful shades thy downy couch inclose,
> And soft solicitation courts repose,
> Amidst the drowsy charms of dull delight,
> Year chases year with unremitted flight,

> Till Want now following, fraudulent and slow,
> Shall spring to seize thee, like an ambushed foe."

From this hubbub of words pass to the original. "Go to the Ant, thou Sluggard; consider her ways, and be wise : which having no guide, overseer, or ruler, provideth her meat in the summer, and gathereth her food in the harvest. How long wilt thou sleep, O Sluggard? when wilt thou arise out of thy sleep? Yet a little sleep, a little slumber, a little folding of the hands to sleep. So shall thy poverty come as one that travelleth, and thy want as an armed man." Proverbs, chap. vi.

One more quotation, and I have done. It is from Cowper's Verses supposed to be written by Alexander Selkirk : —

> " Religion! what treasure untold
> Resides in that heavenly word!
> More precious than silver and gold,
> Or all that this earth can afford.
> But the sound of the church-going bell
> These valleys and rocks never heard,
> Ne'er sighed at the sound of a knell,
> Or smiled when a Sabbath appeared.

> " Ye winds, that have made me your sport,
> Convey to this desolate shore
> Some cordial, endearing report
> Of a land I must visit no more.
> My Friends, do they now and then send
> A wish or a thought after me?
> O tell me I yet have a friend,
> Though a friend I am never to see."

This passage is quoted as an instance of three different styles of composition. The first four lines are poorly expressed; some Critics would call the language prosaic; the fact is, it would be bad prose, so bad, that it is scarcely worse in metre. The epithet " church-going " applied to a bell, and that by so chaste a writer as Cowper, is an instance of the strange abuses which Poets have introduced into their language, till they and their Readers take them as matters of course, if they do not single them out expressly as objects of admiration. The two lines " Ne'er sighed at the sound," &c., are, in my opinion, an instance of the language of passion wrested from its proper use, and, from the mere circumstance of the composition being in metre, applied upon an occasion that does not justify such violent expressions; and I should condemn the passage, though perhaps few Readers will agree with me, as vicious poetic diction. The last stanza is throughout admirably expressed · it would be equally good whether in prose or verse, except that the Reader has an exquisite pleasure in seeing such natural language so naturally connected with metre. The beauty of this stanza tempts me to conclude with a principle which ought never to be lost sight of, and which has been my chief guide in all I have said, — namely, that in works *of imagination and sentiment,* for of these only have I been treating, in proportion as ideas and feelings are valuable, whether the composition be in prose or in verse, they require and exact one and the same language. Metre is but adventitious to composition, and the phraseology for which that passport is necessary, even where it may be graceful at all, will be little valued by the judicious.

ESSAY, SUPPLEMENTARY TO THE PREFACE.

With the young of both sexes, Poetry is, like love, a passion; but, for much the greater part of those who have been proud of its power over their minds, a necessity soon arises of breaking the pleasing bondage; or it relaxes of itself; — the thoughts being occupied in domestic cares, or the time engrossed by business. Poetry then becomes only an occasional recreation; while to those whose existence passes away in a course of fashionable pleasure, it is a species of luxurious amusement. In middle and declining age, a scattered number of serious persons resort to Poetry, as to religion, for a protection against the pressure of trivial employments, and as a consolation for the afflictions of life. And, lastly, there are many, who, having been enamored of this art in their youth, have found leisure, after youth was spent, to cultivate general literature; in which Poetry has continued to be comprehended *as a study.*

Into the above classes the Readers of Poetry may be divided; Critics abound in them all; but

from the last only can opinions be collected of absolute value, and worthy to be depended upon, as
prophetic of the destiny of a new work. The
young, who in nothing can escape delusion, are
especially subject to it in their intercourse with
Poetry. The cause, not so obvious as the fact is
unquestionable, is the same as that from which
erroneous judgments in this art, in the minds of
men of all ages, chiefly proceed ; but upon youth
it operates with peculiar force. The appropriate
business of Poetry, (which, nevertheless, if genuine, is as permanent as pure science,) her appropriate employment, her privilege and her *duty*,
is to treat of things not as they *are*, but as they
appear ; not as they exist in themselves, but
as they *seem* to exist to the *senses*, and to the
passions. What a world of delusion does this acknowledged obligation prepare for the inexperienced ! what temptations to go astray are here
held forth for them whose thoughts have been little
disciplined by the understanding, and whose feelings revolt from the sway of reason !— When a
juvenile Reader is in the height of his rapture
with some vicious passage, should experience
throw in doubts, or common sense suggest suspi-
cions, a lurking consciousness that the realities of
the Muse are but shows, and that her liveliest ex-
citements are raised by transient shocks of conflicting feeling and successive assemblages of contradictory thoughts, is ever at hand to justify

extravagance, and to sanction absurdity.   But, it may be asked, as these illusions are unavoidable, and, no doubt, eminently useful to the mind as a process, what good can be gained by making observations, the tendency of which is to diminish the confidence of youth in its feelings, and thus to abridge its innocent and even profitable pleasures? The reproach implied in the question could not be warded off, if youth were incapable of being delighted with what is truly excellent; or if these errors always terminated of themselves in due season. But with the majority, though their force be abated, they continue through life.   Moreover, the fire of youth is too vivacious an element to be extinguished or damped by a philosophical remark; and, while there is no danger that what has been said will be injurious or painful to the ardent and the confident, it may prove beneficial to those who, being enthusiastic, are at the same time modest and ingenuous.   The intimation may unite with their own misgivings to regulate their sensibility, and to bring in, sooner than it would otherwise have arrived, a more discreet and sound judgment.

If it should excite wonder that men of ability, in later life, whose understandings have been rendered acute by practice in affairs, should be so easily and so far imposed upon when they happen to take up a new work in verse, this appears to be the cause, — that, having discontinued their attention to Poetry, whatever progress may have been

made in other departments of knowledge, they have
not, as to this art, advanced in true discernment beyond the age of youth.   If, then, a new poem fall
in their way, whose attractions are of that kind which
would have enraptured them during the heat of
youth, the judgment not being improved to a degree that they shall be disgusted, they are dazzled ; and prize and cherish the faults for having
had power to make the present time vanish before
them, and to throw the mind back, as by enchant-
ment, into the happiest season of life.   As they
read, powers seem to be revived, passions are re-
generated, and pleasures restored.   The book
was probably taken up after an escape from the
burden of business, and with a wish to forget the
world, and all its vexations and anxieties.   Having obtained this·wish, and so much more, it is natural that they should make report as they have felt.

If Men of mature age, through want of practice, be thus easily beguiled into admiration of
absurdities, extravagances, and misplaced ornaments, thinking it proper that their understandings
should enjoy a holiday, while they are unbending
their minds with verse, it may be expected that
such Readers will resemble their former selves
also in strength of prejudice, and an inaptitude to
be moved by the unostentatious beauties of a pure
style.   In the higher Poetry, an enlightened
Critic chiefly looks for a reflection of the wisdom
of the heart and the grandeur of the imagination.

Wherever these appear, simplicity accompanies them; Magnificence herself, when legitimate, depending upon a simplicity of her own, to regulate her ornaments. But it is a well-known property of human nature, that our estimates are ever governed by comparisons, of which we are conscious with various degrees of distinctness. Is it not, then, inevitable, (confining these observations to the effects of style merely,) that an eye, accustomed to the glaring hues of diction by which such Readers are caught and excited, will for the most part be rather repelled than attracted by an original Work, the coloring of which is disposed according to a pure and refined scheme of harmony? It is in the fine arts as in the affairs of life, no man can *serve* (i. e. obey with zeal and fidelity) two Masters.

As Poetry is most just to its own divine origin when it administers the comforts and breathes the spirit of religion, they who have learned to perceive this truth, and who betake themselves to reading verse for sacred purposes, must be preserved from numerous illusions to which the two Classes of Readers, whom we have been considering, are liable. But, as the mind grows serious from the weight of life, the range of its passions is contracted accordingly; and its sympathies become so exclusive, that many species of high excellence wholly escape, or but languidly excite, its notice. Besides, men who read from religious or moral inclinations, even when the subject is of that kind which they approve, are beset with misconceptions and mistakes peculiar to themselves. Attaching so much importance to the truths which interest them, they are prone to overrate the Authors by whom those truths are expressed and enforced. They come prepared to impart so much passion to the Poet's language, that they remain unconscious how little, in fact, they receive from it. And, on the other hand, religious faith is to him who holds it so momentous a thing, and error appears to be attended with such tremendous consequences, that, if opinions touching upon religion occur which the Reader condemns, he not only cannot sympathize with them, however animated the expression, but there is, for the most part, an end put to all satisfaction and enjoyment. Love, if it before existed, is converted into dislike; and the heart of the Reader is set against the Author and his book. — To these excesses, they, who from their professions ought to be the most guarded against them, are perhaps the most liable; I mean those sects whose religion, being from the calculating understanding, is cold and formal. For when Christianity, the religion of humility, is founded upon the proudest faculty of our nature, what can be expected but contradictions? Accordingly, believers of this cast are at one time contemptuous; at another, being troubled as they are and must be, with inward misgivings, they are jealous and suspicious; — and at all seasons they are under temptation to supply, by the heat with which they defend their tenets, the animation which is wanting to the constitution of the religion itself.

Faith was given to man that his affections, detached from the treasures of time, might be inclined to settle upon those of eternity; — the elevation of his nature, which this habit produces on earth, being to him a presumptive evidence of a future state of existence, and giving him a title to partake of its holiness. The religious man values what he sees chiefly as an " imperfect shadowing forth " of what he is incapable of seeing. The concerns of religion refer to indefinite objects, and are too weighty for the mind to support them without relieving itself by resting a great part of the burden upon words and symbols. The commerce between Man and his Maker cannot be carried on but by a process where much is represented in little, and the Infinite Being accommodates himself to a finite capacity. In all this may be perceived the affinity between Religion and Poetry; between Religion, making up the deficiencies of reason by faith, — and Poetry, passionate for the instruction of reason; between Religion, whose element is infinite, and whose ultimate trust is the supreme of things, submitting herself to circumscription, and reconciled to substitutions, — and Poetry, ethereal and transcendent, yet incapable to sustain her existence without sensuous incarnation. In this community of nature may be perceived also the lurking incitements of kindred error ; — so that we shall find that no poetry has been more subject to distortion, than that species, the argument and scope of which is religious ; and no lovers of the art have gone farther astray than the pious and the devout.

Whither then shall we turn for that union of qualifications which must necessarily exist before the decisions of a critic can be of absolute value ? For a mind at once poetical and philosophical; for a critic whose affections are as free and kindly as the spirit of society, and whose understanding is severe as that of dispassionate government ? Where are we to look for that initiatory composure of mind which no selfishness can disturb ; for a natural sensibility that has been tutored into correctness without losing anything of its quickness ; and for active faculties, capable of answering the demands which an Author of original imagination shall make upon them, associated with a judgment that cannot be duped into admiration by aught that is unworthy of it ? Among those, and those only, who, never having suffered their youthful love of poetry to remit much of its force, have applied to the consideration of the laws of this art the best power of their understandings. At the same time it must be observed, that, as this Class comprehends the only judgments which are trustworthy, so does it include the most erroneous and perverse. For to be mistaught is worse than to be untaught; and no perverseness equals that which is supported by system, no errors are so difficult to root out as those which the understanding has pledged its credit to uphold. In this class are contained censors, who, if they be pleased with what is good, are pleased with it only by imperfect glimpses, and upon false principles; who, should they generalize rightly to a certain point, are sure to suffer for it in the end; who, if they stumble upon a sound rule, are fettered by misapplying it, or by straining it too far, being incapable of perceiving when it ought to yield to one of higher order. In it are found critics too petulant to be passive to a genuine poet, and too feeble to grapple with him; — men who take upon them to report of the course which *he* holds whom they are utterly unable to accompany, — confounded if he turn quick upon the wing, dismayed if he soar steadily "into the region"; — men of palsied imaginations and indurated hearts; in whose minds all healthy action is languid, who therefore feed as the many direct them, or, with the many, are greedy after vicious provocatives; — judges, whose censure is auspicious, and whose praise ominous! In this class meet together the two extremes of best and worst.

The observations presented in the foregoing series are of too ungracious a nature to have been made without reluctance; and, were it only on this account, I would invite the reader to try them by the test of comprehensive experience. If the number of judges who can be confidently relied upon be in reality so small, it ought to follow that partial notice only, or neglect, perhaps long continued, or attention wholly inadequate to their merits, must have been the fate of most works in the higher departments of Poetry; and that, on the other hand, numerous productions have blazed into popularity, and have passed away, leaving scarcely a trace behind them: it will be further found, that when Authors shall have at length raised themselves into general admiration, and maintained their ground, errors and prejudices have prevailed concerning their genius and their works, which the few who are conscious of those errors and prejudices would deplore, if they were not recompensed by perceiving that there are select Spirits for whom it is ordained that their fame shall be in the world an existence like that of Virtue, which owes its being to the struggles it makes, and its vigor to the enemies whom it provokes; — a vivacious quality, ever doomed to meet with opposition, and still triumphing over it; and, from the nature of its dominion, incapable of being brought to the sad conclusion of Alexander, when he wept that there were no more worlds for him to conquer.

Let us take a hasty retrospect of the poetical

literature of this country for the greater part of
the last two centuries, and see if the facts support
these inferences.

Who is there that now reads the " Creation " of
Dubartas? Yet all Europe once resounded with
his praise ; he was caressed by kings ; and, when
his Poem was translated into our language, the
Faery Queene faded before it. The name of
Spenser, whose genius is of a higher order than
even that of Ariosto, is at this day scarcely known
beyond the limits of the British Isles. And if the
value of his works is to be estimated from the attention now paid to them by his countrymen,
compared with that which they bestow on those
of some other writers, it must be pronounced
small indeed.

> " The laurel, meed of mighty conquerors
> And poets *sage*," —

are his own words ; but his wisdom has, in this
particular, been his worst enemy : while its oppo-
site, whether in the shape of folly or madness, has
been *their* best friend. But he was a great power-
er, and bears a high name : the laurel has been
awarded to him.

A dramatic Author, if he write for the stage,
must adapt himself to the taste of the audience, or
they will not endure him ; accordingly the mighty
genius of Shakespeare was listened to. The people were delighted : but I am not sufficiently

versed in stage antiquities to determine whether they did not flock as eagerly to the representation of many pieces of contemporary Authors, wholly undeserving to appear upon the same boards. Had there been a formal contest for superiority among dramatic writers, that Shakespeare, like his predecessors Sophocles and Euripides, would have often been subject to the mortification of seeing the prize adjudged to sorry competitors, becomes too probable, when we reflect that the admirers of Settle and Shadwell were, in a later age, as numerous, and reckoned as respectable in point of talent, as those of Dryden. At all events, that Shakespeare stooped to accommodate himself to the People, is sufficiently apparent; and one of the most striking proofs of his almost omnipotent genius is, that he could turn to such glorious purpose those materials which the prepossessions of the age compelled him to make use of. Yet even this marvellous skill appears not to have been enough to prevent his rivals from having some advantage over him in public estimation; else how can we account for passages and scenes that exist in his works, unless upon a supposition that some of the grossest of them, a fact which in my own mind I have no doubt of, were foisted in by the Players, for the gratification of the many?

But that his Works, whatever might be their reception upon the stage, made but little impression upon the ruling Intellects of the time, may be inferred from the fact that Lord Bacon, in his multifarious writings, nowhere either quotes or alludes to him.* His dramatic excellence enabled him to resume possession of the stage after the Restoration ; but Dryden tells us that in his time two of the plays of Beaumont and Fletcher were acted for one of Shakespeare's. And so faint and limited was the perception of the poetic beauties of his dramas in the time of Pope, that, in his Edition of the Plays, with a view of rendering to the general reader a necessary service, he printed between inverted commas those passages which he thought most worthy of notice.

At this day, the French Critics have abated nothing of their aversion to this darling of our Nation: "the English, with their bouffon de Shakespeare," is as familiar an expression among them as in the time of Voltaire. Baron Grimm is the only French writer who seems to have perceived his infinite superiority to the first names of the French Theatre; an advantage which the Parisian Critic owed to his German blood and German education. The most enlightened Italians, though well acquainted with

---

* The learned Hakewill (a third edition of whose book bears date 1635), writing to refute the error " touching Nature's perpetual and universal decay," cites triumphantly the names of Ariosto, Tasso, Bartas, and Spenser, as instances that poetic genius had not degenerated; but he makes no mention of Shakespeare.

our language, are wholly incompetent to measure the proportions of Shakespeare. The Germans only of foreign nations are approaching
towards a knowledge and feeling of what he
is. In some respects they have acquired a
superiority over the fellow-countrymen of the
Poet: for among us it is a current, I might
say an established opinion, that Shakespeare is
justly praised when he is pronounced to be "a
wild, irregular genius, in whom great faults are
compensated by great beauties." How long may
it be before this misconception passes away, and
it becomes universally acknowledged that the
judgment of Shakespeare in the selection of his
materials, and in the manner in which he has
made them, heterogeneous as they often are, constitute a unity of their own, and contribute all to
one great end, is not less admirable than his
imagination, his invention, and his intuitive
knowledge of human nature?

There is extant a small volume of miscellaneous poems, in which Shakespeare expresses his own
feelings in his own person. It is not difficult to
conceive that the Editor, George Steevens, should
have been insensible to the beauties of one portion
of that volume, the Sonnets; though in no part
of the writings of this Poet is found, in an equal
compass, a greater number of exquisite feelings
felicitously expressed. But, from regard to the
Critic's own credit, he would not have ventured

to talk of an * act of Parliament not being strong enough to compel the perusal of those little pieces, if he had not known that the people of England were ignorant of the treasures contained in them: and if he had not, moreover, shared the too common propensity of human nature to exult over a supposed fall into the mire of a genius whom he had been compelled to regard with admiration, as an inmate of the celestial regions, — "there sitting where he durst not soar."

Nine years before the death of Shakespeare, Milton was born; and early in life he published several small Poems, which, though on their first appearance they were praised by a few of the judicious, were afterwards neglected to that degree, that Pope in his youth could borrow from them without risk of its being known. Whether these Poems are at this day justly appreciated, I will not undertake to decide: nor would it imply a severe reflection upon the mass of readers to suppose the contrary; seeing that a man of the acknowledged genius of Voss, the German poet, could suffer their spirit to evaporate; and could change their character, as is done in the translation

---

* This flippant insensibility was publicly reprehended by Mr. Coleridge in a course of Lectures upon Poetry given by him at the Royal Institution. For the various merits of thought and language in Shakespeare's Sonnets, see Numbers 27, 29, 30, 32, 33, 54, 64, 66, 68, 73, 76, 86, 91, 92, 93, 97, 98, 105, 107, 108, 109, 111, 113, 114, 116, 117, 129, and many others.

made by him of the most popular of those pieces. At all events, it is certain that these Poems of Milton are now much read, and loudly praised; yet were they little heard of till more than 150 years after their publication; and of the Sonnets, Dr. Johnson, as appears from Boswell's Life of him, was in the habit of thinking and speaking as contemptuously as Steevens wrote upon those of Shakespeare.

About the time when the Pindaric Odes of Cowley and his imitators, and the productions of that class of curious thinkers whom Dr. Johnson has strangely styled Metaphysical Poets, were beginning to lose something of that extravagant admiration which they had excited, the Paradise Lost made its appearance. " Fit audience find, though few," was the petition addressed by the Poet to his inspiring Muse. I have said elsewhere that he gained more than he asked; this I believe to be true; but Dr. Johnson has fallen into a gross mistake when he attempts to prove, by the sale of the work, that Milton's Countrymen were "*just* to it " upon its first appearance. Thirteen hundred copies were sold in two years; an uncommon example, he asserts, of the prevalence of genius in opposition to so much recent enmity as Milton's public conduct had excited. But be it remembered, that, if Milton's political and religious opinions, and the manner in which he announced them, had raised him many enemies, they had procured him numerous friends ; who, as all personal danger was passed away at the time of publication, would be eager to procure the master-work of a man whom they revered, and whom they would be proud of praising. Take, from the number of purchasers, persons of this class, and also those who wished to possess the Poem as a religious work, and but few I fear would be left who sought for it on account of its poetical merits. The demand did not immediately increase ; " for," says Dr. Johnson, " many more readers " (he means persons in the habit of reading poetry) " than were supplied at first, the Nation did not afford."   How careless must a writer be who can make this asser- tion in the face of so many existing title-pages to belie it !   Turning to my own shelves, I find the folio of Cowley, seventh edition, 1681.   A book near it is Flatman's Poems, fourth edition, 1686; Waller, fifth edition, same date.   The Poems of Norris of Bemerton not long after went, I believe, through nine editions.   What further demand there might be for these works I do not know ; but I well remember, that, twenty-five years ago, the booksellers' stalls in London swarmed with the folios of Cowley. This is not mentioned in dispar- agement of that able writer and amiable man ; but merely to show that, if Milton's work were not more read, it was not because readers did not exist at the time.   The early editions of the Para- dise Lost were printed in a shape which allowed them to be sold at a low price, yet only three thousand copies of the Work were sold in eleven years; and the Nation, says Dr. Johnson, had been satisfied from 1623 to 1664, that is, forty-one years, with only two editions of the Works of Shakespeare, which probably did not together make one thousand copies; facts adduced by the critic to prove the "paucity of Readers."—There were readers in multitudes; but their money went for other purposes, as their admiration was fixed elsewhere. We are authorized, then, to affirm, that the reception of the Paradise Lost, and the slow progress of its fame, are proofs as striking as can be desired, that the positions which I am attempting to establish are not erroneous.*—How amusing to shape to one's self such a critique as a Wit of Charles's days, or a Lord of the Miscellanies or trading Journalist of King William's time, would have brought forth, if he had set his faculties industriously to work upon this Poem, everywhere impregnated with *original* excellence.

So strange indeed are the obliquities of admiration, that they whose opinions are much influenced by authority will often be tempted to think that

---

* Hughes is express upon this subject: in his dedication of Spenser's Works to Lord Somers, he writes thus: "It was your Lordship's encouraging a beautiful edition of Paradise Lost that first brought that incomparable Poem to be generally known and esteemed."

there are no fixed principles* in human nature for this art to rest upon. I have been honored by being permitted to peruse in MS. a tract composed between the period of the Revolution and the close of that century. It is the Work of an English Peer of high accomplishments, its object to form the character and direct the studies of his son. Perhaps nowhere does a more beautiful treatise of the kind exist. The good sense and wisdom of the thoughts, the delicacy of the feelings, and the charm of the style, are, throughout, equally conspicuous. Yet the Author, selecting among the Poets of his own country those whom he deems most worthy of his son's perusal, particularizes only Lord Rochester, Sir John Denham, and Cowley. Writing about the same time, Shaftesbury, an author at present unjustly depreciated, describes the English Muses as only yet lisping in their cradles.

The arts by which Pope, soon afterwards, contrived to procure to himself a more general and a higher reputation than perhaps any English Poet ever attained during his lifetime, are known to the judicious. And as well known is it to them, that the undue exertion of those arts is the cause why Pope has for some time held a rank in literature,

---

* This opinion seems actually to have been entertained by Adam Smith, the worst critic, David Hume not excepted, that Scotland, a soil to which this sort of weed seems natural, has produced.

to which, if he had not been seduced by an over-love of immediate popularity, and had confided more in his native genius, he never could have descended. He bewitched the nation by his melody, and dazzled it by his polished style, and was himself blinded by his own success. Having wandered from humanity in his Eclogues, with boyish inexperience, the praise which these compositions obtained tempted him into a belief that Nature was not to be trusted, at least in Pastoral Poetry. To prove this by example, he put his friend Gay upon writing those Eclogues which their author intended to be burlesque. The instigator of the work, and his admirers, could perceive in them nothing but what was ridiculous. Nevertheless, though these Poems contain some detestable passages, the effect, as Dr. Johnson well observes, "of reality and truth became conspicuous, even when the intention was to show them grovelling and degraded." The Pastorals, ludicrous to such as prided themselves upon their refinement, in spite of those disgusting passages, "became popular, and were read with delight, as just representations of rural manners and occupations."

Something less than sixty years after the publication of the Paradise Lost appeared Thomson's Winter; which was speedily followed by his other Seasons. It is a work of inspiration; much of it is written from himself, and nobly from himself. How was it received? "It was no sooner read," says one of his contemporary biographers, "than universally admired: those only excepted who had not been used to feel or to look for anything in poetry, beyond a *point* of satirical or epigrammatic wit, a smart *antithesis* richly trimmed with rhyme, or the softness of an *elegiac* complaint. To such his manly classical spirit could not readily commend itself; till, after a more attentive perusal, they had got the better of their prejudices, and either acquired or affected a truer taste. A few others stood aloof, merely because they had long before fixed the articles of their poetical creed, and resigned themselves to an absolute despair of ever seeing anything new and original. These were somewhat mortified to find their notions disturbed by the appearance of a poet, who seemed to owe nothing but to nature and his own genius. But, in a short time, the applause became unanimous; every one wondering how so many pictures, and pictures so familiar, should have moved them but faintly to what they felt in his descriptions. His digressions too, the overflowings of a tender, benevolent heart, charmed the reader no less; leaving him in doubt, whether he should more admire the Poet or love the Man."

This case appears to bear strongly against us: but we must distinguish between wonder and legitimate admiration. The subject of the work is the changes produced in the appearances of nature by the revolution of the year: and, by undertaking to write in verse, Thomson pledged himself to treat his subject as became a Poet. Now it is remarkable that, excepting the nocturnal Reverie of Lady Winchilsea, and a passage or two in the Windsor Forest of Pope, the poetry of the period intervening between the publication of the Paradise Lost and the Seasons does not contain a single new image of external nature; and scarcely presents a familiar one from which it can be inferred that the eye of the Poet had been steadily fixed upon his object, much less that his feelings had urged him to work upon it in the spirit of genuine imagination. To what a low state knowledge of the most obvious and important phenomena had sunk, is evident from the style in which Dryden has executed a description of Night in one of his Tragedies, and Pope his translation of the celebrated moonlight scene in the Iliad. A blind man, in the habit of attending accurately to descriptions casually dropped from the lips of those around him, might easily depict these appearances with more truth. Dryden's lines are vague, bombastic, and senseless;* those of Pope,

---

* Cortes *alone in a night-gown.*

All things are hushed as Nature's self lay dead;
The mountains seem to nod their drowsy head.
The little Birds in dreams their songs repeat,
And sleeping Flowers beneath the Night-dew sweat:
Even Lust and Envy sleep; yet Love denies
Rest to my soul, and slumber to my eyes.

Dryden's Indian Emperor.

though he had Homer to guide him, are throughout false and contradictory. The verses of Dryden, once highly celebrated, are forgotten; those of Pope still retain their hold upon public estimation, — nay, there is not a passage of descriptive poetry, which at this day finds so many and such ardent admirers. Strange to think of an enthusiast, as may have been the case with thousands, reciting those verses under the cope of a moonlight sky, without having his raptures in the least disturbed by a suspicion of their absurdity! — If these two distinguished writers could habitually think that the visible universe was of so little consequence to a poet, that it was scarcely necessary for him to cast his eyes upon it, we may be assured that those passages of the elder poets which faithfully and poetically describe the phenomena of nature were not at that time holden in much estimation and that there was little accurate attention paid to those appearances.

Wonder is the natural product of Ignorance; and as the soil was *in such good condition* at the time of the publication of the Seasons, the crop was doubtless abundant. Neither individuals nor nations become corrupt all at once, nor are they enlightened in a moment. Thomson was an inspired poet, but he could not work miracles; in cases where the art of seeing had in some degree been learned, the teacher would further the proficiency of his pupils, but he could do little *more*; though so far does vanity assist men in acts of self-deception, that many would often fancy they recognized a likeness when they knew nothing of the original. Having shown that much of what his biographer deemed genuine admiration must in fact have been blind wonderment, how is the rest to be accounted for?—Thomson was fortunate in the very title of his Poem, which seemed to bring it home to the prepared sympathies of every one: in the next place, notwithstanding his high powers, he writes a vicious style; and his false ornaments are exactly of that kind which would be most likely to strike the undiscerning. He likewise abounds with sentimental commonplaces, that, from the manner in which they were brought forward, bore an imposing air of novelty. In any well-used copy of the Seasons the book generally opens of itself with the rhapsody on love, or with one of the stories (perhaps Damon and Musidora); these also are prominent in our collections of Extracts, and are the parts of his Work, which, after all, were probably most efficient in first recommending the author to general notice. Pope, repaying praises which he had received, and wishing to extol him to the highest, only styles him "an elegant and philosophical Poet"; nor are we able to collect any unquestionable proofs that the true characteristics of Thomson's genius as an imaginative poet * were perceived, till the elder Warton, almost forty years after the publication of the Seasons, pointed them out by a note in his Essay on the Life and Writings of Pope. In the Castle of Indolence (of which Gray speaks so coldly) these characteristics were almost as conspicuously displayed, and in verse more harmonious and diction more pure. Yet that fine Poem was neglected on its appearance, and is at this day the delight only of a few.

When Thomson died, Collins breathed forth his regrets in an Elegiac Poem, in which he pronounces a poetical curse upon *him* who should regard with insensibility the place where the Poet's remains were deposited. The Poems of the mourner himself have now passed through innumerable editions, and are universally known; but if, when Collins died, the same kind of imprecation had been pronounced by a surviving admirer, small is the number whom it would not have comprehended. The notice which his poems attained during his lifetime was so small, and of course the sale so insignificant, that not long before his death he deemed it right to repay to the bookseller the

* Since these observations upon Thomson were written, I have perused the second edition of his Seasons, and find that even *that* does not contain the most striking passages which Warton points out for admiration: these, with other improvements, throughout the whole work, must have beer added at a later period.

sum which he had advanced for them, and threw the edition into the fire.

Next in importance to the Seasons of Thomson, though at considerable distance from that work in order of time, come the Reliques of Ancient English Poetry; collected, new-modelled, and in many instances (if such a contradiction in terms may be used) composed by the Editor, Dr. Percy. This work did not steal silently into the world, as is evident from the number of legendary tales that appeared not long after its publication; and had been modelled, as the authors persuaded themselves, after the old Ballad. The Compilation was however ill suited to the then existing taste of city society; and Dr. Johnson, 'mid the little senate to which he gave laws, was not sparing in his exertions to make it an object of contempt. The critic triumphed, the legendary imitators were deservedly disregarded, and, as undeservedly, their ill-imitated models sank, in this country, into temporary neglect; while Bürger, and other able writers of Germany, were translating, or imitating, these Reliques, and composing, with the aid of inspiration thence derived, Poems which are the delight of the German nation. Dr. Percy was so abashed by the ridicule flung upon his labors from the ignorance and insensibility of the persons with whom he lived, that though while he was writing under a mask he had not wanted resolution to follow his genius into the regions of true simplicity and genuine pathos (as is evinced by the exquisite ballad of Sir Cauline and by many other pieces), yet when he appeared in his own person and character as a poetical writer, he adopted, as in the tale of the Hermit of Warkworth, a diction scarcely in any one of its features distinguishable from the vague, the glossy, and unfeeling language of his day. I mention this remarkable fact * with regret, esteeming the genius of Dr. Percy in this kind of writing superior to that of any other man by whom in modern times it has been cultivated. That even Bürger (to whom Klopstock gave, in my hearing, a commendation which he denied to Goethe and Schiller, pronouncing him to be a genuine poet, and one of the few among the Germans whose works would last) had not the fine sensibility of Percy, might be shown from many passages, in which he has deserted his original only to go astray. For example,

> Now daye was gone, and night was come,
> And all were fast asleepe,

* Shenstone, in his Schoolmistress, gives a still more remarkable instance of this timidity. On its first appearance, (see D'Israeli's 2d Series of the Curiosities of Literature,) tho Poem was accompanied with an absurd prose commentary, showing, as indeed some incongruous expressions in the text imply, that the whole was intended for burlesque. In subsequent editions, the commentary was dropped, and the People have since continued to read in seriousness, doing for the Author what he had not courage openly to venture upon himself.

> All save the Lady Emeline,
> Who sate in her bowre to weepe:
>
> And soone she heard her true Love's voice
> Low whispering at the walle,
> Awake, awake, my dear Ladye,
> 'T is I thy true-love call.

Which is thus tricked out and dilated:

> Als nun die Nacht Gebirg' und Thal
> Vermummt in Rabenschatten,
> Und Hochburgs Lampen überall
> Schon ausgeflimmert hatten,
> Und alles tief entschlafen war;
> Doch nur das Fräulein immerdar,
> Voll Fieberangst, noch wachte,
> Und seinen Ritter dachte:
> Da horch! Ein süsser Liebeston
> Kam leis' empor geflogen.
> "Ho, Trudchen, ho! Da bin ich schon!
> Frisch auf! Dich angezogen!"

But from humble ballads we must ascend to heroics.

All hail, Macpherson! hail to thee, Sire of Ossian! The Phantom was begotten by the snug embrace of an impudent Highlander upon a cloud of tradition,—it travelled southward, where it was greeted with acclamation, and the thin Consistence took its course through Europe, upon the breath of popular applause. The Editor of the "Reliques" had indirectly preferred a claim to the praise of invention, by not concealing that his supplementary labors were considerable! how selfish his conduct, contrasted with that of the disinterested Gael, who, like Lear, gives his kingdom away, and is content to become a pensioner upon his own issue for a beggarly pittance!—'Open this far-famed Book!—I have done so at random, and the beginning of the "Epic Poem Temora," in eight Books, presents itself. "The blue waves of Ullin roll in light. The green hills are covered with day. Trees shake their dusky heads in the breeze. Gray torrents pour their noisy streams. Two green hills with aged oaks surround a narrow plain. The blue course of a stream is there. On its banks stood Cairbar of Atha. IIis spear supports the king; the red eyes of his fear are sad. Cormac rises on his soul with all his ghastly wounds." Precious memorandums from the pocket-book of the blind Ossian!

If it be unbecoming, as I acknowledge that for the most part it is, to speak disrespectfully of Works that have enjoyed for a length of time a widely spread reputation, without at the same time producing irrefragable proofs of their unworthiness, let me be forgiven upon this occasion.— Having had the good fortune to be born and reared in a mountainous country, from my very childhood I have felt the falsehood that pervades the volumes imposed upon the world under the name of Ossian. From what I saw with my own eyes, I knew that the imagery was spurious. In Nature everything is distinct, yet nothing defined into absolute independent singleness. In Macpherson's work, it is exactly the reverse; everything (that is not stolen) is in this manner defined, insulated, dislocated, deadened, — yet nothing distinct. It will always be so when words are substituted for things. To say that the characters never could exist, that the manners are impossible, and that a dream has more substance than the whole state of society, as there depicted, is doing nothing more than pronouncing a censure which Macpherson defied, when, with the steeps of Morven before his eyes, he could talk so familiarly of his Car-borne heroes ; — of Morven, which, if one may judge from its appearance at the distance of a few miles, contains scarcely an acre of ground sufficiently accommodating for a sledge to be trailed along its surface. — Mr. Malcolm Laing has ably shown that the diction of this pretended translation is a motley assemblage from all quarters ; but he is so fond of making out parallel passages as to call poor Macpherson to account for his " *ands* " and his " *buts* " ! and he has weakened his argument by conducting it as if he thought that every striking resemblance was a *conscious* plagiarism. It is enough that the coincidences are too remarkable for its being probable or possible that they could arise in different minds without communication between them. Now as the Translators of the Bible, and Shakespeare, Milton, and Pope, could not be indebted to Macpherson, it follows that he must have owed his fine

feathers to them; unless we are prepared gravely
to assert, with Madame de Staël, that many of
the characteristic beauties of our most celebrated
English Poems are derived from the ancient Fin-
gallian; in which case the modern translator
would have been but giving back to Ossian his
own. — It is consistent that Lucien Buonaparte,
who could censure Milton for having surrounded
Satan in the infernal regions with courtly and regal splendor, should pronounce the modern Ossian
to be the glory of Scotland; — a country that has
produced a Dunbar, a Buchanan, a Thomson,
and a Burns! These opinions are of ill omen for
the Epic ambition of him who has given them to
the world.

Yet, much as those pretended treasures of antiquity have been admired, they have been wholly
uninfluential upon the literature of the Country.
No succeeding writer appears to have caught from
them a ray of inspiration; no author, in the least
distinguished, has ventured formally to imitate
them, — except the boy, Chatterton, on their first
appearance. He had perceived, from the successful trials which he himself had made in literary
forgery, how few critics were able to distinguish
between a real ancient medal and a counterfeit of
modern manufacture; and he set himself to the
work of filling a magazine with *Saxon Poems*, —
counterparts of those of Ossian, as like his as one
of his misty stars is to another. This incapability

to amalgamate with the literature of the Island, is, in my estimation, a decisive proof that the book is essentially unnatural; nor should I require any other to demonstrate it to be a forgery, audacious as worthless. — Contrast, in this respect, the effect of Macpherson's publication with the Reliques of Percy, so unassuming, so modest in their pretensions! — I have already stated how much Germany is indebted to this latter work; and for our own country, its poetry has been absolutely redeemed by it. I do not think that there is an able writer in verse of the present day who would not be proud to acknowledge his obligations to the Reliques; I know that it is so with my friends; and, for myself, I am happy in this occasion to make a public avowal of my own.

Dr. Johnson, more fortunate in his contempt of the labors of Macpherson than those of his modest friend, was solicited not long after to furnish Prefaces biographical and critical for the works of some of the most eminent English Poets. Tho booksellers took upon themselves to make the collection; they referred probably to the most popular miscellanies, and, unquestionably, to their books of accounts; and decided upon the claim of authors to be admitted into a body of the most eminent, from the familiarity of their names with the readers of that day, and by the profits, which, from the sale of his works, each had brought and was bringing to the Trade. The Editor was allowed a limited exercise of discretion, and the Authors whom he recommended are scarcely to be mentioned without a smile.   We open the volume of Prefatory Lives, and to our astonishment the *first* name we find is that of Cowley!— What is become of the morning-star of English Poetry?   Where is the bright Elizabethan constellation?   Or, if names be more acceptable than images, where is the ever-to-be-honored Chaucer? where is Spenser? where Sidney? and, lastly, where he, whose rights as a poet, contradistinguished from those which he is universally allowed to possess as a dramatist, we have vindicated,— where Shakespeare? — These, and a multitude of others not unworthy to be placed near them, their contemporaries and successors, we have *not*.   But in their stead, we have (could better be expected when precedence was to be settled by an abstract of reputation at any given period made, as in this case before us?) Roscommon, and Stepney, and Phillips, and Walsh, and Smith, and Duke, and King, and Spratt,— Halifax, Granville, Sheffield, Congreve, Broome, and other reputed Magnates,— metrical writers utterly worthless and useless, except for occasions like the present, when their productions are referred to as evidence what a small quantity of brain is necessary to procure a considerable stock of admiration, provided the aspirant will accommodate himself to the likings and fashions of his day.

As I do not mean to bring down this retrospect

to our own times, it may with propriety be closed at the era of this distinguished event. From the literature of other ages and countries, proofs equally cogent might have been adduced, that the opinions announced in the former part of this Essay are founded upon truth. It was not an agreeable office, nor a prudent undertaking, to declare them ; but their importance seemed to render it a duty. It may still be asked, where lies the particular relation of what has been said to these volumes ? — The question will be easily answered by the discerning Reader who is old enough to remember the taste that prevailed when some of these poems were first published, seventeen years ago ; who has also observed to what degree the poetry of this Island has since that period been colored by them ; and who is further aware of the unremitting hostility with which, upon some principle or other, they have each and all been opposed. A sketch of my own notion of the constitution of Fame has been given ; and, as far as concerns myself, I have cause to be satisfied. The love, the admiration, the indifference, the slight, the aversion, and even the contempt, with which these Poems have been received, knowing, as I do, the source within my own mind from which they have proceeded, and the labor and pains which, when labor and pains appeared needful, have been bestowed upon them, must all, if I think consistently, be received as pledges and tokens, bearing the same general impression, though widely different in value; — they are all proofs that for the present time I have not labored in vain; and afford assurances, more or less authentic, that the products of my industry will endure.

If there be one conclusion more forcibly pressed upon us than another by the review which has been given of the fortunes and fate of poetical Works, it is this, — that every author, as far as he is great and at the same time *original*, has had the task of *creating* the taste by which he is to be enjoyed: so has it been, so will it continue to be. This remark was long since made to me by the philosophical Friend for the separation of whose Poems from my own I have previously expressed my regret. The predecessors of an original Genius of a high order will have smoothed the way for all that he has in common with them, — and much he will have in common; but for what is peculiarly his own, he will be called upon to clear and often to shape his own road, — he will be in the condition of Hannibal among the Alps.

And where lies the real difficulty of creating that taste by which a truly original poet is to be relished? Is it in breaking the bonds of custom, in overcoming the prejudices of false refinement, and displacing the aversions of inexperience? Or, if he labor for an object which here and elsewhere I have proposed to myself, does it consist in divesting the reader of the pride that induces him to dwell upon those points wherein men differ from each other, to the exclusion of those in which all men are alike, or the same; and in making him ashamed of the vanity that renders him insensible of the appropriate excellence which civil arrangements, less unjust than might appear, and Nature illimitable in her bounty, have conferred on men who may stand below him in the scale of society? Finally, does it lie in establishing that dominion over the spirits of readers by which they are to be humbled and humanized, in order that they may be purified and exalted?

If these ends are to be attained by the mere communication of *knowledge*, it does *not* lie here. — TASTE, I would remind the reader, like IMAGINATION, is a word which has been forced to extend its services far beyond the point to which philosophy would have confined them. It is a metaphor, taken from a *passive* sense of the human body, and transferred to things which are in their essence *not* passive, — to intellectual *acts* and *operations*. The word Imagination has been overstrained, from impulses honorable to mankind, to meet the demands of the faculty which is perhaps the noblest of our nature. In the instance of Taste, the process has been reversed; and from the prevalence of dispositions at once injurious and discreditable, being no other than that selfishness which is the child of apathy, — which, as Nations decline in productive and creative power, makes them value themselves upon a presumed refinement of judging. Poverty of language is the primary cause of the use which we make of the word Imagination; but the word Taste has been stretched to the sense which it bears in modern Europe by habits of self-conceit, inducing that inversion in the order of things whereby a passive faculty is made paramount among the faculties conversant with the fine arts. Proportion and congruity, the requisite knowledge being supposed, are subjects upon which taste may be trusted ; it is competent to this office ; — for in its intercourse with these the mind is *passive*, and is affected painfully or pleasurably as by an instinct. But the profound and the exquisite in feeling, the lofty and universal in thought and imagination, — or, in ordinary language, the pathetic and the sublime, — are neither of them, accurately speaking, objects of a faculty which could ever without a sinking in the spirit of Nations have been designated by the metaphor, *Taste*. And why? Because without the exertion of a coöperating *power* in the mind of the Reader, there can be no adequate sympathy with either of these emotions: without this auxiliary impulse, elevated or profound passion cannot exist.

Passion, it must be observed, is derived from a word which signifies *suffering ;* but the connection which suffering has with effort, with exertion, and *action*, is immediate and inseparable. How strikingly is this property of human nature exhibited by the fact, that, in popular language, to be in a passion, is to be angry ! — But

> " Anger in hasty *words* or *blows*
> Itself discharges on its foes."

To be moved, then, by a passion, is to be excited, often to external, and always to internal effort; whether for the continuance and strengthening of the passion, or for its suppression, accordingly as the course which it takes may be painful or pleasurable. If the latter, the soul must contribute to its support, or it never becomes vivid, and soon languishes, and dies. And this brings us to the point. If every great poet with whose writings men are familiar, in the highest exercise of his genius, before he can be thoroughly enjoyed, has to call forth and to communicate *power*, this service, in a still greater degree, falls upon an original writer, at his first appearance in the world. — Of genius the only proof is the act of doing well what is worthy to be done, and what was never done before: of genius, in the fine arts, the only infallible sign is the widening the sphere of human sensibility, for the delight, honor, and benefit of human nature. Genius is the introduction of a new element into the intellectual universe: or, if that be not allowed, it is the application of powers to objects on which they had not before been exercised, or the employment of them in such a manner as to produce effects hitherto unknown. What is all this, but an advance, or a conquest, made by the soul of the poet? Is it to be supposed that the reader can make progress of this kind, like an Indian prince or general, stretched on his palanquin, and borne by his slaves? No; he is invigorated and inspirited by his leader, in order that he may exert himself; for he cannot proceed in quiescence, he cannot be carried like a dead weight. Therefore, to create taste is to call forth and bestow power, of which knowledge is the effect; and *there* lies the true difficulty.

As the pathetic participates of an *animal* sensation, it might seem that, if the springs of this emotion were genuine, all men, possessed of competent knowledge of the facts and circumstances, would be instantaneously affected. And doubtless in the works of every true poet will be found passages of that species of excellence, which is proved by effects immediate and universal. But there are emotions of the pathetic that are simple and direct, and others that are complex and revolutionary; some to which the heart yields with gentleness, others against which it struggles with pride; these varieties are infinite as the combinations of circumstance and the constitutions of character. Remember, also, that the medium through which, in poetry, the heart is to be affected, is language; a thing subject to endless fluctuations and arbitrary associations. The genius of the poet melts these down for his purpose ; but they retain their shape and quality to him who is not capable of exerting, within his own mind, a corresponding energy.   There is also a meditative, as well as a human, pathos ; an enthusiastic, as well as an ordinary, sorrow ; a sadness that has its seat in the depths of reason, to which the mind cannot sink gently of itself, but to which it must descend by treading the steps of thought.   And for the sublime, — if we consider what are the cares that occupy the passing day, and how remote is the practice and the course of life from the sources of sublimity, in the soul of Man, can it be wondered that there is little existing preparation for a poet charged with a new mission to extend its kingdom, and to augment and spread its enjoyments ?

Away, then, with the senseless iteration of the word *popular*, applied to new works in poetry, as if there were no test of excellence in this first of the fine arts but that all men should run after its productions, as if urged by an appetite, or constrained by a spell ! — The qualities of writing best fitted for eager reception are either such as startle the world into attention by their audacity and extravagance ; or they are chiefly of a superficial kind, lying upon the surfaces of manners ; or arising out of a selection and arrangement of incidents, by which the mind is kept upon the stretch of curiosity, and the fancy amused without the trouble of thought   but in everything which is to send the soul into herself, to be admonished of her weakness, or to be made conscious of her power, — wherever life and nature are described as operated upon by the creative or abstracting virtue of the imagination, —wherever the instinctive wisdom of antiquity and her heroic passions uniting, in the heart of the poet, with the meditative wisdom of later ages, have produced that accord of sublimated humanity, which is at once a history of the remote past and a prophetic enunciation of the remotest future, — *there* the poet must reconcile himself for a season to few and scattered hearers. — Grand thoughts, (and Shakespeare must often have sighed over this truth,) as they are most naturally and most fitly conceived in solitude, so can they not be brought forth in the midst of plaudits, without some violation of their sanctity.   Go to a silent exhibition of the productions of the sister Art, and be convinced that the qualities which dazzle at first sight, and kindle the admiration of the multitude, are essentially different from those by which permanent influence is secured.   Let us not shrink from following up these principles as far as they will carry us, and conclude with observing, that there never has been a period, and perhaps never will be, in which vicious poetry, of some kind or other, has not excited more zealous admiration, and been far more generally read, than good ; but this advantage attends the good, that the *individual*, as well as the species, survives from age to age; whereas, of the depraved, though the species be immortal, the individual quickly *perishes ;* the object of present admiration vanishes, being supplanted by some other as easily produced; which, though no better, brings with it at least the irritation of novelty, — with adaptation, more or less skilful, to the changing humors of the majority of those who are most at leisure to regard poetical works when they first solicit their attention.

Is it the result of the whole, that, in the opinion of the writer, the judgment of the People is not to be respected ? The thought is most injurious; and, could the charge be brought against him, he would repel it with indignation. The People have already been justified, and their eulogium pronounced by implication, when it was said above, that, of *good* poetry, the *individual*, as well as the species, *survives.* And how does it survive but through the People ? What preserves it but their intellect and their wisdom?

" Past and Future are the wings
On whose support, harmoniously conjoined,
Moves the great Spirit of human knowledge."
MS.

The voice that issues from this Spirit is that Vox Populi which the Deity inspires. Foolish must he be who can mistake for this a local acclamation, or a transitory outcry,—transitory though it be for years, local though from a Nation. Still more lamentable is his error who can believe that there is anything of divine infallibility in the clamor of that small though loud portion of the community, ever governed by factitious influence, which, under the name of the PUBLIC, passes itself, upon the unthinking, for the PEOPLE. Towards the Public, the Writer hopes that he feels as much deference as it is entitled to: but to the People, philosophically characterized, and to the embodied spirit of their knowledge, so far as it exists and moves, at the present, faithfully supported by its two wings, the past and the future, his devout respect, his reverence, is due. He offers it willingly and readily; and, this done, takes leave of his Readers, by assuring them, that, if he were not persuaded that the contents of these volumes, and the Work to which they are subsidiary, evince something of the " Vision and the Faculty divine," and that, both in words and things, they will operate, in their degree, to extend the domain of sensibility for the delight, the honor, and the benefit of human nature, notwithstanding the many happy hours which he has employed in their composition, and the manifold comforts and enjoyments they have procured to him, he would not, if a wish could do it, save them from immediate destruction; — from becoming at this moment, to the world, as a thing that had never been.

1815.

DEDICATION.

PREFIXED TO THE EDITION OF 1815

TO

SIR GEORGE HOWLAND BEAUMONT, Bart.

My dear Sir George, —

Accept my thanks for the permission given me to dedicate these volumes to you. In addition to a lively pleasure derived from general considerations, I feel a particular satisfaction; for, by inscribing these Poems with your Name, I seem to myself in some degree to repay, by an appropriate honor, the great obligation which I owe to one part of the Collection, — as having been the means of first making us personally known to each other. Upon much of the remainder, also, you have a peculiar claim, — for some of the best pieces were composed under the shade of your own groves, upon the classic ground of Coleorton; where I was animated by the recollection of those illustrious Poets of your name and family, who were born in that neighborhood; and, we may be assured, did not wander with indifference by the dashing stream of Grace Dieu, and among the rocks that diversify the forest of Charnwood.—Nor is there any one to whom such parts of this Collection as have been inspired or colored by the beautiful Country from which I now address you, could be presented with more propriety than to yourself,—to whom it has suggested so many admirable pictures. Early in life, the sublimity and beauty of this region excited your admiration; and I know that you are bound to it in mind by a still strengthening attachment.

Wishing and hoping that this Work, with the embellishments it has received from your pencil,* may survive as a lasting memorial of a friendship, which I reckon among the blessings of my life,

I have the honor to be,

My dear Sir George,

Yours most affectionately and faithfully,

WILLIAM WORDSWORTH.

RYDAL MOUNT, WESTMORELAND,
February 1, 1815.

* The state of the plates has, for some time, not allowed them to be repeated.

THE powers requisite for the production of poetry are: first, those of Observation and Description, — i. e. the ability to observe with accuracy things as they are in themselves, and with fidelity to describe them, unmodified by any passion or feeling existing in the mind of the describer; whether the things depicted be actually present to the senses, or have a place only in the memory. This power, though indispensable to a Poet, is one which he employs only in submission to necessity, and never for a continuance of time: as its exercise supposes all the higher qualities of the mind to be passive, and in a state of subjection to external objects, much in the same way as a translator or engraver ought to be to his original. 2dly, Sensibility, — which, the more exquisite it is, the wider will be the range of a poet's perceptions; and the more will he be incited to observe objects, both as they exist in themselves and as re-acted upon by his own mind. (The distinction between poetic and human sensibility has been marked in the character of the Poet delineated in

the original Preface.)   3dly, Reflection,—which
makes the Poet acquainted with the value of actions, images, thoughts, and feelings ; and assists
the sensibility in perceiving their connection with
each other.   4thly, Imagination and Fancy,—to
modify, to create, and to associate.   5thly, Invention,—by which characters are composed out of
materials supplied by observation ; whether of the
Poet's own heart and mind, or of external life and
nature ; and such incidents and situations produced as are most impressive to the imagination,
and most fitted to do justice to the characters, sentiments, and passions, which the Poet undertakes
to illustrate.   And, lastly, Judgment,—to decide
how and where, and in what degree, each of these
faculties ought to be exerted; so that the less
shall not be sacrificed to the greater ; nor the
greater, slighting the less, arrogate, to its own injury, more than its due.   By judgment, also, is
determined what are the laws and appropriate
graces of every species of composition.*

The materials of Poetry, by these powers col
lected and produced, are cast, by means of various
moulds, into divers forms.   The moulds may be
enumerated, and the forms specified, in the following order.   1st, The Narrative,—including the
Epopœia, the Historic Poem, the Tale, the Ro-

* As sensibility to harmony of numbers, and the power of
producing it, are invariably attendants upon the faculties
above specified, nothing has been said upon those requisites.

mance, the Mock-heroic, and, if the spirit of Homer will tolerate such neighborhood, that dear production ·of our days, the Metrical Novel. Of this Class, the distinguishing mark is, that the Narrator, however liberally his speaking agents be introduced, is himself the source from which everything primarily flows. Epic Poets, in order that their mode of composition may accord with the elevation of their subject, represent themselves as *singing* from the inspiration of the Muse, " Arma virumque *cano* "; but this is a fiction, in modern times, of slight value; the Iliad or the Paradise Lost would gain little in our estimation by being chanted. The other poets who belong to this class are commonly content to *tell* their tale ; — so that of the whole it may be affirmed that they neither require nor reject the accompaniment of music.

2dly, The Dramatic, — consisting of Tragedy, Historic Drama, Comedy, and Masque, in which the Poet does not appear at all in his own person, and where the whole action is carried on by speech and dialogue of the agents ; music being admitted only incidentally and rarely. The Opera may be placed here, inasmuch as it proceeds by dialogue ; though, depending, to the degree that it does, upon music, it has a strong claim to be ranked with the lyrical. The characteristic and impassioned Epistle, of which Ovid and Pope have given examples, considered as a species of monodrama, may, without impropriety, be placed in this class.

3dly, The Lyrical, — containing the Hymn, the Ode, the Elegy, the Song, and the Ballad; in all which, for the production of their *full* effect, an accompaniment of music is indispensable.

4thly, The Idyllium,—descriptive chiefly either of the processes and appearances of external nature, as the Seasons of Thomson; or of characters, manners, and sentiments, as are Shenstone's Schoolmistress, The Cotter's Saturday Night of Burns, The Twa Dogs of the same Author; or of these in conjunction with the appearances of Nature, as most of the pieces of Theocritus, the Allegro and Penseroso of Milton, Beattie's Minstrel, Goldsmith's Deserted Village. The Epitaph, the Inscription, the Sonnet, most of the epistles of poets writing in their own persons, and all locodescriptive poetry, belong to this class.

5thly, Didactic, — the principal object of which is direct instruction; as the Poem of Lucretius, the Georgics of Virgil, The Fleece of Dyer, Mason's English Garden, &c.

And, lastly, Philosophical Satire, like that of Horace and Juvenal; personal and occasional Satire rarely comprehending sufficient of the general in the individual to be dignified with the name of poetry.

Out of the three last has been constructed a composite order, of which Young's Night

Thoughts, and Cowper's Task, are excellent examples.

It is deducible from the above, that poems, apparently miscellaneous, may with propriety be arranged either with reference to the powers of mind *predominant* in the production of them; or to the mould in which they are cast; or, lastly, to the subjects to which they relate. From each of these considerations, the following Poems have been divided into classes; which, that the work may more obviously correspond with the course of human life, and for the sake of exhibiting in it the three requisites of a legitimate whole, a beginning, a middle, and an end, have been also arranged, as far as it was possible, according to an order of time, commencing with Childhood, and terminating with Old Age, Death, and Immortality. My guiding wish was, that the small pieces of which these volumes consist, thus discriminated, might be regarded under a twofold view; as composing an entire work within themselves, and as adjuncts to the philosophical Poem, " The Recluse." This arrangement has long presented itself habitually to my own mind. Nevertheless, I should have preferred to scatter the contents of these volumes at random, if I had been persuaded that, by the plan adopted, anything material would be taken from the natural effect of the pieces, individually, on the mind of the unreflecting Reader. I trust there is a sufficient variety in each class to prevent this; while, for him who reads with reflection, the arrangement will serve as a commentary unostentatiously directing his attention to my purposes, both particular and general. But, as I wish to guard against the possibility of misleading by this classification, it is proper first to remind the Reader, that certain poems are placed according to the powers of mind, in the production of them; *predominant*, which implies the exertion of other faculties in less degree. Where there is more imagination than fancy in a poem, it is placed under the head of Imagination, and *vice versâ*. Both the above classes might without impropriety have been enlarged from that consisting of " Poems founded on the Affections "; as might this latter from those, and from the class " proceeding from Sentiment and Reflection." The most striking characteristics of each piece, mutual illustration, variety, and proportion, have governed me throughout.   ·

None of the other classes, except those of Fancy and Imagination, require any particular notice.   But a remark of general application may be made.   All Poets, except the dramatic, have been in the practice of feigning that their works were composed to the music of the harp or lyre: with what degree of affectation this has been done in modern times, I leave to the judicious to determine.   For my own part, I have not been disposed to violate probability so far, or to make such a large demand upon the Reader's charity. Some of these pieces are essentially lyrical; and therefore cannot have their due force without a supposed musical accompaniment; but, in much the greatest part, as a substitute for the classic lyre or romantic harp, I require nothing more than animated or impassioned recitation, adapted to the subject. Poems, however humble in their kind, if they be good in that kind, cannot read themselves; the law of long syllable and short must not be so inflexible, — the letter of metre must not be so impassive to the spirit of versification,— as to deprive the Reader of all voluntary power to modulate, in subordination to the sense, the music of the poem ; — in the same manner as his mind is left at liberty, and even summoned, to act upon its thoughts and images. But, though the accompaniment of a musical instrument be frequently dispensed with, the true Poet does not therefore abandon his privilege distinct from that of the mere Proseman :—

> " He murmurs near the running brooks
> A music sweeter than their own."

Let us come now to the consideration of the words Fancy and Imagination, as employed in the classification of the following Poems. " A man," says an intelligent author, " has imagination in proportion as he can distinctly copy in idea the impressions of sense : it is the faculty which

images within the mind the phenomena of sensa
tion. A man has fancy in proportion as he can
call up, connect, or associate, at pleasure, those
internal images ($\phi a \nu \tau \acute{a} \zeta \epsilon \iota \nu$ is to cause to appear)
so as to complete ideal representations of absent
objects. Imagination is the power of depicting,
and fancy of evoking and combining. The imagination is formed by patient observation ; the fancy
by a voluntary activity in shifting the scenery of
the mind. The more accurate the imagination, the
more safely may a painter, or a poet, undertake a
delineation, or a description, without the presence
of the objects to be characterized. The more ver-
satile the fancy, the more original and striking
will be the decorations produced." — *British Syno-
nymes discriminated, by W. Taylor.*

Is not this as if a man should undertake to supply an account of a building, and be so intent
upon what he had discovered of the foundation, as
to conclude his task without once looking up at
the superstructure ? Here, as in other instances
throughout the volume, the judicious Author's
mind is enthralled by Etymology ; he takes up
the original word as his guide and escort, and too
often does not perceive how soon he becomes its
prisoner, without liberty to tread in any path but
that to which it confines him. It is not easy to
find out how imagination, thus explained, differs
from distinct remembrance of images ; or fancy
from quick and vivid recollection of them: each

is nothing more than a mode of memory. If the two words bear the above meaning, and no other, what term is left to designate that faculty of which the Poet is " all compact," — he whose eye glances from earth to heaven, whose spiritual attributes body forth what his pen is prompt in turning to shape? or what is left to characterize Fancy, as insinuating herself into the heart of objects with creative activity? — Imagination, in the sense of the word as giving title to a class of the following Poems, has no reference to images that are merely a faithful copy, existing in the mind, of absent external objects; but is a word of higher import, denoting operations of the mind upon those objects, and processes of creation or of composition, governed by certain fixed laws. I proceed to illustrate my meaning by instances. A parrot *hangs* from the wires of his cage by his beak or by his claws; or a monkey from the bough of a tree by his paws or his tail. Each creature does so literally and actually. In the first Eclogue of Virgil, the Shepherd, thinking of the time when he is to take leave of his farm, thus addresses his goats: —

" Non ego vos posthac viridi projectus in antro
Dumosa *pendere* procul do rupe videbo."

————— " half-way down
Hangs one who gathers samphire,"

is the well-known expression of Shakespeare, de-

'ineating an ordinary image upon the cliffs cf
Dover. In these two instances is a slight exertion
of the faculty which I denominate Imagination, in
the use of one word: neither the goats nor the
samphire-gatherer do literally hang, as does the
parrot or the monkey; but, presenting to the
senses something of such an appearance, the mind
in its activity, for its gratification, contemplates
them as hanging.

> " As when far off at sea a fleet descried
> *Hangs* in the clouds, by equinoctial winds   .
> Close sailing from Bengala, or the isles
> Of Ternate or Tidore, whence merchants bring
> Their spicy drugs; they on the trading flood
> Through the wide Ethiopian to the Cape
> Ply, stemming nightly toward the Pole: so seemed
> Far off the flying Fiend."

Here is the full strength of the imagination involved in the word *hangs*, and exerted upon the
whole image: First, the fleet, an aggregate cf
many ships, is represented as one mighty person,
whose track, we know and feel, is upon the
waters; but, taking advantage of its appearance
to the senses, the Poet dares to represent it as
hanging in the clouds, both for the gratification
of the mind in contemplating the image itself,
and in reference to the motion and appearance
of the sublime objects to which it is compared.

From impressions of sight we will pass to those

of sound; which, as they must necessarily be of a
less definite character, shall be selected from these
volumes: —

" Over his own sweet voice the Stock-dove *broods* " ;

of the same bird,

> " His voice was *buried* among trees,
>   Yet to be come at by the breeze ";

> " O Cuckoo ! shall I call thee *Bird,*
>   Or but a wandering *Voice?* "

The stock-dove is said to *coo*, a sound well imitating the note of the bird ; but, by the intervention of the metaphor *broods*, the affections are called
in by the imagination to assist in marking the
manner in which the bird reiterates and prolongs
her soft note, as if herself delighting to listen to it,
and participating of a still and quiet satisfaction,
like that which may be supposed inseparable
from the continuous process of incubation.   " His
voice was buried among trees," a metaphor expressing the love of *seclusion* by which this Bird
is marked ; and characterizing its note as not par-
taking of the shrill and the piercing, and therefore
more easily deadened by the intervening shade ;
yet a note so peculiar and withal so pleasing, that
the breeze, gifted with that love of the sound
which the Poet feels, penetrates the shades in
which it is entombed, and conveys it to the ear
of the listener.

> ' Shall I call thee Bird,
>   Or but a wandering Voice? "

This concise interrogation characterizes the seeming ubiquity of the voice of the cuckoo, and dis-
possesses the creature almost of a corporeal ex·
istence; the Imagination being tempted to this
exertion of her power by a consciousness-in the
memory that the cuckoo is almost perpetually heard
throughout the season of spring, but seldom becomes an object of sight.

Thus far of images independent of each other,
and immediately endowed by the mind with properties that do not inhere in them, upon an incite-
ment from properties and qualities the existence
of which is inherent and obvious.   These processes
of imagination are carried on either by conferring
additional properties upon an object, or abstracting
from it some of those which it actually possesses,
and thus enabling it to react upon the mind
which hath performed the process, like a new
existence.

I pass from the Imagination acting upon an
individual image, to a consideration of the same
faculty employed upon images in a conjunction by
which they modify each other.   The Reader has
already had a fine instance before him in the
passage quoted from Virgil, where the apparently
perilous situation of the goat, hanging upon the
shaggy precipice, is contrasted with that of the
shepherd contemplating it from the seclusion of

the cavern in which he lies stretched at ease and
in security. Take these images separately, and
how unaffecting the picture compared with that
produced by their being thus connected with, and
opposed to, each other !

> " As a huge stone is sometimes seen to lie
>   Couched on the bald top of an eminence,
>   Wonder to all who do the same espy
>   By what means it could thither come, and whence,
>   So that it seems a thing endued with sense,
>   Like a sea-beast crawled forth, which on a shelf
>   Of rock or sand reposeth, there to sun himself.
>
> " Such seemed this Man ; not all alive or dead,
>   Nor all asleep, in his extreme old age.
>
>   .   .   .   .   .
>
>   Motionless as a cloud the old Man stood,
>   That heareth not the loud winds when they call,
>   And moveth altogether if it move at all."

In these images, the conferring, the abstracting,
and the modifying powers of the Imagination, immediately and mediately acting, are all brought
into conjunction. The stone is endowed with
something of the power of life to approximate it to
the sea-beast; and the sea-beast stripped of some
of its vital qualities to assimilate it to the stone;
which intermediate image is thus treated for the
purpose of bringing the original image, that of the
stone, to a nearer resemblance to the figure and
condition of the aged Man ; who is divested of so
much of the indications of life and motion as to
bring him to the point where the two objects unite

and coalesce in just comparison. After what has been said, the image of the cloud need not be commented upon.

Thus far of an endowing or modifying power: but the Imagination also shapes and *creates ;* and how? By innumerable processes; and in none does it more delight, than in that of consolidating numbers into unity, and dissolving and separating unity into number, — alternations proceeding from, and governed by, a sublime consciousness of the soul in her own mighty and almost divine powers. Recur to the passage already cited from Milton. When the compact Fleet, as one Person, has been introduced "sailing from Bengala." "They," i. e. the " merchants," representing the fleet resolved into a multitude of ships, "ply" their voyage towards the extremities of the earth: "so" (referring to the word "As " in the commencement) "seemed the flying Fiend"; the image of his Person acting to recombine the multitude of ships into one body, — the point from which the comparison set out. "So seemed," and to whom seemed? To the heavenly Muse who dictates the poem, to the eye of the Poet's mind, and to that of the Reader, present at one moment in the wide Ethiopian, and the next in the solitudes, then first broken in upon, of the infernal regions !

"Modo me Thebis, modo ponit Athenis."

Hear again this mighty Poet, — speaking of the

Messiah going forth to expel from heaven the rebellious angels : —

> " Attended by ten thousand thousand Saints
> He onward came : far off his coming shone," —

the retinue of Saints, and the Person of the Messiah himself, lost almost and merged in the splendor of that indefinite abstraction, " his coming " !

As I do not mean here to treat this subject further than to throw some light upon the present volumes, and especially upon one division of them, I shall spare myself and the Reader the trouble of considering the Imagination as it deals with thoughts and sentiments, as it regulates the composition of characters, and determines the course of actions : I will not consider it (more than I have already done by implication) as that power which, in the language of one of my most esteemed Friends, " draws all things to one ; which makes things animate or inanimate, beings with their attributes, subjects with their accessories, take one color and serve to one effect." *   The grand storehouse of enthusiastic and meditative Imagination, of poetical, as contradistinguished from human and dramatic Imagination, are the prophetic and lyrical parts of the Holy Scriptures, and the works of Milton ; to which I cannot forbear to add those of Spenser.   I select these writers in preference to

* Charles Lamb upon the genius of Hogarth.

those of ancient Greece and Rome, because the anthropomorphitism of the Pagan religion subjected the minds of the greatest poets in those countries too much to the bondage of definite form; from which the Hebrews were preserved by their abhorrence of idolatry. This abhorrence was almost as strong in our great epic Poet, both from circumstances of his life and from the constitution of his mind. However imbued the surface might be with classical literature, he was a Hebrew in soul; and all things tended in him towards the sublime. Spenser, of a gentler nature, maintained his freedom by aid of his allegorical spirit, at one time inciting him to create persons out of abstractions; and at another, by a superior effort of genius, to give the universality and permanence of abstractions to his human beings, by means of attributes and emblems that belong to the highest moral truths and the purest sensations, — of which his character of Una is a glorious example. Of the human and dramatic Imagination the words of Shakespeare are an inexhaustible source.

> "I tax not you, ye Elements, with unkindness;
> I never gave you kingdoms, called you Daughters!"

And if, bearing in mind the many Poets distinguished by this prime quality, whose names I omit to mention, yet justified by recollection of the insults which the ignorant, the incapable, and the presumptuous have heaped upon these and my other writings, I may be permitted to anticipate the judgment of posterity upon myself, I shall declare (censurable, I grant, if the notoriety of the fact above stated does not justify me) that I have given, in these unfavorable times, evidence of exertions of this faculty upon its worthiest objects, the external universe, the moral and religious sentiments of Man, his natural affections, and his acquired passions; which have the same ennobling tendency as the productions of men, in this kind, worthy to be holden in undying remembrance.

To the mode in which Fancy has already been characterized as the power of evoking and combining, or, as my friend Mr. Coleridge has styled it, " the aggregate and associative power," my objection is only that the definition is too general. To aggregate and to associate, to evoke and combine, belong as well to the Imagination as to the Fancy; but either the materials evoked and combined are different; or they are brought together under a different law, and for a different purpose. Fancy does not require that the materials which she makes use of should be susceptible of change in their constitution, from her touch; and, where they admit of modification, it is enough for her purpose if it be slight, limited, and evanescent. Directly the reverse of these, are the desires and demands of the Imagination. She recoils from everything but the plastic, the pliant, and the indefinite.   She leaves it to Fancy to describe Queen Mab as coming,

> "In shape no bigger than an agate-stone
> On the fore-finger of an alderman."

Having to speak of stature, she does not tell you that her gigantic Angel was as tall as Pompey's Pillar; much less that he was twelve cubits, or twelve hundred cubits, high; or that his dimensions equalled those of Teneriffe or Atlas; because these, and if they were a million times as high it would be the same, are bounded.   The expression is, " His stature reached the sky !" the illimitable firmament! — When the Imagination frames a comparison, if it does not strike on the first presentation, a sense of the truth of the likeness, from the moment that it is perceived, grows — and continues to grow — upon the mind; the resemblance depending less upon outline of form and feature, than upon expression and effect; less upon casual and outstanding, than upon inherert and internal, properties: moreover, the images invariably modify each other. — The law under which the processes of Fancy are carried on is as capricious as the accidents of things, and the effects are surprising, playful, ludicrous, amusing, tender, or pathetic, as the objects happen to be appositely produced or fortunately combined. Fancy depends upon the rapidity and profusion with which she scatters her thoughts and images; trusting that their number, and the felicity with which they are linked together, will make amends for the want of individual value : or she prides herself upon the curious subtilty and the successful elaboration with which she can detect their lurking affinities. If she can win you over to her purpose, and impart to you her feelings, she cares not how unstable or transitory may be her influence, knowing that it will not be out of her power to resume it upon an apt occasion.   But the Imagination is conscious of an indestructible dominion ; — the Soul may fall away from it, not being able to sustain its grandeur ; but, if once felt and acknowledged, by no act of any other faculty of the mind can it be relaxed, impaired, or diminished. — Fancy is given to quicken and to beguile the temporal part of our nature, Imagination to incite and to support the eternal. — Yet is it not the less true that Fancy, as she is an active, is also, under her own laws and in her own spirit, a creative faculty. In what manner Fancy ambitiously aims at a rivalship with Imagination, and Imagination stoops to work with the materials of Fancy, might be illustrated from the compositions of all eloquent writers, whether in prose or verse ; and chiefly from those of our own Country. Scarcely a page of the impassioned parts of Bishop Taylor's Works can be opened that shall not afford examples. — Referring the Reader to those inestimable volumes. I will content myself with placing a conceit (ascribed

to Lord Chesterfield) in contrast with a passage
from the Paradise Lost : —

" The dews of the evening most carefully shun,
    They are the tears of the sky for the loss of the sun."

After the transgression of Adam, Milton, with
other appearances of sympathizing Nature, thus
marks the immediate consequence : —

" Sky lowered, and, muttering thunder, some sad drops
    Wept at completion of the mortal sin."

The associating link is the same in each instance :
Dew and rain, not distinguishable from the liquid
substance of tears, are employed as indications of
sorrow. A flash of surprise, is the effect in the
former case ; a flash of surprise, and nothing
more ; for the nature of things does not sustain
the combination. In the latter, the effects from
the act, of which there is this immediate consequence and visible sign, are so momentous, that
the mind acknowledges the justice and reasonable-
ness of the sympathy in nature so manifested ;
and the sky weeps drops of water as if with human eyes, as " Earth had before trembled from
her entrails, and Nature given a second groan."
Finally, I will refer to Cotton's " Ode upon
Winter," an admirable composition, though stained
with some peculiarities of the age in which he
lived, for a general illustration of the characteris-

tics of Fancy.   The middle part of this ode contains a most lively description of the entrance of Winter, with his retinue, as "a palsied king," and yet a military monarch, — advancing for conquest with his army; the several bodies of which, and their arms and equipments, are described with a rapidity of detail, and a profusion of *fanciful* comparisons, which indicate on the part of the poet extreme activity of intellect, and a corresponding hurry of delightful feeling.   Winter retires from the foe into his fortress, where

> "a magazine
> Of sovereign juice is cellared in;
> Liquor that will the siege maintain,
> Should Phœbus ne'er return again."

Though myself a water-drinker, I cannot resist the pleasure of transcribing what follows, as an instance still more happy of Fancy employed in the treatment of feeling, than, in its preceding passages, the Poem supplies of her management of forms.

> "'T is that, that gives the poet rage,
> And thaws the gellied blood of age;
> Matures the young, restores the old,
> And makes the fainting coward bold.

> " It lays the careful head to rest,
> Calms palpitations in the breast,
> Renders our lives' misfortune sweet;

> .   .   .   .   .

" Then let the chill Sirocco blow,
  And gird us round with hills of snow,
  Or else go whistle to the shore,
  And make the hollow mountains roar,

" Whilst we together jovial sit
  Careless, and crowned with mirth and wit,
  Where, though bleak winds confine us home,
  Our fancies round the world shall roam.

' We 'll think of all the Friends we know,
  And drink to all worth drinking to;
  When having drunk all thine and mine,
  We rather shall want healths than wine.

" But where Friends fail us, we 'll supply
  Our friendships with our charity;
  Men that remote in sorrows live,
  Shall by our lusty brimmers thrive.

" We 'll drink the wanting into wealth,
  And those that languish into health,
  The afflicted into joy; the opprest
  Into security and rest.

' The worthy in disgrace shall find
  Favor return again more kind,
  And in restraint who stifled lie,
  Shall taste the air of liberty.

' The brave shall triumph in success,
  The lover shall have mistresses,
  Poor, unregarded Virtue, praise,
  And the neglected Poet, bays.

' Thus shall our healths do others good,
  Whilst we ourselves do all we would;
  For, freed from envy and from care,
  What would we be but what we are? "

When I sat down to write this Preface, it was my intention to have made it more comprehensive; but, thinking that I ought rather to apologize for detaining the reader so long, I will here conclude.

POSTSCRIPT.

1835.

In the present volume, as in those that have preceded it, the reader will have found occasionally opinions expressed upon the course of public affairs, and feelings giving vent to as national interests excited them. Since nothing, I trust, has been uttered but in the spirit of reflective patriotism, those notices are left to produce their own effect; but, among the many objects of general concern, and the changes going forward, which I have glanced at in verse, are some especially affecting the lower orders of society: in reference to these, I wish here to add a few words in plain prose.

Were I conscious of being able to do justice to those important topics, I might avail myself of the periodical press for offering anonymously my thoughts, such as they are, to the world; but I feel that, in procuring attention, they may derive some advantage, however small, from my name, in addition to that of being presented in a less fugitive shape. It is also not impossible that the state of mind which some of the foregoing poems may have produced in the reader will dispose him to receive more readily the impression which I desire to make, and to admit the conclusions I would establish.

1. The first thing that presses upon my attention is the Poor-Law Amendment Act. I am aware of the magnitude and complexity of the subject, and the unwearied attention which it has received from men of far wider experience than my own; yet I cannot forbear touching upon one point of it, and to this I will confine myself, though not insensible to the objection which may reasonably be brought against treating a portion of this, or any other great scheme of civil polity, separately from the whole. The point to which I wish to draw the reader's attention is, that *all* persons who cannot find employment, or procure wages sufficient to support the body in health and strength, are entitled to a maintenance by law.

This dictate of humanity is acknowledged in the Report of the Commissioners: but is there not room for apprehension that some of the regulations of the new act have a tendency to render the principle nugatory by difficulties thrown in the way of applying it? If this be so, persons will not be wanting to show it, by examining the provisions of the act in detail, — an attempt which would be quite out of place here; but it will not, therefore, be deemed unbecoming in one who fears that the prudence of the head may, in framing some of those provisions, have supplanted the wisdom of the heart, to enforce a principle which cannot be violated without infringing upon one of the most precious rights of the English people, and opposing one of the most sacred claims of civilized humanity.

There can be no greater error, in this department of legislation, than the belief that this principle does by necessity operate for the degradation of those who claim, or are so circumstanced as to make it likely they may claim, through laws founded upon it, relief or assistance. The direct contrary is the truth: it may be unanswerably maintained, that its tendency is to raise, not to depress; by stamping a value upon life, which can belong to it only where the laws have placed men who are willing to work, and yet cannot find employment, above the necessity of looking, for protection against hunger and other natural evils, either to individual and casual charity, to despair and death, or to the breach of law by theft, or violence.

And here, as in the Report of the Commisioners, the fundamental principle has been recognized, I am not at issue with them any farther than I am compelled to believe that their " remedial measures " obstruct the application of it more than the interests of society require.

And, calling to mind the doctrines of political

economy which are now prevalent, I cannot forbear to enforce the justice of the principle, and to insist upon its salutary operation.

And first for its justice : If self-preservation be the first law of our nature, would not every one in a state of nature be morally justified in taking to himself that which is indispensable to such preservation, where, by so doing, he would not rob another of that which might be equally indispensable to *his* preservation ?   And if the value of life be regarded in a right point of view, may it not be questioned whether this right of preserving life, at any expense short of endangering the life of another, does not survive man's entering into the social state ; whether this right can be surrendered or forfeited, except when it opposes the divine law, upon any supposition of a social compact, or of any convention for the protection of mere rights of property ?

But, if it be not safe to touch the abstract question of man's right in a social state to help himself even in the last extremity, may we not still contend for the duty of a Christian government, standing *in loco parentis* towards all its subjects, to make such effectual provision, that no one shall be in danger of perishing either through the neglect or harshness of its legislation ?   Or, waiving this, is it not indisputable that the claim of the state to the allegiance, involves the protection, of the subject ?   And, as all rights in one party impose a correlative duty upon another, it follows that the right of the state to require the services of its members, even to the jeoparding of their lives in the common defence, establishes a right in the people (not to be gainsaid by utilitarians and economists) to public support, when, from any cause, they may be unable to support themselves.

Let us now consider the salutary and benign operation of this principle. Here we must have recourse to elementary feelings of human nature, and to truths which from their very obviousness are apt to be slighted, till they are forced upon our notice by our own sufferings or those of others. In the Paradise Lost, Milton represénts Adam, after the Fall, as exclaiming, in the anguish of his soul, —

> " Did I request Thee, Maker, from my clay
> To mould me man; did I solicit Thee
> From darkness to promote me?
> .   .   .   .   .   My will
> Concurred not to my being."

Under how many various pressures of misery have men been driven thus, in a strain touching upon impiety, to expostulate with the Creator! and under few so afflictive as when the source and origin of earthly existence have been brought back to the mind by its impending close in the pangs of destitution. But as long as, in our legislation, due weight shall be given to this principle, no man will be forced to bewail the gift of life in hopeless want of the necessaries of life.

Englishmen have, therefore, by the progress of civilization among them, been placed in circumstances more favorable to piety and resignation to the divine will, than the inhabitants of other countries, where a like provision has not been established. And as Providence, in this care of our countrymen, acts through a human medium, the objects of that care must, in like manner, be more inclined towards a grateful love of their fellow-men. Thus, also, do stronger ties attach the people to their country, whether while they tread its soil, or, at a distance, think of their native land as an indulgent parent, to whose arms even they who have been imprudent and undeserving may, like the prodigal son, betake themselves, without fear of being rejected.

Such is the view of the case that would first present itself to a reflective mind ; and it is in vain to show, by appeals to experience, in contrast with this view, that provisions founded upon the principle have promoted profaneness of life, and dispositions the reverse of philanthropic, by spreading idleness, selfishness, and rapacity : for these evils have arisen, not as an inevitable consequence of the principle, but for want of judgment in framing laws based upon it ; and, above all, from faults in the mode of administering the law. The mischief that has grown to such a height from granting relief in cases where proper vigilance would have shown that it was not required, or in bestowing it in undue measure, will be urged by no truly enlightened statesman as a sufficient reason for banishing the principle itself from legislation.

Let us recur to the miserable states of consciousness that it precludes.

There is a story told, by a traveller in Spain, of a female who, by a sudden shock of domestic calamity, was driven out of her senses, and ever after looked up incessantly to the sky, feeling that her fellow-creatures could do nothing for her relief. Can there be Englishmen who, with a good end in view, would, upon system, expose their brother Englishmen to a like necessity of looking upwards only ; or downwards to the earth, after it shall contain no spot where the destitute can demand, by civil right, what by right of nature they are entitled to ?

Suppose the objects of our sympathy not sunk into this blank despair, but wandering about as strangers in streets and ways, with the hope of succor from casual charity ; what have we gained by such a change of scene? Woful is the condition of the famished Northern Indian, dependent, among winter snows, upon the chance-passage of a herd of deer, from which one, if brougnt down by his rifle-gun, may be made the means of keeping him and his companions alive. As miserable is that of some savage Islander, who, when the land has ceased to afford him sustenance, watches for food which the waves may cast up, or in vain endeavors to extract it from the inexplorable deep.   But neither of these is in a state of wretchedness comparable to that which is so often endured in civilized society: multitudes, in all ages, have known it, of whom may be said:—

> "Homeless, near a thousand homes they stood,
> And near a thousand tables pined, and wanted food."

Justly might I be accused of wasting time in an uncalled-for attempt to excite the feelings of the reader, if systems of political economy, widely spread, did not impugn the principle, and if the safeguards against such extremities were left unimpaired.   It is broadly asserted by many, that every man who endeavors to find work, *may* find it: were this assertion capable of being verified, there still would remain a question, what kind of work, and how far may the laborer be fit for it? For if sedentary work is to be exchanged for standing, and some light and nice exercise of the fingers, to which an artisan has been accustomed all his life, for severe labor of the arms, the best efforts would turn to little account, and occasion would be given for the unthinking and the unfeeling unwarrantably to reproach those who are put upon such employment, as idle, froward, and unworthy of relief, either by law or in any other way! Were this statement correct, there would indeed be an end of the argument, the principle here maintained would be superseded. But, alas! it is far otherwise. That principle, applicable to the benefit of all countries, is indispensable for England, upon whose coast families are perpetually deprived of their support by shipwreck, and where large masses of men are so liable to be thrown out of their ordinary means of gaining bread, by changes in commercial intercourse, subject mainly or solely to the will of foreign powers; by new discoveries in arts and manufactures; and by reckless laws, in conformity with theories of political economy, which, whether right or wrong in the abstract, have proved a scourge to tens of thousands, by the abruptness with which they have been carried into practice.

But it is urged, — Refuse altogether compulsory relief to the able-bodied, and the number of those who stand in need of relief will steadily diminish, through a conviction of an absolute necessity for greater forethought, and more prudent care of a man's earnings. Undoubtedly it would, but so also would it, and in a much greater degree, if the legislative provisions were retained, and parochial relief administered under the care of the upper classes, as it ought to be. For it has been invariably found, that wherever the funds have been raised and applied under the superintendence of gentlemen and substantial proprietors, acting in vestries, and as overseers, pauperism has diminished accordingly. Proper care in that quarte would effectually check what is felt in some districts to be one of the worst evils in the poor law system, namely, the readiness of small and needy proprietors to join in imposing rates that seemingly subject them to great hardships, while, in fact, this is done with a mutual understanding, that the relief each is ready to bestow upon his still poorer neighbors will be granted to himself, or his relatives, should it hereafter be applied for.

But let us look to inner sentiments of a nobler quality, in order to know what we have to build upon. Affecting proofs occur in every one's experience, who is acquainted with the unfortunate and the indigent, of their unwillingness to derive their subsistence from aught but their own funds or labor, or to be indebted to parochial assistance for the attainment of any object, however dear to them. A case was reported, the other day, from a coroner's inquest, of a pair who through the space of four years had carried about their dead infant from house to house, and from lodging to lodging, as their necessities drove them, rather than ask the parish to bear the expense of its interment: —the poor creatures lived in the hope of one day being able to bury their child at their own cost. It must have been heart-rending to see and hear the mother, who had been called upon to account for the state in which the body was found, make this deposition. By some, judging coldly, if not harshly, this conduct might be imputed to an unwarrantable pride, as she and her husband had, it is true, been once in prosperity. But examples, where the spirit of independence works with equal strength though not with like miserable accompaniments, are frequently to be found even yet among the humblest peasantry and mechanics. There is not, then, sufficient cause for doubting that a like sense of honor may be revived among the people, and their ancient habits of independence restored, without resorting to those severities which the new Poor Law Act has introduced.

But even if the surfaces of things only are to be examined, we have a right to expect that lawgivers should take into account the various tempers and dispositions of mankind : while some are led, by the existence of a legislative provision, into idleness and extravagance, the economical virtues might be cherished in others by the knowledge that, if all their efforts fail, they have in the Poor Laws a " refuge from the storm and a shadow from the heat." Despondency and distraction are no friends to prudence : the springs of industry will relax, if cheerfulness be destroyed by anxiety ; without hope men become reckless, and have a sullen pride in adding to the heap of their own wretchedness. He who feels that he is abandoned by his fellow-men will be almost irresistibly driven to care little for himself ; will lose his self-respect accordingly, and with that loss, what remains to him of virtue ?

With all due deference to the particular experience and general intelligence of the individuals who framed the Act, and of those who in and out of Parliament have approved of and supported it, it may be said, that it proceeds too much upon the presumption that it is a laboring man's own fault if he be not, as the phrase is, beforehand with the world. But the most prudent are liable to be thrown back by sickness, cutting them off from labor, and causing to them expense: and who but has observed how distress creeps upon multitudes without misconduct of their own; and merely from a gradual fall in the price of labor, without a correspondent one in the price of provisions; so that men who may have ventured upon the marriage state with a fair prospect of maintaining their families in comfort and happiness, see them reduced to a pittance which no effort of theirs can increase? Let it be remembered, also, that there are thousands with whom vicious habits of expense are not the cause why they do not store up their gains; but they are generous and kind-hearted, and ready to help their kindred and friends; moreover, they have a faith in Providence, that those who have been prompt to assist others will not be left destitute, should they themselves come to need. By acting from these blended feelings, numbers have rendered themselves incapable of standing up against a sudden reverse. Nevertheless, these men, in common with all who have the misfortune to be in want, if many theorists had their wish, would be thrown upon one or other of those three sharp points of condition before adverted to, from which the intervention of law has hitherto saved them.

All that has been said tends to show how the principle contended for makes the gift of life more valuable, and has, it may be hoped, led to the conclusion that its legitimate operation is to make men worthier of that gift: in other words, not to degrade, but to exalt human nature. But the subject must not be dismissed without adverting to the indirect influence of the same principle upon the moral sentiments of a people among whom it is embodied in law. In our criminal jurisprudence there is a maxim, deservedly eulogized, that it is better that ten guilty persons should escape, than that one innocent man should suffer; so, also, might it be maintained, with regard to the Poor Laws, that it is better for the interests of humanity among the people at large, that ten undeserving should partake of the funds provided, than that one morally good man, through want of relief, should either have his principles corrupted, or his energies destroyed; than that such a one should either be driven to do wrong, or be cast to the earth in utter hopelessness. In France, the English maxim of criminal jurisprudence is reversed; there, it is deemed better that ten innocent men should suffer, than one guilty escape: in France, there is no universal provision for the poor; and we may judge of the small value set upon human life in the metropolis of that country, by merely noticing the disrespect with which, after death, the body is treated, not by the thoughtless vulgar, but in schools of anatomy, presided over by men allowed to be, in their own art and in physical science, among the most enlightened in the world. In the East, where countries are overrun with population as with a weed, infinitely more respect is shown to the remains of the deceased; and what a bitter mockery is it, that this insensibility should be found where civil polity is so busy in minor regulations, and ostentatiously careful to gratify the luxurious propensities, whether social or intellectual, of the multitude! Irreligion is, no doubt, much concerned with this offensive disrespect shown to the bodies of the dead in France; but it is mainly attributable to the state in which so many of the living are left by the absence of compulsory provision for the indigent, so humanely established by the law of England.

Sights of abject misery, perpetually recurring, harden the heart of the community. In the perusal of history, and of works of fiction, we are not indeed, unwilling to have our commiseration excited by such objects of distress as they present to us; but, in the concerns of real life, men know that such emotions are not given to be indulged for their own sakes : there, the conscience declares to them that sympathy must be followed by action ; and if there exist a previous conviction that the power to relieve is utterly inadequate to the demand, the eye shrinks from communication with wretchedness, and pity and compassion languish, like any other qualities that are deprived of their natural aliment. Let these considerations be duly weighed by those who trust to the hope that an increase of private charity, with all its advantages of superior discrimination, would more than compensate for the abandonment of those principles the wisdom of which has been here insisted upon. How discouraging, also, would be the sense of injustice, which could not fail to arise in the minds of the well disposed, if the burden of supporting the poor, a burden of which the selfish have hitherto by compulsion borne a share, should now, or hereafter, be thrown exclusively upon the benevolent.

By having put an end to the Slave-Trade and Slavery, the British people are exalted in the scale of humanity ; and they cannot but feel so, if they look into themselves, and duly consider their relation to God and their fellow-creatures. That was a noble advance ; but a retrograde movement will assuredly be made, if ever the principle, which has been here defended, should be either avowedly abandoned or but ostensibly retained.

But, after all, there may be little reason to apprehend permanent injury from any experiment that may be tried. On the one side will be human nature rising up in her own defence, and on the other prudential selfishness acting to the same purpose, from a conviction that, without a compulsory provision for the exigencies of the laboring multitude, that degree of ability to regulate the price of labor, which is indispensable for the reasonable interest of arts and manufactures, cannot in Great Britain be upheld.

II. In a poem of the foregoing collection, allusion is made to the state of the workmen congregated in manufactories. In order to relieve many of the evils to which that class of society are subject, and to establith a better harmony between them and their employers, it would be well to repeal such laws as prevent the formation of joint-stock companies. There are, no doubt, many and great obstacles to the formation and salutary working of these societies, inherent in the mind of those whom they would obviously benefit. But the combinations of masters to keep down, unjustly, the price of labor, would be fairly checked by them, as far as they were practicable ; they would encourage economy, inasmuch as they would enable a man to draw profit from his savings, by investing them in buildings or machinery for processes of manufacture with which he was habitually connected. His little capital would then be working for him while he was at rest or asleep; he would more clearly perceive the necessity of capital for carrying on great works; he would better learn to respect the larger portions of it in the hands of others; he would be less tempted to join in unjust combinations; and, for the sake of his own property, if not for higher reasons, he would be slow to promote local disturbance, or endanger public tranquillity; he would, at least, be loth to act in that way *knowingly:* for it is not to be denied that such societies might be nurseries of opinions unfavorable to a mixed constitution of government, like that of Great Britain. The democratic and republican spirit which they might be apt to foster would not, however, be dangerous in itself, but only as it might act without being sufficiently counterbalanced, either by landed proprietorship, or by a Church extending itself so as to embrace an ever-growing and ever-shifting population of mechanics and artisans. But if the tendencies of such societies would be to make the men prosper who might belong to them, rulers and legislators should rejoice in the result, and do their duty to the state by upholding and extending the influence of that Church to which it owes, in so great a measure, its safety, its prosperity, and its glory.

This, in the temper of the present times, may be difficult, but it is become indispensable, since large towns in great numbers have sprung up

and others have increased tenfold, with little or
no dependence upon the gentry and the landed
proprietors ; and apart from those mitigated feudal institutions, which, till of late, have acted so
powerfully upon the composition of the House of
Commons.   Now it may be affirmed, that, in
quarters where there is not an attachment to the
Church, or the landed aristocracy, and a pride in
supporting them, *there* the people will dislike both,
and be ready, upon such incitements as are perpetually recurring, to join in attempts to overthrow
them.   There is no neutral ground here : from
want of due attention to the state of society in large
towns and manufacturing districts, and ignorance
or disregard of these obvious truths, innumerable well-meaning persons became zealous sup-
porters of a Reform Bill, the qualities and powers
of which, whether destructive or constructive, they
would otherwise have been afraid of; and even
the framers of that bill, swayed as they might be
by party resentments and personal ambition, could
not have gone so far, had not they too been lam-
entably ignorant or neglectful of the same truths
both of fact and philosophy.

But let that pass; and let no opponent of the
bill be tempted to compliment his own foresight,
by exaggerating the mischiefs and dangers that
have sprung from it: let not time be wasted in
profitless regrets ; and let those party distinctions
vanish to their very names that have separated

men who, whatever course they may have pursued, have ever had a bond of union in the wish to save the limited monarchy, and those other institutions that have, under Providence, rendered for so long a period of time this country the happiest and worthiest of which there is any record since the foundation of civil society.

III. A philosophic mind is best pleased when looking at religion in its spiritual bearing; as a guide of conduct, a solace under affliction, and a support amid the instabilities of mortal life: but the Church having been forcibly brought by political considerations to my notice, while treating of the laboring classes, I cannot forbear saying a few words upon that momentous topic.

There is a loud clamor for extensive change in that department. The clamor would be entitled to more respect, if they who are the most eager to swell it with their voices were not generally the most ignorant of the real state of the Church, and the service it renders to the community. *Reform* is the word employed. Let us pause and consider what sense it is apt to carry, and how things are confounded by a lax use of it. The great religious Reformation, in the sixteenth century, did not profess to be a new construction, but a restoration of something fallen into decay, or put out of sight. That familiar and justifiable use of the word seems to have paved the way for fallacies

with respect to the term Reform, which it is difficult
to escape from.   Were we to speak of improvement, and the correction of abuses, we should run
less risk of being deceived ourselves, or of misleading others.   We should be less likely to fall
blindly into the belief, that the change demanded
is a renewal of something that has existed before,
and that therefore we have experience on our
side ; nor should we be equally tempted to beg
the question, that the change for which we are
eager must be advantageous.   From generation to
generation, men are the dupes of words ; and it is
painful to observe, that so many of our species
are most tenacious of those opinions which they
have formed with the least consideration.   They
who are the readiest to meddle with public affairs,
whether in church or state, fly to generalities, that
they may be eased from the trouble of thinking
about particulars ; and thus is deputed to mechanical instrumentality the work which vital knowledge only can do well.

" Abolish pluralities, have a resident incumbent
in every parish," is a favorite cry ; but, without
adverting to other obstacles in the way of this
specious scheme, it may be asked what benefit
would accrue from its *indiscriminate* adoption, to
counterbalance the harm it would introduce, by
nearly extinguishing the order of curates, unless
the revenues of the Church should grow with the
population, and be greatly increased in many

thinly peopled districts, especially among the parishes of the North.

The order of curates is so beneficial, that some particular notice of it seems to be required in this place. For a church poor as, relatively to the numbers of people, that of England is, and probably will continue to be, it is no small advantage to have youthful servants, who will work upon the wages of hope and expectation. Still more advantageous is it to have, by means of this order, young men scattered over the country, who, being more detached from the temporal concerns of the benefice, have more leisure for improvement and study, and are less subject to be brought into secular collision with those who are under their spiritual guardianship. The curate, if he reside at a distance from the incumbent, undertakes the requisite responsibilities of a temporal kind, in that modified way which prevents him, as a new-comer, from being charged with selfishness : while it prepares him for entering upon a benefice of his own, with something of a suitable experience. If he should act under and in coöperation with a resident incumbent, the gain is mutual. His studies will probably be assisted ; and his training, managed by a superior, will not be liable to relapse in matters of prudence, seemliness, or in any of the highest cares of his functions ; and by way of return for these benefits to the pupil, it will often happen that the zeal of a middle-aged or declining

incumbent will be revived, by being in near communion with the ardor of youth, when his own
efforts may have languished through a melancholy consciousness that they have not produced
as much good among his flock as, when he first
entered upon the charge, he fondly hoped.

Let one remark, and that not the least important, be added. A curate, entering for the first
time upon his office, comes from college after a
course of expense, and with such inexperience in
the use of money, that, in his new situation, he is
apt to fall unawares into pecuniary difficulties.
If this happens to him, much more likely is it to
happen to the youthful incumbent; whose relations, to his parishioners and to society, are more
complicated ; and, his income being larger and
independent of another, a costlier style of living
is required of him by public opinion. If embar-
rassment should ensue, and with that unavoidably
some loss of respectability, his future usefulness
will be proportionably impaired : not so with the
curate, for he can easily remove and start afresh,
with a stock of experience and an unblemished
reputation ; whereas the early indiscretions of an
incumbent, being rarely forgotten, may be im-
pediments to the efficacy of his ministry for the
remainder of his life. The same observations
would apply with equal force to doctrine. A
young minister is liable to errors, from his notions
being either too lax, or overstrained. In both

cases it would prove injurious that the error should be remembered, after study and reflection, with advancing years, shall have brought him to a clearer discernment of the truth, and better judgment in the application of it.

It must be acknowledged, that, among the regulations of ecclesiastical polity, none at first view are more attractive than that which prescribes for every parish a resident incumbent.   How agreeable to picture to one's self, as has been done by poets and romance-writers, from Chaucer down to Goldsmith, a man devoted to his ministerial office, with not a wish or a thought ranging beyond the circuit of its cares!   Nor is it in poetry and fiction only that such characters are found; they are scattered, it is hoped not sparingly, over real life, especially in sequestered and rural districts, where there is but small influx of new inhabitants, and little change of occupation.   The spirit of the Gospel, unaided by acquisitions of profane learning and experience in the world, — that spirit, and the obligations of the sacred office, may, in such situations, suffice to effect most of what is needful. But for the complex state of society that prevails in England, much more is required, both in large towns, and in many extensive districts of the country.   A minister there should not only be irreproachable in manners and morals, but accomplished in learning, as far as is possible without sacrifice of the least of his pastoral duties.   As necessary, perhaps more so, is it that he should be a citizen as well as a scholar; thoroughly acquainted with the structure of society, and the constitution of civil government, and able to reason upon both with the most expert; all ultimately in order to support the truths of Christianity, and to diffuse its blessings.

A young man coming fresh from the place of his education cannot have brought with him these accomplishments; and if the scheme of equalizing church incomes, which many advisers are much bent upon, be realized, so that there should be little or no secular inducement for a clergyman to desire a removal from the spot where he may chance to have been first set down; surely not only opportunities for obtaining the requisite qualifications would be diminished, but the motives for desiring to obtain them would be proportionably weakened. And yet these qualifications are indispensable for the diffusion of that knowledge, by which alone the political philosophy of the New Testament can be rightly expounded, and its precepts adequately enforced. In these times, when the press is daily exercising so great a power over the minds of the people, for wrong or for right as may happen, *that* preacher ranks among the first of benefactors, who, without stooping to the direct treatment of current politics and passing events, can furnish infallible guidance through the delusions that surround them; and who, appealing to the sanctions of Scripture, may place the grounds of its injunctions in so clear a light, that disaffection shall cease to be cultivated as a laudable propensity, and loyalty cleansed from the dishonor of a blind and prostrate obedience.

It is not, however, in regard to civic duties alone, that this knowledge in a minister of the Gospel is important; it is still more so for softening and subduing private and personal discontents. In all places, and at all times, men have gratuitously troubled themselves, because their survey of the dispensations of Providence has been partial and narrow; but now that readers are so greatly multiplied, men judge as they are *taught*, and repinings are engendered everywhere, by imputations being cast upon the government; and are prolonged or aggravated by being ascribed to misconduct or injustice in rulers, when the individual himself only is in fault. If a Christian pastor be competent to deal with these humors, as they may be dealt with, and by no members of society so successfully, both from more frequent and more favorable opportunities of intercourse, and by aid of the authority with which he speaks, he will be a teacher of moderation, a dispenser of the wisdom that blunts approaching distress by submission to God's will, and lightens, by patience, grievances which cannot be removed.

We live in times when nothing, of public good at least, is generally acceptable, but what we believe can be traced to preconceived intention, and specific acts and formal contrivances of human understanding. A Christian instructor thoroughly accomplished would be a standing restraint upon such presumptuousness of judgment, by impressing the truth that,

> In the unreasoning progress of the world,
> A wiser spirit is at work for us,
> A better eye than ours.   MS.

Revelation points to the purity and peace of a future world; but our sphere of duty is upon earth; and the relations of impure and conflicting things to each other must be understood, or we shall be perpetually going wrong, in all but goodness of intention; and goodness of intention will itself relax through frequent disappointment. How desirable, then, is it, that a minister of the Gospel should be versed in the knowledge of existing facts, and be accustomed to a wide range of social experience! Nor is it less desirable for the purpose of counterbalancing and tempering in his own mind that ambition with which spiritual power is as apt to be tainted as any other species of power which men covet or possess.

It must be obvious that the scope of the argument is to discourage an attempt which would introduce into the Church of England an equality of income, and station, upon the model of that of Scotland. The sounder part of the Scottish nation

know what good their ancestors derived from their
Church, and feel how deeply the living generation
is indebted to it.   They respect and love it, as accommodated in so great a measure to a compara-
tively poor country, through the far greater portion of which prevails a uniformity of employment;
but the acknowledged deficiency of theological
learning among the clergy of that Church is easily
accounted for by this very equality.   What else
may be wanting there, it would be unpleasant to
inquire, and might prove invidious to determine :
one thing, however, is clear, that in all countries
the temporalities of the Church Establishment
should bear an analogy to the state of society, otherwise it cannot diffuse its influence through the
whole community.   In a country so rich and luxurious as England, the character of its clergy must
unavoidably sink, and their influence be everywhere impaired,— if individuals from the upper
ranks, and men of leading talents, are to have no
inducements to enter into that body but such as are
purely spiritual.   And this " tinge of secularity "
is no reproach to the clergy, nor does it imply a
deficiency of spiritual endowments.   Parents and
guardians, looking forward to sources of honorable maintenance for their children and wards,
often direct their thoughts early towards the
Church, being determined partly by outward circumstances, and partly by indications of seriousness, or intellectual fitness.   It is natural that a

boy or youth, with such a prospect before him, should turn his attention to those studies, and be led into those habits of reflection, which will in some degree tend to prepare him for the duties he is hereafter to undertake. As he draws nearer to the time when he will be called to these duties, he is both led and compelled to examine the Scriptures. He becomes more and more sensible of their truth. Devotion grows in him; and what might begin in temporal considerations will end (as in a majority of instances we trust it does) in a spiritual-mindedness not unworthy of that Gospel, the lessons of which he is to teach, and the faith of which he is to inculcate. Not inappositely may be here repeated an observation, which, from its obviousness and importance, must have been frequently made, namely, that the impoverishing of the clergy, and bringing their incomes much nearer to a level, would not cause them to become less worldly-minded: the emoluments, howsoever reduced, would be as eagerly sought for, but by men from lower classes in society; men who, by their manners, habits, abilities, and the scanty measure of their attainments, would unavoidably be less fitted for their station, and less competent to discharge its duties.

Visionary notions have in all ages been afloat upon the subject of best providing for the clergy; notions which have been sincerely entertained by good men, with a view to the improvement of that order, and eagerly caught at and dwelt upon by the designing, for its degradation and disparagement. Some are beguiled by what they call the *voluntary system*, not seeing (what stares one in the face at the very threshold) that they who stand in most need of religious instruction are unconscious of the want, and therefore cannot reasonably be expected to make any sacrifice in order to supply it. Will the licentious, the sensual, and the depraved take from the means of their gratifications and pursuits, to support a discipline that cannot advance without uprooting the trees that bear the fruit which they devour so greedily? Will *they* pay the price of that seed whose harvest is to be reaped in an invisible world? A voluntary system for the religious exigencies of a people numerous and circumstanced as we are! Not more absurd would it be to expect that a knot of boys should draw upon the pittance of their pocket-money to build schools, or out of the abundance of their discretion be able to select fit masters to teach and keep them in order! Some, who clearly perceive the incompetence and folly of such a scheme for the agricultural part of the people, nevertheless think it feasible in large towns, where the rich might subscribe for the religious instruction of the poor. Alas! they know little of the thick darkness that spreads over the streets and alleys of our large towns. The parish of Lambeth, a few years since, contained not more than one church and three or four small proprietary chapels, while dissenting chapels, of every denomination, were still more scantily found there; yet the inhabitants of the parish amounted at that time to upwards of fifty thousand. Were the parish church and the chapels of the Establishment existing there an *impediment* to the spread of the Gospel among that mass of people? Who shall dare to say so? But if any one, in the face of the fact which has just been stated, and in opposition to authentic reports to the same effect from various other quarters, should still contend, that a voluntary system is sufficient for the spread and maintenance of religion, we would ask, What kind of religion? Wherein would it differ, among the many, from deplorable fanaticism?

For the preservation of the Church Establishment, all men, whether they belong to it or not, could they perceive their true interest, would be strenuous: but how inadequate are its provisions for the needs of the country! and how much is it to be regretted, that, while its zealous friends yield to alarms on account of the hostility of dissent, they should so much overrate the danger to be apprehended from that quarter, and almost overlook the fact that hundreds of thousands of our fellow-countrymen, though formally and nominally of the Church of England, never enter her places of worship, neither have they communication with her ministers! This deplorable state of things was partly produced by a decay of zeal among the rich and influential, and partly by a want of due expansive power in the constitution of the Establishment as regulated by law. Private benefactors, in their efforts to build and endow churches, have been frustrated, or too much impeded, by legal obstacles : these, where they are unreasonable or unfitted for the times, ought to be removed ; and, keeping clear of intolerance and injustice, means should be used to render the presence and powers of the Church commensurate with the wants of a shifting and still-increasing population.

This cannot be effected, unless the English Government vindicate the truth, that, as her Church exists for the benefit of all (though not in equal degree), whether of her communion or not, all should be made to contribute to its support. If this ground be abandoned, cause will be given to fear that a moral wound may be inflicted upon the heart of the English people, for which a remedy cannot be speedily provided by the utmost efforts which the members of the Church will themselves be able to make.

But let the friends of the Church be of good courage. Powers are at work, by which, under Divine Providence, she may be strengthened and the sphere of her usefulness extended ; not by alterations in her Liturgy, accommodated to this or that demand of finical taste, not by cutting off this

or that from her Articles or Canons, to which the
scrupulous or the overweening may object.   Covert schism, and open nonconformity, would survive
after alterations, however promising in the eyes
of those whose subtilty had been exercised in
making them.   Latitudinarianism is the parhelion
of liberty of conscience, and will ever successfully
lay claim to a divided worship.   Among Presby-
terians, Socinians, Baptists, and Independents,
there will always be found numbers who will tire
of their several creeds, and some will come over
to the Church.   Conventicles may disappear, con-
gregations in each denomination may fall into decay or be broken up, but the conquests which the
National Church ought chiefly to aim at lie among
the thousands and tens of thousands of the unhap-
py outcasts who grow up with no religion at all.
The wants of these cannot but be feelingly remembered.   Whatever may be the disposition of
the new constituencies under the reformed Parliament, and the course which the men of their choice
may be inclined or compelled to follow, it may be
confidently hoped that individuals, acting in their
private capacities, will endeavor to make up for
the deficiencies of the legislature.   Is it too much
to expect that proprietors of large estates, where
the inhabitants are without religious instruction,
or where it is sparingly supplied, will deem it
their duty to take part in this good work; and
that thriving manufacturers and merchants will,

in their several neighborhoods, be sensible of the like obligation, and act upon it with generous rivalry?

Moreover, the force of public opinion is rapidly increasing: and some may bend to it, who are not so happy as to be swayed by a higher motive; especially they who derive large incomes from lay-impropriations, in tracts of country where ministers are few and meagrely provided for. A claim still stronger may be acknowledged by those who, round their superb habitations, or elsewhere, walk over vast estates which were lavished upon their ancestors by royal favoritism, or purchased at insignificant prices after church spoliation; such proprietors, though not conscience-stricken (there is no call for that), may be prompted to make a return for which their tenantry and dependents will learn to bless their names. An impulse has been given; an accession of means from these several sources, coöperating with a *well*-considered change in the distribution of some parts of the property at present possessed by the Church, a change scrupulously founded upon due respect to law and justice, will, we trust, bring about so much of what her friends desire, that the rest may be calmly waited for, with thankfulness for what shall have been obtained.

Let it not be thought unbecoming in a layman, to have treated at length a subject with which the clergy are more intimately conversant. All may, without impropriety, speak of what deeply concerns all; nor need an apology be offered for going over ground which has been trod before so ably and so often: without pretending, however, to anything of novelty, either in matter or manner, something may have been offered to view which will save the writer from the imputation of having little to recommend his labor, but goodness of intention.

It was with reference to thoughts and feelings expressed in verse, that I entered upon the above notices, and with verse I will conclude. The passage is extracted from my manuscripts, written above thirty years ago: it turns upon the individual dignity which humbleness of social condition does not preclude, but frequently promotes. It has no direct bearing upon clubs for the discussion of public affairs, nor upon political or trade-unions; but if a single workman — who, being a member of one of those clubs, runs the risk of becoming an agitator, or who, being enrolled in a union, must be left without a will of his own, and therefore a slave — should read these lines, and be touched by them, I should indeed rejoice; and little would I care for losing credit as a poet with intemperate critics, who think differently from me upon political philosophy or public measures, if the sober-minded admit that, in general views, my affections have been moved, and my imagination exercised, under and *for* the guidance of reason.

" Here might I pause, and bend in reverence
To Nature, and the power of human minds;
To men as they are men within themselves.
How oft high service is performed within,
When all the external man is rude in show;
Not like a temple rich with pomp and gold,
But a mere mountain chapel that protects
Its simple worshippers from sun and shower!
Of these, said I, shall be my song; of these,
If future years mature me for the task,
Will I record the praises, making verse
Deal boldly with substantial things, — in truth
And sanctity of passion speak of these,
That justice may be done, obeisance paid
Where it is due.   Thus haply shall I teach,
Inspire, through unadulterated ears
Pour rapture, tenderness, and hope; my theme
No other than the very heart of man,
As found among the best of those who live,
Not unexalted by religious faith,
Nor uninformed by books, good books, though few,
In Nature's presence: thence may I select
Sorrow that is not sorrow, but delight,
And miserable love that is not pain
To hear of, for the glory that redounds
Therefrom to human kind, and what we are.
Be mine to follow with no timid step
Where knowledge leads me; it shall be my pride
That I have dared to tread this holy ground,
Speaking no dream, but things oracular,
Matter not lightly to be heard by those
Who to the letter of the outward promise
Do read the invisible soul; by men adroit
In speech, and for communion with the world .
Accomplished, minds whose faculties are then
Most active when they are most eloquent,
And elevated most when most admired.
Men may be found of other mould than these;
Who are their own upholders, to themselves

Encouragement and energy and will;
Expressing liveliest thoughts in lively words
As native passion dictates.   Others, too,
There are, among the walks of homely life,
Still higher, men for contemplation framed;
Shy, and unpractised in the strife of phrase;
Meek men, whose very souls perhaps would sink
Beneath them, summoned to such intercourse.
Theirs is the language of the heavens, the power,
The thought, the image, and the silent joy:
Words are but under-agents in their souls;
When they are grasping with their greatest strength,
They do not breathe among them; this I speak
In gratitude to God, who feeds our hearts
For his own service, knoweth, loveth us,
When we are unregarded by the world."

INDEX TO THE POEMS.

INDEX TO THE FIRST LINES.

END OF VOL. V.